ONE
CHANCE

The One Chance Series

One Chance

Two Secrets

ONE
CHANCE

SARAH FRANK

BeaLu Books

ISBN 978-0-9990924-0-8 (Hardback Edition)
ISBN 978-0-9990924-1-5 (Paperback Edition)

Library of Congress Control Number 2017963315

Publisher's Cataloging-in-Publication Data
provided by Five Rainbows Cataloging Services

Names: Frank, Sarah Irene.
Title: One chance / Sarah Frank.
Description: Tampa : BeaLu Books, 2018. | Series: One chance, bk. 1. | Summary: Join a group of orphans as they journey back in time to find out why Sandy's parents abandoned her. | Grades 4-7.
Identifiers: LCCN 2017963315 | ISBN 978-0-9990924-0-8 (hardcover) | ISBN 978-0-9990924-1-5 (pbk.) | ISBN 978-0-9990924-2-2 (ebook)
Subjects: LCSH: Time travel--Fiction. | Middle school students--Fiction. | Orphans--Fiction. | Abandoned children--Fiction. | Mystery and detective stories. | BISAC: JUVENILE FICTION / Time Travel. | JUVENILE FICTION / Family / Orphans & Foster Homes. | JUVENILE FICTION / Mysteries & Detective Stories. | JUVENILE FICTION / Action & Adventure / General.
Classification: LCC PZ7.1.F745 On 2018 (print) | LCC PZ7.1.F745 (ebook) | DDC [Fic]--dc23.

Book cover and design by Tara Raymo • creativelytara.com

Printed in the United States of America
January 2018 - First Edition Hardback and Paperback

BeaLu Books
Tampa, Florida

www.BeaLuBooks.com

For my family,
thanks for all the love and support.

For my friends,
thanks for always being there for me.

For my teachers and counselors,
thanks for helping me find my way.

For all the people that helped this book get published,
thanks for making my dreams come true.

ONE
CHANCE

ONE

Prologue: Germany, 12 years ago

World-renowned scientist, Dr. Ava Petris, collapsed into her office chair with a loud sigh. She rubbed her eyes, removed her shoes, and massaged her aching feet, then applied pressure to the tense muscles of her neck. Finally, a time to relax. As she began to recline in her chair, the phone rang. Dr. Petris eyed it from across the room. With a reluctant groan, she took a deep breath and stood up. One look at the caller ID told her to ignore it. With a roll of her eyes, Dr. Petris walked slowly around her office, her fingers running across the white oak shelves mounted on the wall. Her eyes glanced from frame to frame displaying her greatest achievements and awards. Her works were among the most important discoveries in scientific history. Universities around the world studied her work.

Back at her desk, she opened a file titled 'Confidential—Stone Properties' on her computer and reviewed it for what felt like the millionth time. This project was easily the most exciting one she had undertaken, but also the most difficult. Dr. Petris knew she was on the brink of something—maybe even the most important discovery in the history of science—but she couldn't quite get there. The project was unusual because it confused her, but the confusion only motivated her more.

The German government classified Dr. Petris's project as TOP SECRET. Her orders came directly from Chancellor Schmidt himself. He allowed her to hire two scientists to assist her and insisted she has a bodyguard.

The amazing opportunity to work with two of Germany's top scientists thrilled Dr. Petris. Yet, an unbelievable amount of pressure rested on her shoulders now. Dr. Petris inhaled and exhaled, her hands folded across her stomach and her glasses perched on the bridge of her nose.

Tomorrow would be a new day, a new chance.

• • •

Dr. Petris awoke to the sound of heavy rain and crackling thunder. She hauled herself to her feet and made herself a strong cup of coffee. After throwing on some of her most comfortable clothes and her lab coat, she continued to get ready for the day. On her way to work, accompanied by her bodyguard, Brutus Ebbe, Dr. Petris couldn't get the project out of her mind.

She went through the security retina scan and fingerprint identification to get to her lab. Arriving at her lab's door, she unlocked it and flicked on the light as she stepped into the room. Maybe today would be the day she solved the mystery of the Stone of Discedo. Maybe today would finally be the day when she activated it.

The Stone of Discedo sat on the metal lab table, its powerful abilities locked. The overhead lamp illuminated the emerald rock, the light bouncing off its surface. The stone was roughly the size of a tennis ball but had more potential power than a nuclear bomb. There it sat—capable of changing the world. Yet, her inability to access the stone's potential made the stone no more valuable than an ordinary rock. To everyone else, Dr. Petris masked her frustration, but there was no lying to herself.

Brutus stood near the back door, watching Dr. Petris intently. Was he watching her, or what she was doing? Was there even a difference? Ava didn't mind the attention, especially from him. Did Chancellor Schmidt give her a bodyguard because she was incapable of defending herself? Or maybe he was not protecting her; maybe he was protecting the Stone of Discedo.

Whatever the reason, Ava was glad he was there. Brutus was tough and muscular, not to mention smart and respectful of her and her co-workers. In the four months, Brutus shielded her from prying eyes, provided moral support, and while he never said it, seemed to genuinely care about her and her project. Although their jobs didn't require much communication, there was certainly a connection between them. She had never had a relationship before, as work was always her top priority but maybe, just maybe, Brutus might be the first and only exception.

Scientists Nicolaus Bert and Peter Herrmann arrived and crowded around the lab table as the three of them examined the Stone of Discedo.

"Hmmm . . .," Nicolaus muttered as he shifted his gaze between a hand-held magnetometer and the emerald green stone. "Very strong magnetism." Nicolaus began to read off measurements, and Peter jotted them down.

"Get me the tweezers," Dr. Petris ordered, not moving her eyes off the stone. Nicolaus took no time in grabbing them from the table of instruments and handing them to her, careful not to poke her. Ava set right to work, her latex gloves maneuvering gingerly around the precious rock. Just then, there was a knock on the lab door.

Brutus stepped towards the door and looked through the peephole. It was a rare event that people visited the lab. In fact, Dr. Petris couldn't recall any visits at all. Brutus nodded and opened the door. A stout, potbellied man stepped into the room. The man was balding, and what was left of his hair was steel gray and cut very short. In his hand was a security pass. Dr. Petris, the other scientists, Brutus, and the chancellor of Germany were the only ones with security clearance and passes to the lab.

"Chancellor Schmidt!" Ava exclaimed. She removed her gloves as she shook his hand. The chancellor's hand grazed hers, his skin as pale and cold as ice.

"Ava, what a pleasure it is to see you," said Chancellor Schmidt. "How is my project coming along?"

"Lately, we have been working on researching the stone's history. Today, we took more notes about its physical characteristics, but I'm afraid I have nothing new to report. We still don't know how to activate it."

"Refresh my memory," Chancellor Schmidt said, leaning against the wall. "About the history, I mean."

"We've still got a long way to go," Ava added, hesitant to share the information. Most of her potential leads had turned out to be dead ends.

Chancellor Schmidt smiled, but it didn't quite reach his cold eyes. "Ava, I decided to entrust this information to my vice-chancellor, and I need you to explain it to him."

Ava chewed on her lip. Her eyes flitted to Brutus, who merely winked. "My apologies, Chancellor, but I can't come with you today. I . . . I have plans. I—"

"I was not going to ask you to come with me, Miss Petris," Chancellor Schmidt said. "I ask you to wait for my explanation before you jump to conclusions."

"My apologies."

"I'm going to record you explaining the project. I daresay you know more about it than I do."

"Yes, sir. What time or day this week works for you?" Ava asked, removing her glasses and setting them on the table. She took out a small pad of paper and a pen to note the date and time.

"Now!" he ordered. "We have no time to waste. This stone's magic is priceless. It could make Germany the most powerful nation in the world—"

"This project is for scientific purposes," Ava interrupted. "And for scientific purposes only."

"Yes, well . . ." the chancellor's voice died, unsure of what to say. She questioned whether those were his intentions.

"Chancellor, you're not planning on using the Stone of Discedo to intimidate other countries or change hist—"

"No, of course not," the Chancellor said a little too quickly. "Nothing like that."

Ava raised an eyebrow, questioning the truth to his words.

Chancellor Schmidt pulled a small, black recording device out of his suit pocket. "Well, Ava, I am a busy man with a tight schedule. I want you to explain the project, and its . . . backstory for my vice-chancellor to understand the project and its entirety." He seemed to be picking his words with caution. "Go ahead."

Ava, surprised but always quick on her feet, looked straight into the video camera and began, "It all started a year ago. My partner, Sophia Edgar, and I heard about this . . . mythical stone and decided to try to find it. It disappeared in England, around the 1350's. The stories stated an artist, Elias Prewell, had kept it for years and then fell ill with the Black Plague. The word *discedo* is a Latin word meaning 'departure.' We think he named it 'The Stone of Discedo' because it takes you from your timeline." Ava paused briefly and adjusted her glasses. "Elias knew he was close to death, so he decided to hide the stone in one of his sculptures. Sophia and I took a trip to the UK and researched him. Before his death, he had three statues he'd been working on in his studio. One was never finished, the second was in Edward III's castle, and the third was in an art gallery, which burned down in the late 1400's.

Sophia speculated the stone was likely hidden in the statue located in Edward III's castle. She reasoned if Elias truly didn't want the stone found, it would be in the place no one could get to it. The statue moved to the British Museum, in London, sometime in the 1700's. Sophia suggested we confide in someone who worked at the museum our suspicions about the Stone of Discedo. Then we would get their permission to examine the statue. But we weren't sure who we could trust with the secret. No one could know. While I don't condone thievery, there seemed to be no other option. The project had to be kept a secret. We had to steal the stone if it was in fact in the statue."

"Of course," the Chancellor agreed.

"After researching the museum, we decided to visit it. We found a storage closet in the museum and hid there until the museum closed. We located the statue of the knight we believed hid the Stone of Discedo. On the back of the knight's foot, there was an engraving. It said 'tempus itinerantar' meaning 'travel through time.' Below the engraving was a little hole we used to open a small door slightly larger than a tennis ball. Inside, we found the stone."

"In the knight's foot?"

"Nobody really looks at the back of a statue's feet," she explained. "It was by far the most inconspicuous place."

"So, Elias Prewell didn't want the stone to be found?"

Ava nodded. She wasn't sure how much information the Chancellor wanted, nor how much information to give.

"He didn't want the Stone to be found accidentally."

"Right. Continue," the Chancellor said.

Ava looked straight into the camera again and continued the story. "We were able to remove the stone, and then we headed back to the closet to wait for the museum to open the next morning. About an hour after it opened, we left. Sophia and I exited the museum, leaving no one the wiser. That afternoon we left the country. Upon returning to Germany, a group of men attacked us. Their faces were unrecognizable, but they had distinctive snake tattoos on their necks. Somehow, they knew we had the stone," Ava said fighting tears. "We were running away from the men, sprinting as fast as we could. The men had guns, they were shooting at us, bullets were flying this way and that. We kept running, as fast as our legs could carry us—"

"I do not need a play by play," the Chancellor said. "I need you to talk more about the stone and the project." Ava ignored him.

"One of the bullets hit Sophia. I couldn't even turn around to help her or get her body. I had to keep running. Once I escaped, I promised myself I would activate the Stone of Discedo, not just for me, but for Sophia too. Later, I discovered the men who attacked us were with Simon Moreno, a notorious and mysterious villain. Nobody really knows much about him, other than the fact that he is a criminal. I was terrified. With no one left to turn to, I went to you, Chancellor Schmidt, my old childhood friend. After I shared with you the history, we agreed to help each other." Ava smiled at the Chancellor, trying to melt his icy stare.

"Continue," he said.

"*Project Stone Activation* commenced four months ago. Essentially, we are trying to figure out how to activate the stone's powers. According to legend, when the stone is activated, it can allow a person to travel back in time. We theorize that, if the legend holds true, the stone can bend the space-time continuum and, well, slingshot people back to an earlier time. However, this project presents us with challenges. The Stone of Discedo is . . . inactivated. We anticipate—"

Suddenly, the laboratory door blew open with a BANG! Three black-clad men entered clutching guns. One of the men walked ahead of the other two; his gloved hand raised holding a gun, his finger wrapped around the trigger. It would only take the tiniest amount of pressure . . . Instinctively, Brutus stepped in front of Ava and began to pull out his own gun. Before Brutus was able to get his gun out, there was a gunshot; the bullet sliced through the air. Brutus groaned in pain as he crashed to the floor. Ava took a few seconds to process what had happened. She blinked, trying to clear her mind. The sound of the gunshot still ringing in the air.

The Chancellor shrieked and ran for the back door, dropping the recording device. One of the other black-clad men reached down and picked it up. Another one of the men raised his handgun and pulled the trigger. Bullets obliterated the air. There was no time to react. A bullet hit Chancellor Schmidt squarely in the back of his head. The Chancellor slammed into the ground, bleeding profusely.

Ava's heart raced, practically pumping out of her chest as she tried to evaluate what was happening. Then it hit her. These were the same people who killed Sophia, Simon Moreno and his men. She spotted the tattoos on each of their necks and knew for sure it was them. She would never forget those tattoos or faces.

Ava looked over at Brutus, desperate to help him. The Chancellor was dead, and Brutus was dying. Any attempt made by the others to save Brutus would only get them killed. Another gunshot struck Nicolaus's ear as he, Peter, and Ava ducked below the table which was closed in on three sides. Breathing heavily, their hearts racing faster than ever before, Peter and Ava gasped at the sight of the blood dripping down Nicolaus's arm.

Ava could hear footsteps coming closer. She closed her eyes and prayed Moreno's men wouldn't kill them too. The footsteps stopped. Ava could hear the rapid breathing of one of the men.

He was standing right by the table they were under. Ava held her breath. What were they doing?

Moments later, she heard the footsteps receding from the lab table, and the breathing becoming more distant. However, it seemed one man remained in the room. The man was muttering something, but his words were too soft for Ava to hear. She kept her eyes closed and her body still.

Footsteps died as the last man ran away. Ava waited a moment, then took a mirror out of her pocket. She held it up, using the reflection to make sure the men were gone. The room seemed clear.

"They're gone," Ava whispered. Nicolaus, clutching his blood-stained ear, and Peter stood up. All three scientists were pale and shaky. Chancellor Schmidt was motionless on the ground and Brutus . . . oh, Brutus.

Ava knelt next to Brutus. "You risked your life," she whispered, holding Brutus's head gently in her hands. His skin got paler and paler as the blood drained from his body. Brutus's tufts of black hair stood straight up, his scalp stained red. His blood smeared Ava's hands, but she didn't seem to notice or care. Peter and Nicolaus were frozen on their feet, unblinking and unmoving, watching in horror as their fearless boss broke down in tears.

"It was my job," Brutus gasped for breath, "to protect you all . . . from Simon Moreno and . . . Charles Moo . . ." He went limp before he could finish. Ava laid his head down on the ground, using her sleeve to stem her tears. Brutus was gone forever.

"He sacrificed himself to save me," she sobbed. Ava wiped more tears from her eyes.

"Ava?" Nicolaus asked, his voice trembling as he tried to stem the blood flow. Peter, his hands shaking, was dialing for help. Ava continued to cry silently; tears fell onto her cheeks, running down her paled face. Her eyes traveled to the lab table in front of Nicolaus and Peter. She gasped, her heart racing faster. Somehow, part of her had been expecting this, yet the other part couldn't believe it. The lab table was empty.

The Stone of Discedo had been stolen.

TWO

South Toheeden, Ohio
Twelve years later . . .

I stood in front of a cracked vanity mirror, gazing at my
reflection. I saw a slender girl with hair the color of wet
sand and a face splattered with freckles below ocean blue eyes.
I pulled away from my reflection and eased a brush through my
hair. Swiftly, I pulled it into a braid, leaving loose strands tucked
behind my ears. I changed into a fresh pair of jeans and a plain
T-shirt.

My eyes traveled to the small window in my bedroom, fixed
on the sun outside. I walked slowly over to the window sill and
pressed my face up against the cool glass. The sun poked up above
the tree line, rising gracefully into the beautiful spring sky. The
blooming flowers were glistening with morning dew and swaying
slightly in the wind. South Toheeden, Ohio had always been a
peaceful small town, and was, for the most part, nothing out of
the ordinary.

• • •

The dull violet paint peeled off my bedroom walls exposing ugly bits of drywall. The room was confined and smelled of mothballs, which littered the floor of the tiny closet. I'd gotten used to all of it though. For the past eight years, I lived here, at Ms. Evelyn Marsh's house. Ms. Evelyn was a cold woman who gave me what I needed, but never anything more.

The only reason I was ever given for why I had to live here was the same story I'd heard a million times. Eight years ago, my parents dropped me off with the Supters, family friends, for a promised duration of five days but they never returned. The Supter family was nice enough, but after two weeks, they called the state's social workers. The social workers picked me up, and for some reason unknown to me, dropped me here, with Ms. Evelyn.

I didn't have any other family that I knew of, but I didn't understand why I'd been left with Ms. Evelyn. At times, I wondered if maybe she'd been a friend of my parents, but her abrasive personality made that almost impossible for me to believe. Why I couldn't go to another foster home outside of South Toheeden, I didn't know, but I did know there had to be a reason why I was dumped here.

I sat down on my bed and hugged my doll, Jessie, the last thing my parents had given me before they left. A single tear escaped my eye and rolled down my cheek. I pressed Jessie close to my heart; she was the faintest connection to my parents. However, she felt small and insufficient in my hands, but then again, at least she was something. A source of comfort, of consolation. She eased the feeling of loneliness. I cuddled her close and kissed her forehead. More tears made their way down my face, wet against Jessie's dress. Jessie helped, but I needed more. I needed a real person to talk to, to hug, to get advice from. I needed my parents.

The thought was ripped from my mind when my bedroom door opened. There she stood. Ms. Evelyn. She was a lady of average height and weight, her raven black hair always up in a clean and easy bun. Her skin was pale and unblemished. She wore very little to no makeup, and her outfits were plain and simple. Ms. Evelyn's posture was always ramrod straight, and her thin-rimmed glasses always perched on the bridge of her nose.

"Pack your stuff!" Ms. Evelyn ordered. "All of it. You'll be moving to the orphanage tomorrow."

"I—what?" I asked, bewildered.

"You are moving to the orphanage. I've already notified your teachers."

"Wait, what—"

"This will be your last day at Mountain View Middle School and your last day living under my roof. Get packed up!"

"But why do I have to move?"

Ms. Evelyn didn't answer. Instead, she left and slammed my bedroom door closed. I didn't know what to think. After eight years . . . I had to move? Why? Had I done something that made Ms. Evelyn want to get rid of me? It had been eight years, more than 2/3 of my life, living here and suddenly . . . I had to move? And why was I just being told now? Why hadn't Ms. Evelyn told me a month ago, or even a week ago? I mean, I guess she'd mentioned it a while ago as an option, a faint possibility, but now I had to move. Ms. Evelyn hadn't mentioned the idea of an orphanage in a couple of months! And then, all she had told me was the orphanage was run by her sister, Ms. Abigail, and it was zoned for Rolling Hills Middle School. That was it, a slight mention only in passing. Why had I not been given any warning? I doubted I would be able to handle living in an orphanage. It would make everything seem more real.

Fresh tears began flowing. I couldn't stop them even if I wanted to. Sobbing, I began to pack my suitcase. Once I was finished, I packed the rest of my stuff in my crimson drawstring backpack. The fabric of the bag was faded and discolored, but it was just as useful as it had been when I got it from my mom so many years ago. Every time I looked at it I remembered parts of her. From what I could recall, she looked exactly like me. My mother had blond hair the color of wet sand, and ocean blue eyes. Every day I wondered if she or my father was alive. He was more of a shadowy figure in my memories; I could never quite form a clear picture of him in my head. "Tall, dark, and handsome" I remember my mother saying.

Looking at that faded backpack . . . made me think of her, of my family. I always wondered if my parents were alive, and if they were, then why couldn't they come get me? And if they were dead, how come no one told me? I blinked away tears and turned off the light, trying hard to forget all the terrible experiences I had gone through here. I'd dealt with depression and loneliness, among many other things. The whole time I'd been here I struggled with the mystery of my parents' disappearance. The question I've asked a million times but has never been answered.

"SANDY! Come down here! I have a list of chores for you!" Ms. Evelyn shouted, yanking me from my thoughts. I rolled my eyes. Grabbing my bag, I said goodbye to my bedroom, knowing I would have a new life starting tomorrow. That meant today was the last day of an old one.

THREE

The bell rang to start my last day at Mountain View Middle School. People walked around, chatting with friends, laughing and having a good time, but no one paid any attention to me. Not that that was out of the ordinary, but today was a special day. However, I was quick to figure out it was only special to me.

My third-period teacher, Mr. Phillips, was easily my favorite. Mr. Phillips was always smiling, and he had a gentle, fatherly spirit about him.

"Sandy," Mr. Phillips said, "I've been told it's your last day here! I'm sorry to hear that. What school will you be transferring to?"

"Rolling Hills, I think," I replied, setting my books on my desk. I sighed a long, loud, and sorrowful sigh. I knew I'd miss this class. Mr. Phillips gave a small, wry smile.

"All of us at Mountain View will miss you. I hope you do well at Rolling Hills," he told me. "Oddly enough, we have a new student starting today. His name is Brian Moore." As if on cue, a boy with startlingly blue eyes that seemed to have a twinkle in them entered the room. Brian's eyebrows raised for a split second out of what I assumed was surprise. He blinked twice and then focused his eyes determinedly on the floor.

There was something familiar about Brian, but I couldn't quite put my finger on it. Undoubtedly, I had met him before, but where? Why did he look so familiar? I studied him for a few moments, and the answer suddenly dawned on me. Brian had been in my third-grade class at Dry River Elementary School. Why was he pretending he didn't know me? Maybe he had just forgotten. Brian's messenger bag hung loosely from his shoulder; he hugged his history books close to his chest.

"Hi, I'm Sandy. I don't know if you remember me or not, but we went to elementary school together. It's nice to see you again," I said, extending my hand. Brian, although seeming reluctant, put his out in response. Even though I shook his hand with vigor and enthusiasm, he still averted his eyes. It was at this point Mr. Phillips returned to his desk.

"I don't know you," he muttered. Brian looked at the desks behind me, the linoleum floor, even the classroom door. At anything other than me.

"Sure, you do! You just don't remember me. I was in your third-grade class! I think we even sat next to each other."

"I don't know anybody named Sandy," said Brian, still avoiding my eyes.

"You don't remember me?"

"Sorry, but no, I don't."

"You seem . . ." I began, stopping in my tracks. I didn't want to be rude. "Is there anything I can do to help?"

"I'm fine, okay?"

"Well if you say so," I said with a small shrug. I wondered

what made Brian change so drastically in three years. Did I mix him up with someone else? No, that couldn't be right. How many other Brian Moores could there be? Especially in the small town of South Toheeden, Ohio? I remembered him as friendly and smart, and a host of other positive things. Something wasn't right. I was sure of it.

"Have a seat. Class will begin in a moment," Mr. Phillips said brightly. I took my seat between Brian and my friend Ida. I could feel Brian's gaze on the back of my neck. What was going on?

"What did you get for number three?" Ida asked me. "I just want to check."

"D."

"Oh, talking about your grades?" A girl named Jasmine said with her usual note of sass. She flipped her hair over her shoulder and smirked. Jasmine blinked, and I noticed how long and thick her eyelashes were, the obvious product of too much mascara.

"Just for the record, Sandy and I are both honor roll students," Ida responded in a cool voice, "but I don't think you can say the same."

Jasmine, unable to think of a comeback quickly enough, made a face at us. Then she glared at me, eyes narrowed as if she knew what I was thinking.

"Why don't you leave us alone and mind your own business?" suggested Ida. Jasmine turned away. Ida smiled with satisfaction and winked at me. Then she flipped her fierce red hair over her shoulder, just like Jasmine had done. I could see Jasmine roll her eyes and a small smile appeared on my lips.

At the beginning of lunch, I met my friends at our table in

the cafeteria. Ida showed me her scrapbook, but I wasn't paying too much attention to her or to anything else. My mind was elsewhere.

My fifth-period class was language arts taught by Mrs. Resnick. Today, she wore a black Pittsburgh Steelers jersey.

Our class met in the library, and by the time I got there, it was almost impossible to find a seat by a computer. Luckily, there was a seat open in the corner. I ran over to it before someone else could snatch it. Mrs. Resnick told us to pick a topic and research it.

About five minutes in, something caught my eye. In the opposite corner was Brian. He saw me staring and walked towards the other wall. About five minutes after the class settled, I asked Mrs. Resnick if I could check out a book.

"Go ahead," she said. I thanked her and walked over to where Brian was perusing the bookshelves. He was obviously searching for something specific. In his hand, he held three books.

Is the Space-Time Continuum Open for Travel?

Magic vs. Science

Time Travel: Fact or Fiction?

"You can only check out two books at once," I told him.

"I know," he snapped.

"Then why do you—"

"Sandy, it's none of your business. Go back to your computer."

"No." I wasn't sure why I said 'no,' but I did. I had this funny, indescribable feeling that something was going on.

"Sandy, I can't tell you anything."

"Can't or won't?"

Brian sighed and shook his head. "Fine. We'll have to meet

somewhere right after sixth period."

"But I'll miss part of seventh period!" I quietly protested. "I could get in huge trouble!" The Brian I knew in elementary school would never suggest anything like this.

"Listen, Sandy, I'm a good student. Believe me when I tell you neither one of us wants to miss class. But some things are more important."

"Yes, but—"

"I would never do anything I thought would get me—or you—in major trouble. Just ask your sixth-period teacher a question after class, so you can stay late and ask for a pass. Use the pass when you go back to seventh period. After meeting me, of course," Brian told me. "If you do it right, it'll work. I've done it at my old school."

"How come we can't meet after school?" I asked, frowning.

"I have my first day of band practice after school today, and probably every day after school while I catch up." Brian turned to go as he added, "And I also have a bunch of other stuff going on."

"Okay, well where are we going to meet?"

"Can you think of anywhere?"

"Maybe Room 209 the empty classroom. Nobody ever goes in there."

"Alright." Brian was grinning slightly with satisfaction as he turned towards the checkout desk.

With that, I headed back to my computer. I couldn't concentrate on my research paper, as my mind was buzzing. What was Brian hiding?

The bell rang to end fifth period, and I met my friends at

Ida's hallway locker. Next period was gym, the only class other than lunch where I could talk with Ida and one of my other best friends, Olivia. As much as I hated the class itself, I appreciated getting to spend time with them. During the insanity of the school hallways, it was difficult to find time to catch up.

"We're starting a new sport today," Ida told us, digging through her hall locker.

"Yeah. Too bad soccer is over," Olivia sighed. "I actually enjoyed it. Who would've thought that I, of all people, would like a sport?"

"I loved the soccer unit, but I got bitten by so many ants," Ida said, indicating a row of red bumps on her ankle. "Thirteen bites, and everyone knows thirteen is an unlucky number." Olivia and I laughed, and Ida gave us a *really face*. Then Ida slammed her locker shut so hard, her locker mirror fell out and cracked as it hit the floor.

"AH!" Ida shouted. "A broken mirror! That's seven years of bad luck!" She grabbed a container of salt out of her locker.

"Ida, why do you have—" I began to ask, but my question was soon answered. Ida sprinkled some salt into her palm and tossed it over her shoulder.

"Can one of you throw away that mirror?" Ida asked. "I don't want to touch it in case I get even more bad luck."

"I'll get it," I said. I stooped down to pick up Ida's broken mirror. It occurred to me I had yet to tell them I was changing schools because I was too distracted at lunch. I took a deep breath and told them everything.

"What?!" Ida exclaimed. "You're kidding!"

"Sandy, are you serious?" asked Olivia.

"Yeah," I said. I wanted to shrink, to disappear. Expressions of sadness, shock, disappointment, and even confusion appeared on their faces.

At last, Ida spoke. "Well, then we have to make today the best day possible for you!" I smiled and was hugging them when I spotted Brian leaving the boys' bathroom.

"Hold on guys. I gotta—I'll be right back," I said. Olivia nodded, and Ida shrugged. "Brian! Wait up!"

"What do you want?" Brian asked.

"Nothing, really. Just to ask if you're alright. Finding all your classes okay?"

"Yeah. And for the last time, I'm fine."

"You seem kind of . . . different," I said. "Just nervous?"

"I have my reasons," Brian muttered to the floor, "none of which concern you. I'm going to be late," he added, walking away.

"Sandy? We're going to be late too. Let's go," said Olivia.

"See you later, Sandy," Brian said.

I began to object, but he walked away. Only reluctantly, I followed my friends to gym class. We entered the locker rooms, and after I changed quickly, I left the loud and busy locker room for the gym.

The gym was a high-ceilinged room illuminated by four colossal windows. Shimmering afternoon sunlight played across the bleachers. The last group of kids entered the gym from the locker room, my friends among them. Olivia was spinning a volleyball on her pointer finger, and Ida was bumping one up and down in the air.

"Alright, it's the first day of our volleyball unit. Everyone, find a partner and get on opposite sides of the net. Make sure one of you has a ball, and the other one doesn't." Like always, I partnered with Ida, and Olivia partnered with our friend Amanda. Jasmine and her posse of friends were beside us.

"We're going to start by bumping. Put your hands out in front of you like so," Coach David instructed, showing us the proper form. I locked my arms and cupped my hands, mimicking the coach. "Now, if you have a ball, serve it to your partner. Partners, bump the ball back to them." Ida served the ball to me, and I bumped it back, aiming for her chest. Unfortunately, as usual, my aim was way off. The ball grazed the top of the net and plummeted to the ground, just beyond reach from Ida. Ida dove to the ground and bumped the ball over the net, saving it from touching the floor.

"Wow," I said. "Have you played volleyball before?"

Ida blushed, her red cheeks matching her hair, "A little bit. Thanks."

As Ida began to help me with serving, Jasmine and her click strutted over.

"Would you look at that?" Jasmine said. "It's one more thing I'm better at than you!" One of her friends handed her a volleyball, and she tossed it into the air and spiked it forcefully over the net.

"You may be a bit better at volleyball, but Sandy is better at a lot of things," snapped Ida.

"Yeah? Like what?"

Before Ida could even answer, Coach David blew the whistle. Everyone in our class gathered around him, Jasmine and

Ida exchanging looks all the while.

"Everyone run four laps around the gym," ordered the coach.

Halfway through the first lap, I was among the last group of kids. I hated laps because it made me seem even slower. Once all the athletic kids finished, they would watch us, the non-athletic kids, pant until we were done.

Ida and Olivia were towards the front, and I could see their heads bobbing up and down.

At the start of the third lap, Amanda was just ahead of me, with Jasmine running in between us. Then everything seemed to happen in slow motion: Jasmine began to run faster as she passed Amanda, and her left foot collided with Amanda's right foot causing her to trip and fall onto the polished hardwoods. I stopped and knelt next to Amanda as Jasmine and her posse ran around us.

"Are you okay?" I asked.

"No," she sobbed. Tears filled her eyes and spilled down her face. "My ankle hurts."

"You probably sprained it," I told her. "Can you stand?"

"I don't think so," Amanda said, wiping tears from her eyes.

"Here, let me help you," I offered, extending a hand. I pulled Amanda upright. She draped one arm around me for support and hopped over to the first row of the splintered bleachers. Ida and Olivia immediately sprinted over to us.

Olivia's eyebrows jumped into the air. "What happened?"

"Amanda sprained her ankle," I explained. "Olivia, can you tell Coach David to call the nurse?"

"Sure."

The nurse arrived with the wheelchair as PE came to an end. I gave Amanda a quick hug before running to the locker room. I hastily changed back into my regular clothes and remembered the promise I made to Brian. A risky promise, sure, but I had my fingers crossed it would pay off.

Ida and Olivia were waiting for me. "Guys, you go ahead without me. I have to ask Coach a question," I told them.

"What about?" Ida demanded.

"Oh, you know . . . stuff."

"Very specific," Ida said. "Alright, I guess we'll see you later." The bell rang, and Ida and Olivia left the locker room. I found Coach David still in the gym.

"Um, Coach?" I asked.

"Yes?" the coach said, dumping the volleyballs into a basket without looking at me.

"Can I ask you a question?" I knew I sounded as nervous as I felt.

"Yeah, okay," Coach David agreed, still not turning to face me.

"Well, um, I was wondering . . ." Come on, Sandy, think of something, anything . . . Lying had never been one of my strengths. "I wanted to know . . ."

"Yes?" Coach David turned around and raised an eyebrow.

"For volleyball, what are we supposed to use to, um, hit the ball? Like, where on our arms?"

"You use your forearms," Coach David answered. "Now go to class."

"Can I have a pass?" I asked. "My next class is pretty far from here—"

"Well, Sandy, I—"

"Please?" I needed this to work so I could meet Brian and keep my conduct grade intact.

"Sandy—" Coach David protested. Then he sighed and said, "I guess so." He handed me a blue slip of paper with his messy signature on it.

"Thanks, Coach."

"You're welcome," he said. The tardy bell rang as I exited the gym, giving me a feeling I was unaccustomed to—*rebelliousness*.

I reached room 209, clutching the little blue slip of paper which protected my conduct grade.

It was a stark room with rows of chairs and splintered desks pushed up against the far wall. According to Mrs. Resnick, no teacher had used this classroom in years.

Brian was already there, perched cross-legged on a desk near the back, fastening the strap on his backpack absentmindedly. He gazed out of the window with lazy interest. Another spring shower had wrapped itself around South Toheeden.

"Hey," I greeted him, laying my drawstring bag on the floor.

"Hey," he replied. "I'm going to do my best to make this quick."

"Alright," I nodded. "Go ahead." Again, I wondered why we had to meet in a private room? What could possibly be this important? I looked up from my pass, and my eyes caught his. His eyes were bright blue and intelligent-looking. I instantly felt a sense of trust towards him, and in what he was saying.

Brian began, "It all started at my old school, Valley Heights." I snorted but disguised it as a hoarse cough. "What's so funny?" he demanded.

"N-nothing. It's just the name is—never mind. Continue."

"Anyway, I went to my locker after lunch, and it was cracked open. Someone had broken in. I opened my locker, expecting a note or a prank, but instead, there was a stone."

"A stone? In your locker? What does it look like?"

"Shhhh!" Brian hissed. "What if someone heard you?"

"Sorry."

"It's emerald green, and about the size of a tennis ball but it has uneven edges."

"Is it sharp? What does it feel like?"

"Well it's not sharp, the edges are actually kind of dull and the texture . . . It's kind of rough. The stone's color though . . . it's this gorgeous emerald green, as deep as can be."

"But why would someone break into your locker and—"

"I've been wondering the same thing," Brian interrupted me. He slid off the desk and began to pace. "Why would someone break into my locker and plant a stone there?"

"And why you?"

"Exactly. I haven't got a clue why it was planted on me of all people. When I first found the stone, I didn't know what it was, but I knew it was special. I drove myself crazy, spending all my evenings researching, trying to figure out what it was and how it got in my locker. I mean, after all, someone had to have broken in to put it there."

"So? What did you find out?"

"I discovered it's called the Stone of Discedo, and theoretically, it can travel through time."

"It can time travel?" I repeated.

"Let me start at the beginning. Twelve years ago, there was an armed robbery in a German science lab. Two people— including the Chancellor of Germany— were murdered. One woman went to the hospital due to trauma-induced shock, and I think one man even had part of his ear shot off. The Chancellor's death brought up some interesting things. It was rumored that Germany was working on a TOP SECRET project, a project that would make them the most powerful nation in the world. Supposedly, they had a stone that could potentially allow one to time travel if it was activated. Think about it, you could change anything you wanted to. You could invest in successful companies, prepare for attacks, win wars, stop terrible things from happening, correct wrong decisions, and so much more."

"I can't believe—"

"Most people question if the stone is real or if it's just a rumor. Legend has it that it can time travel, but in order for the user to fix something in their own timeline, they would have to first fix three horrible events in history."

"But we don't know if that's true. We don't know if it actually works?"

"Well to be perfectly honest, I think a lot of people refuse to believe in it because they don't want to believe there is that much power. People believe what they want to believe. Some people don't believe it exists at all, that it's a call for attention or a myth. But there are a lot of people who do believe that the stone exists, and most of them are scared of it. They know that somewhere in the world, someone possesses an incredible amount of power."

"I would be scared too," I admitted. "But is the stone even activated? Do you know if anyone has used it before?"

"Well . . . I used it but . . ." Brian closed his eyes and shook his head, cutting his own sentence short.

"But what?"

"But I messed up," he said, "and I promised myself I would never try to use it again."

"What happened?"

"That's a conversation for another time."

I was a little disappointed. The curiosity was eating me from the inside out.

Brian continued, "Anyway, the people who stole it from that lab in Germany, whoever they are, figured out a way to activate it . . . kind of."

"What do you mean by 'kind of'?"

"They were able to figure out how to activate it, but they weren't able to do it. The men, Simon Moreno, and some other guys, were taken to jail. Notes were found when their hideout was searched. They were all cryptic; one of the notes said, 'by one with a pure heart and even purer intentions.'"

"So, does that mean they couldn't use the Stone of Discedo because they aren't good people?" I raised an eyebrow. "That sounds kind of cliché."

"I didn't come up with it," Brian said, holding up his hands as if surrendering. "And there's no way to be sure that's even what that note was talking about. Apparently, none of the notes were full sentences or thoughts."

"So where did the stone go when Simon Moreno and his men were arrested?"

"That's another thing," Brian said. "Nobody knows. The

stone dropped off the face of the earth. There has been no record of anyone seeing it for the past twelve years. When Simon and his men were arrested, their hideout was searched, but nothing was supposedly found other than the notes. Some people think perhaps someone investigating the hideout took it, while others theorize that Simon Moreno hid it when he realized there was a chance he would be captured. In all my research, I could find no definitive record of where the stone went after Simon Moreno's capture."

"So, the Stone of Discedo just . . . disappeared? For twelve years?" My mouth fell open. Could this be true? Could this be real?

"And twelve years after it disappeared, there it was. In my locker, sitting on my science textbook." Brian rubbed his eyes. "It's hard to believe."

"Wow." The only word I could manage.

"There's more. Anybody found with the stone in their possession will be immediately taken to jail. Possibly for a life sentence."

"Why?"

"Sandy, this stone, the Stone of Discedo, is believed to be capable of rewriting history. It's magic. If someone got ahold of it, if it got into the wrong hands . . . everything could change."

"Yeah, that's true," I agreed.

"Governments all over the world are searching for it," Brian added. "And to think that it's right here. Right here with a twelve-year-old boy in South Toheeden, Ohio."

"I still have some questions."

"I might have some answers."

"What are you going to do with it? Do your parents know? Why don't you tell an authority?"

"SHHHH! Keep it down!" He lowered his voice to a barely-audible whisper, "and yes, I still have it, but no, my, uh, parents don't know. Nobody does. Other than you."

"Why do you still have it? Why don't you plant it on someone else?"

"I can't," Brian shook his head. "I just can't."

"Why not?"

"Because I can't bring the danger upon someone else. I don't want anyone else to suffer like I did, with curiosity, with a huge, huge secret to keep and all the other problems that come with it. Besides, what if I got caught doing it? It's just too risky."

I opened my mouth to ask what problems he had, but instead said, "Yeah, I guess you're right."

"Also, what if it got into the wrong hands?" Brian asked as if it was obvious. "And Sandy, it's magic! Magic! If you had one chance to change something that happened in your life, whatever your heart desired, would you give it up? If you had one chance to change everything, wouldn't you take it?

"Well, I—"

"No, you wouldn't give it up. Besides, there was a reason why it was planted on me. This wasn't some random thing. There has to be a reason why I have it." Silence fell between us.

"This can't be true," I shook my head in denial.

"Well I don't care if you believe me or not," Brian shrugged. "I told you everything, exactly like I promised."

"One question:" I said, even though I had hundreds, "Why did you tell me? Why did you trust me with a secret this big?" Brian's blue eyes froze over, and his face was suddenly stone.

"I needed to tell someone. The secret was just tearing me to pieces. I also knew you were already onto me. I could tell. You saw me checking out those time travel books, and you knew that I was hiding something."

I frowned. "How could you—"

"You have to promise not to tell anyone. Promise?" Brian deflected the question like water glancing off glass.

"I promise," I agreed. I paused and then asked, "How do you pronounce its name again?"

"Dih-see-doh," Brian said, pronouncing each syllable.

"The Stone of Discedo," I said. Even its name sounded magical. While I desperately wanted to ask to see the stone, I withstood the urge to ask, and instead said, "Now we should probably get to class. Who do you have?"

"Mrs. Swenson," he answered, "but first, Sandy, I have to have your word that you won't tell anybody about any of this. If someone finds out, both of us are looking at time in jail."

"You can trust me."

"Good," Brian nodded.

"There's one problem," I said, biting my lip.

"What?" he frowned.

"I'm transferring schools. I don't own a phone. How will we contact each other?"

"Don't worry, I have my ways."

"But—"

"Don't worry, Sandy," he assured me. On that note, he left the room, leaving the rest a mystery.

All I could think about the rest of the day was what Brian told me. I had known he was hiding something, but something that big? I hadn't expected magic! Maybe his parents broke up, or he had a major crush on someone, but I certainly hadn't expected a magical stone.

At dinner that night, I was surprised by a piece of good news. "Sandy, there's been a change in plans. You'll probably be moving to the orphanage on Sunday instead of tomorrow. There was an emergency and my sister Abigail had to take in a new kid. She doesn't have any room right now, but she is optimistic a spot will open in a few days."

"Okay."

I didn't want to go to the orphanage, knowing deep inside the title "orphan" would be a big psychological burden for me. It would make my parents' absence real. Too real. Living with a foster parent like Ms. Evelyn was bad, but being an official orphan would likely feel much worse. But maybe . . . maybe Ms. Abigail would be nicer than Ms. Evelyn, maybe the orphanage would be better than my situation here.

I often wondered why my last name was changed to Marsh because that couldn't have been my real name. That couldn't have been the name put on my birth certificate when I was born . . . right? Living here was always intended to be temporary, or at least that's what I was told, so why had my last name been changed? Everything, even simple things like writing my name at the top of a test, was a reminder I didn't have parents.

I raced upstairs. I had never been so relieved to see the

peeling paint, the tiny bed, or the musty closet. Sure, it wasn't ideal. In fact, I didn't even like being here, yet there was something about going to an orphanage that made me feel sick to my stomach. I was pleased to be able to stay here, at least for a few more days. I sighed, my lips turning upwards into a small smile.

* * *

Within an hour, my feeling of relief wore off, doused by worry. I knew I would still have to move to the orphanage, I just had more time to adjust to the thought. To make things worse, Ms. Evelyn had become progressively more cross. It was obvious she wanted me gone, and Ms. Evelyn didn't care enough about me or my feelings to try and hide it.

At the moment, I was sitting on my bed, leaning against the chipped, white headboard, daydreaming. My mind wandered from topic to topic but kept coming back to Brian and his secret. Could the Stone of Discedo really time travel? Did magic exist? Question after question filled my brain, visions of the stone appearing in my mind. There was only one way to find out if what Brian was saying was legitimate.

After a moment of anxious hesitation, I tip-toed downstairs, scanning the kitchen for Ms. Evelyn. Holding my breath, I peeked into the den. She wasn't in there either, so she had to be in her bedroom. Her door was closed. Cautiously, I pressed my ear to the oak door and waited. The faint noises of the TV could be heard, mingling with Ms. Evelyn's sharp voice.

"Oh. Yes. Sure, I'll hold." I sighed, knowing I had a few minutes before she would hang up, and probably more than that until she would come out of her room.

I entered the dimly lit den illuminated only by the light from a grimy window. The lilac shades were torn in several places. I strode across the room and took a seat at the desk. The computer was old and outdated, but it would serve the purpose I needed.

I opened an internet browser and typed Stone of Discedo into the search bar. I scrolled through web links until I found a reliable source. It took a while, but after reading a few articles, I realized Brian was likely telling the truth. The Stone of Discedo really existed, and therefore, magic did too.

• • •

There was still a little bit of doubt in my mind. The existence of magic wasn't something to be taken lightly. The next day, Wednesday, I decided to ask my science teacher a question. Second-period science, taught by Mr. Bluecrest, was usually exciting and interactive. However, today we were doing an exam review in our groups. The classroom was loud when I raised my hand, knowing nobody would overhear me. Mr. Bluecrest walked over to my desk.

"Sandy, you have a question?" he asked, looking over my shoulder.

"Yeah, but it's not about this," I pointed to the textbook. "It's about something else."

"Sure, what is it?"

"Well, I was wondering . . . is time travel scientifically possible?"

"I'm afraid not," Mr. Bluecrest shook his head. "Time travel is magic, not science. The two don't overlap. Most people don't believe in magic because they fear and doubt the unknown.

Personally, I do believe in something that defies all scientific laws. We may not know what, or why, but we cannot say that the unknown does not exist. Fearing or doubting the unknown is for the close-minded. We don't know what we don't know."

"Okay, thank you. I was just wondering." Mr. Bluecrest went back to his desk, leaving me to my thoughts. So it was true. Magic might really exist.

• • •

At lunch, I sat down next to Ida, Olivia, and Amanda, whose crutches were propped against the table next to her. This was the first time I was able to talk to them all day. Last period, we'd taken a test from bell to bell, and had no time to talk.

"Sandy, I didn't get to ask you earlier, but how come you're here?" Ida asked as soon as I walked in.

"The, um, orphanage was full. I think there was a kid pulled from a bad home or something like that. She needed a place to stay for a few nights before they send her to live with one of her family members out of state."

"How do you know that?" Amanda asked, looking a little puzzled.

"I overheard Ms. Evelyn discussing it on the phone last night. Anyway, the kid needs the spot more than I do."

"How long do you get to stay at Mountain View?" Amanda asked, taking a sip of her lemonade.

"I probably have about three more days here. Today included."

"That's great!" Amanda exclaimed. "We get to spend more time with you!"

"Hey," Ida leaned in, talking in a whisper. "What's up with

that new kid, Brian?"

"Um, heh, what a sudden change of subject," I said.

"Felt like the right time," Ida shrugged.

"Hey, Ida, is the salad any good?" I asked.

"Yeah, Sandy, it's good," Ida narrowed her eyebrows. "Why do you seem so nervous?"

"Oh, um, no reason," I blurted, no longer in control of my tongue. "Just, uh, worried about getting homework tonight."

"That's not it," Ida said. "I think you know something."

"Huh, me? About what?"

"I think you know something about the new kid, Brian," Ida speculated.

"Do you think he's cute?" Olivia asked.

"WHAT?! Me? No way!" I shouted. A couple of people turned to look at me.

"Then why did you start fidgeting when I said his name?" Ida asked.

"Leave her alone," Amanda interrupted. "She doesn't have to tell us anything."

"Whatever," Ida said, spearing a meatball.

"I think I'll go get a drink of water." As I got up, I heard Ida whisper something to the others. I did what Brian asked me to do. I kept the secret, but I wasn't sure if I could lie to my friends again.

When I got back to the table, the others had moved on to a completely different subject. At the table next to us were Jasmine and her posse. Jasmine chatted with her friends as she unwrapped a peanut butter sandwich. Then it hit me.

"Jasmine, throw that away!" I exclaimed.

"Why should I?" Jasmine demanded.

"Amanda has a peanut allergy!"

"I don't see why I shouldn't be able to eat my lunch just because she has an allergy."

"Amanda could die if she even touches a peanut."

"Actually, it's okay," said Amanda.

"Wait . . . so you don't have an allergy anymore?" I asked. I could've sworn she had an allergy.

"Well, kind of." Amanda swallowed her food and then explained, "I did OIT."

"What does that stand for?"

"Oral Immunotherapy. My allergist helped me build up a tolerance for peanuts. Now I can be around them, and I even eat them daily."

In response, Jasmine took a big bite of her sandwich with a smirk plastered on her face.

Ida picked up the conversation where it had left off, "Anyway, so earlier, the janitor was fixing a lightbulb in the hallway, and he was up on a ladder. I mean, everyone knows walking under a ladder is bad luck—"

"You're crazy, you know that, right?" Olivia giggled.

Just then Brian entered the cafeteria, clutching a massive science book in one hand and a lunch tray in the other.

"Hey," he said. He sat down next to Olivia, and her eyebrows jerked upward.

"Oh, um, hi, Brian," Olivia said.

"Olivia, right?" he asked, swallowing his food and washing it down with a swig of chocolate milk.

"Yeah, that's me," she said, sounding even more awkward than before, "and this is, um, Ida and Amanda."

"Forgot our names for a second?" Ida asked, laughing. Olivia's face got even redder. I gave her a quizzical look, but she ignored me.

Our table got quiet. Brian opened a book and began to read while he ate. Olivia glanced up at him every now and then, then shook her head and looked down at her untouched plate of food. I felt as if my thoughts were drowned out by the roar of the other students. The cafeteria was in its usual hectic state, outcries and cursing and food being launched from one side of the lunchroom to the other. I could vaguely hear the teachers calling for order, begging for obedience, but their half-hearted commands didn't faze the students whatsoever.

Brian was hastily spearing mystery meat chunks into his mouth, shoveling down his food with a careless haste that suggested he was in some kind of rush.

"I have to go. I've got stuff to do," he said after his final bite of lunch.

"Like what?" I asked.

"I think you have some idea," Brian replied, slinging his bag over his shoulder with a note of finality. He left, disappearing into the hallway.

"What is it? What is he going to do?" Olivia asked.

"It's nothing," I waved it off. Now it was my turn to avoid Olivia's gaze.

"Tell us," Ida demanded. "We're your friends. You can confide in us."

"I never said I couldn't, but I just can't say," I avoided her burning gaze. "It's not my secret to tell anyway."

"It's fine, guys, she doesn't have to tell us," Amanda said. "It's none of our business."

"I still think you like him," Ida giggled. "You're not fooling anyone." I couldn't fight it. If I disagreed, then what would I tell them? Maybe it was better if they thought I had a crush on him. Then they'd stop bothering me about it. I chuckled to myself as I left the cafeteria.

After fifth period with Mrs. Resnick, I hurried to gym class. Taking one last breath of fresh air, I entered the locker room, immediately consumed by the smell of bleach and body odor.

Ida led the way into the gym where we found Coach David, standing next to a tall, slim woman I'd never seen before. The woman was twirling a metallic whistle on a key ring.

"Gather round, guys," Coach David shouted. "I'd like to introduce you to my new intern, Coach Bates. I'm going to let her take over this period for today. Do whatever she tells you." Coach David motioned to Coach Bates and left the gym.

Coach Bates began to speak, "While I'm here, we're going to play my favorite sport, basketball. Grab a basketball and warm-up with some free shooting."

"This stinks. I actually liked volleyball," Olivia sighed.

Leaning on her crutches, Amanda grinned, "Just try to have fun!"

Olivia shot a contemptuous look at Coach Bates. Ida and I laughed and continued shooting. I had taken about twenty shots and had yet to make a single one. On the other hand, Ida was making basket after basket after basket.

"Can you help me?" I asked Ida. After Ida helped me find the right form, I bent my knees to shoot. My fingers grazed the ball as it left my hand, soared into the air, and fell into the net. Swish. I liked the sound of a swish. It was the sound of success.

At the end of class, Coach Bates blew into her whistle. As the shrill sound echoed around the gymnasium, she shouted, "If you had fun today playing basketball, consider trying out for the local YMCA team! Tryouts are tomorrow after school. Class dismissed."

As the girls headed back to the locker room, abrasive remarks arose regarding the coach, mainly from Jasmine's clique of popular girls.

"Did you see her hair?"

"What an awful lesson!"

"What kind of girl plays basketball?"

"Just because you stink at it doesn't mean every girl does," Ida fired back, clearly offended. "Basketball takes a lot of stamina, agility, and speed, and for your information, I am trying out for the team. If you have a problem with that, we can take it to the court."

"Whatever," Jasmine said, squinting at Ida. With that, Jasmine and her click sauntered from the locker room, whispering something we couldn't hear.

"Stuck up brats," I muttered, my voice rich with contempt.

Ida rolled her eyes, "I hate Jasmine's group."

Amanda shook her head, "They think they're superior like

they are so much better than us."

"Jasmine especially," Olivia added.

"See you guys later." Amanda waved goodbye, as she and Ida went one way and Olivia and I the other way.

I was heading to math when a boy's voice spoke in my ear. "Sandy, follow me." It was Brian. I'd recognize his voice anywhere.

"Brian, I can't be late for seventh period again," I quietly protested. "I don't even have a pass this time."

"There's a substitute in your class. Mrs. Brownsburg won't know. Plus, I promise to give you a fake pass when you go back to class. I have more to tell you. I got this note in my locker." Brian pulled a slip of paper out of his pocket and handed it to me.

STAY AWAY FROM THE GIRL.

I gaped at him, speechless. Finally, I managed, "Wh-when did you find this?"

"Just now," Brian told me, tucking the bit of paper back into his pocket, "and I'm going to find out who wrote it."

"How are you going to do that?"

"Well," Brian began, "I have some ideas. Come with me to room 209 if you want to know what they are."

• • •

"How are you planning to figure out who wrote you that note?" I asked once I closed the door to room 209.

"Well to start, I . . . I think this person knows about the Stone of Discedo, maybe even the same person who planted the stone in my locker in the first place."

"I don't know. That's kind of a leap."

"After finding out that magic exists, I'm not even sure what is and isn't a leap anymore," Brian sighed. "And also, I think you are the girl."

"Me?" I exclaimed. "I'm the girl?"

"Who else? You're the only girl I'm friends with. You're the only person I've really talked to since I transferred here. I can't think of any other girl it could be."

"Oh," I said. "So, I am the girl."

"Maybe someone has a crush on you or wants you all to themselves and thinks I'm an obstacle."

"Ew, no," I said, crinkling my nose and shaking my head. "Besides, you and I don't talk much where people can see anyway. How would anyone know we're friends?"

"I don't know," Brian said. "Then again, it's hard to believe me getting an anonymous note is unrelated to the Stone of Discedo. It can't just be a coincidence."

"I agree."

"Maybe the person who left the note is somehow connected to Valley Heights."

"Why would the person who wrote this have a connection with your old school?"

"Well, I've only been here for a few days, and I haven't talked to anyone other than you. I don't know how anyone could possibly know anything about the Stone of Discedo," Brian answered. He paused for a second, "Unless you told someone."

"No! No, I didn't. I swear. I swear I didn't tell anyone."

Brian sighed, "I believe you."

"Good." I nodded. "Well, what do we do?"

"I think we should try and narrow down who it could be."

"Well, it could be someone who works here, like a teacher or administrator. Maybe someone snuck into the school or signed into the school. Like a visitor or a volunteer."

"We should go check!" Brian and I started off, taking the longer, but less frequented route, ensuring none of the teachers saw us out of class.

The walls in the office were painted a dull pewter gray and in the center of the stark room sat three mahogany desks, two of them occupied, the other empty. The one on the far right belonged to a plump, kind-hearted secretary named Debra McLaughlin.

"Why are you two out of class?" Miss McLaughlin asked, putting a hand over the mouth of the phone and smiling warmly at me.

"Here's our pass," said Brian at once, showing her a sticky-note with some scribbles on it.

"What I meant was why are you here?"

"We, uh," I began, no words coming to mind.

"Sandy forgot her homework, and her mom promised to bring it in for her. We came to see if she'd come yet," Brian lied. I felt my heart drop. Brian had made a big mistake. Both Miss McLaughlin, as the person in charge of student records, and I knew I didn't have a mother or at least not one I could call.

Miss McLaughlin frowned. "Sandy doesn't—" I shook my head at Miss McLaughlin, silently begging her not to tell him.

She recovered smoothly. "Sandy never forgets her homework. And I think . . ." Miss McLaughlin typed something into the computer. "She has culinary for eighth period. I don't believe Chef Kris gives homework."

"Oh, uh . . ." Brian spluttered.

"What are you here for?" she asked us again, her eyes examining Brian. It was as if she was evaluating his honesty. I looked at Brian. He shrugged his shoulders. I decided to go for it.

"Can we look at the list of people who visited the school today?" I asked.

"As a matter of fact, I have it right here. Now normally I don't show this to students, but as you said before, Sandy's mom may have come by . . ." Miss McLaughlin winked at me, and I managed a small smile in return. Brian gratefully took the clipboard in his hand and scanned the list.

"Okay. Not many people have stopped by," he said.

Name	Reason	Check In Time	Check Out Time
Ben Stafford	PTSA Business	12:00	12:40
Cassandra Dane	Other	2:00	
Trevor Stanton	Meeting	2:15	
Lauren Li	Other	2:50	

Brian took a picture of the sign-in sheet with his phone when Miss McLaughlin turned away. When she turned back around, Brian passed Miss McLaughlin the clipboard and said to me, "I found the note at 2:40. Just before seventh period."

"What note, dear?" Miss McLaughlin questioned, slipping the clipboard back into her desk drawer.

"Nothing," I answered. "Thanks for the help, Miss McLaughlin. We better head back to class." Brian and I left the office without another word and began to walk back to room 209.

After we were out of earshot, he whispered, "Trevor Stanton. Maybe it was him who left the note." Trevor Stanton . . . the name sounded familiar.

"Isn't he a school board member?"

"He's the head, I think," Brian answered.

"Okay, but why on earth would he do that?"

"I don't know," Brian said, shaking his head.

"I don't think it was him," I said. "School board members, especially the head, aren't really involved with individual students. Besides, the handwriting on the sign-in sheet didn't seem to match the one on the note."

"He might have been in a rush writing the note or something." Brian suggested, examining it.

"I don't know, but if 'the girl' was referring to me, it can't be Stanton because he doesn't know who I am!"

"Just because you don't know him, doesn't mean he doesn't know you," Brian corrected. "I mean he is the head of the school board."

"There are thousands of students in the county. Do you really think he pays attention to each one of us individually?"

"I guess it's possible. Let's see who we can eliminate that could help. I think we can agree it's not Ben Stafford."

"Who?"

"A PTSA parent that came in at noon."

"Right," I said.

"And it's not Lauren Li," Brian continued. "She signed in after I saw the note in my locker. I still think Mr. Stanton left the note."

"Did you notice that Ms. Dane never signed out? She may still be here. And she put 'other' for the reason." I paused for a second and thought it over. "Then again, I don't know her. Do you?"

"Not in the slightest." Brian opened the door to room 209 and followed me in.

"We don't know any of the people that came into the school today, so I doubt any of them were responsible for the note. Plus, if the writer of the notes doesn't work here, I don't think they would've signed in. If you were leaving a note for someone, you wouldn't want to leave a trace, right? If you were trying to be anonymous, would you really sign in?"

"I think it would be a smart move to sign in," Brian countered. "You would blend in, nobody would suspect you."

"You've got a point there."

"Ugh, there are so many possibilities," Brian sighed, sitting down at a desk.

"I wish it was easier to figure this out. It's all so confusing," I rubbed my head. The room was silent for a moment until I added, "And the weird thing is, we're involved in this big mystery together, and I don't even know you that well."

"That's the weird thing? I would think a magical, time-traveling stone is the weird thing," Brian laughed, "but to each his own." We laughed together for a moment.

"Sandy, I still think it could be Mr. Stanton. Unlike Ms. Dane and the other people who signed in, he could know who we are."

"But probably not," I pointed out. "Why would anyone have the motive to leave you a note? Why does it matter to them anyway? And how would they have found out anything? I think the person who left this note snuck into the school. And to ... to do something like that, sneaking into the school just to leave a note, it must mean that this person cares about one of us. Or the stone. Plus, if someone were to come here and drop off a mysterious note with no name, they wouldn't sign in, would they?"

"Maybe," Brian shrugged, "but then again, everyone has to have a sign-in pass. If someone that doesn't work here is out on campus without a pass, they get sent back to the office."

I shook my head, "Yeah I guess that's true. But still, all the people who signed into school today are total strangers. Whoever left that note probably didn't sign in. I think the person who wrote the note would have snuck in."

Brian sighed. "This is so confusing."

"We can talk more another time. We should get back to class," I suggested. "Wait, how are we going to get to class? Class is more than ten minutes in and I don't even have a pass."

"Here," Brian handed me a sticky note with a fake signature on it.

"Will this work?"

"It better," Brian said. I raised my eyebrows in alarm. "I'm just kidding, Sandy. It'll work."

"Okay," I said, still a little doubtful. "Thanks." I scooped up my crimson drawstring bag and left the room. In a rush to get to class as soon as possible, I darted to my locker and opened it as fast as I could. As soon as I did, a small piece of folded paper fell out. I slowly picked it up and unfolded it. The note was written in the same handwriting as the note Brian received.

DON'T GET INVOLVED IN TROUBLE.

I was speechless. There were so many different possibilities of who it could be. Who left me this note? And why? I now doubted it could be a student, the second note seemed too serious and made no sense coming from someone of the same age. If the first note had been left by someone who had a crush on me, this second note didn't seem to fit. The only other options were visitors and staff. Did the writer of the notes work here? Or did they know how to sneak into the school? Maybe Brian was right, maybe the person who left the notes did sign in, and maybe it was Mr. Stanton. He could know who we were. Somehow, this person was able to get onto campus and know which locker belonged to me and which one belonged to Brian. Or maybe . . . maybe the writer of the note wasn't the same person as the one who left it. Maybe the person who wrote the note got someone, a student, a teacher, an administrator, a janitor, someone who can get on campus without signing in, to deliver the notes. My thoughts were broken up, and I suddenly didn't have time to think about it any longer. I needed to get to class.

Pocketing the note, I grabbed a notebook out of my locker and walked towards Mrs. Brownsburg's class, deep in thought.

• • •

The bell rang to end seventh period, and the thundering of footsteps filled the hallways. As I started walking towards the electives hallway, I spotted Brian walking towards the music suite.

"Brian, I have to tell you something."

"Yeah?"

"I got a note too. It was in my locker. Look." I shoved it into his outstretched hand. "I think it's safe to say it's probably not a student, but still we need to talk."

Brian shook his head, "We don't have time right now."

"Can we meet after school at the Red Bush Café?"

"Not today. I have band after school. How about Sunday?"

"Well, I . . . um . . ." Sunday was the day I moved to the orphanage. Part of me wanted to tell him I'm an orphan, but now just didn't seem like the time. "I'm busy Sunday. How about Saturday?" For a second, I wondered if Ms. Evelyn would be okay with me going out, but then I answered my own question—she'd be happy to get me out of the house and have it all to herself.

"Yeah, sure. Saturday at the Red Bush Café it is. Noon?"

"Sure, I'll see you then."

In eighth period culinary class, I tried to distract myself by helping a group of girls make their ravioli. Cooking was one of the only escapes from reality I had.

Chef Kris would even occasionally let me stay after school to cook or cleanup, which was far better than being home with Ms. Evelyn. Anywhere was better than home. My mind wandered, thinking about the notes, the stone, the move, the whole mystery in general. I soon became lost in the scents of the kitchen.

• • •

The next day, Thursday, had a light rain shower and cloudy skies. In first period history, my mind was elsewhere. Thinking, questioning everything I thought I knew. It was hard to grasp the fact time travel could really exist and a stone enabling it could be in Brian's possession. How did it get from a lab in Germany to America, and then into Brian's possession? Why Brian of all people? Who was leaving these notes, and why? Were they a warning, or a threat? Did the person leaving the notes know about Brian and the stone?

Mr. Mason, the history teacher, always began class with a "Today in History." Once he finished, he asked the class questions; however, the only one who seemed to know the answers was Brian.

"What happened April of 1861?" Mr. Mason questioned. He looked around the room hopefully, but nobody's hand was raised other than Brian's. "Yes, Brian?"

"The Civil War started," Brian answered.

"How did it start?" Mr. Mason queried. This time he didn't even bother scanning the classroom for others to answer. "Yes, Brian?"

"The Civil War started when the Confederates bombarded Union soldiers at Fort Sumter," Brian answered.

"Very good, Brian. Now here's a question for anyone but Brian: Who won the Civil War and what was the result?" He scanned the room, but nobody seemed eager to answer. "Ida?" he asked, even though she hadn't raised her hand.

"Well, um, the Union won . . ."

"And what was the result of that?"

"I don't know," Ida said.

"Okay, then," Mr. Mason sighed, accepting defeat. "Brian?"

"The Union won the war, and slavery was abolished. The country was one again."

"Very good, Brian." I wondered if Mr. Mason would ever get tired of saying that.

"Can anyone tell me what Reconstruction was?" Again, nobody but Brian raised their hand. "Brian?"

"Reconstruction occurred after the Civil War. It was the remaking of the Southern United States."

"Fantastic answer," Mr. Mason said, looking very pleased.

When the time came for lunch, I found myself surrounded by my friends in the cafeteria, talking vehemently about all the assigned homework.

"Sandy?" Brian walked over to me in the lunchroom.

"Hold on, Ida," I said. As I turned to Brian, Ida winked at me.

"Yeah?" I asked him.

"Can I talk to you for a minute?" he sounded desperate. Urgent.

"Sure," I spooned a final scoop of mashed potatoes into my mouth and threw away my trash. I left the cafeteria with Brian tugging me to the same deserted classroom as before.

"What is it?"

"I've been thinking . . . What did Miss McLaughlin mean yesterday? You know, when she was about to say something then changed it? What was that about? Are you hiding something?"

"Umm . . . well . . ." I sat there, unsure whether to trust him with the information. The only other people who knew were Ida, Olivia, and Amanda. "Well," I inhaled deeply, making my decision on the spot, "I don't . . . I don't have a mom." No need to mention my father. Not yet, at least. Having one parent is very different than having none.

"Oh." A mixture of sympathy and sorrow broke over Brian's pale face, and he locked his fingers together in an awkward way. He averted his eyes. "Sandy, I'm really sorry."

I looked at him and wanted to cry. His eyes looked into mine as he slowly lifted his head. I felt a strange sensation like he was reading my mind.

"I have to go now," Brian said finally after a minute of silence. "Ummm . . . Here's my number." He scribbled his name and number on a bit of paper and handed it to me. "See you Saturday. Bye Sandy." He left, and I slipped the paper into my backpack.

I felt overwhelmed, confused, stressed, and exhausted, and wanted more than anything to get away. To escape my life, even for just a small amount of time. I hated that my parents left me, intentional or otherwise. I hated that I would have to leave my friends. I resented the world, and all the people in it who took what they had for granted; people who have parents, a future, and a spot in this world. They don't know what it's like to not have a family. They don't understand what it's like to be alone. I didn't just understand it, I lived it. I sat there, staring at the wall, missing my parents, feeling completely lost, confused, and alone.

• • •

At the end of the day, I went outside to wait in the car line.

I climbed into the backseat of Ms. Evelyn's car. The moment I closed the door, she said, "When we get home, clean the dishes and make dinner. I have stuff to do."

After I dropped my bag on my bed upstairs, I set to work, knowing it wasn't worth it to argue with Ms. Evelyn. With a barely audible, exasperated sigh, I grabbed a soapy sponge and began to scrub.

Once I finished the dishes, I started on dinner. At times, it seemed like just another chore, but cooking was one of my favorite things to do. The constant struggle of forcing down Ms. Evelyn's food gave me reasons to offer to cook dinner almost every night. My food was more than tolerable. It was actually tasty, unlike the nasty chicken fingers or grilled cheese sandwiches Ms. Evelyn made. I'd learned how to cook from watching the Food Network when Ms. Evelyn let me watch TV. Cooking helped me escape the world, to get my mind off things.

I opened the fridge, looking for edible ingredients. I started to make burgers, placing the patties onto the frying pan, my senses captivated by the scent. The smell of the burgers, the sizzling of the hot pan . . . cooking was my safe place. I closed my eyes and inhaled, taking a moment to appreciate what I did have.

Friday was a slow day; nothing seemed to happen. With the minor exceptions of goodbye hugs from my friends, hardly anyone seemed to notice or care I was leaving. Some of my teachers mentioned it to me, Mr. Phillips even gave me a card, but other than that, the day was just like any other. At the end of the day, when I was waiting by the car line for Ms. Evelyn, Brian came up to me.

"Hey, Sandy," he said.

"Brian, I was wondering," lowering my voice to a whisper. "Is there any way I could see the stone? Do you have it with you?"

"Yeah, I have it with me, but that's only because our house gets cleaned every Friday, and sometimes on Tuesdays. I don't want it to be found accidentally. I think you know I can't show it to you, at least not with so many people around."

"Could I come over to your house then?" I asked. "Sorry, I'm not trying to invite myself over, that was rude—"

Brian laughed. "No, it's okay. Sandy, I'm sorry, but when our house is being cleaned, I'm not allowed to have anyone over." He smiled and added, "Not that I've ever really had anyone to invite over anyway."

"It's okay."

"That's my ride, I've got to go. I'll see you tomorrow."

"I hope so," I crossed my fingers, wondering what I would do if Ms. Evelyn said no.

• • •

Saturday morning, I walked downstairs and found Ms. Evelyn in the den on her computer.

"Ms. Evelyn, can I . . . can I walk to the Red Bush Café? I'm supposed to meet a friend . . . it's um, a final school project that we, um, have to finish."

"Hold on a second," Ms. Evelyn pulled out her phone and typed something in. She waited for a second, staring at her phone and then said, "Yes, I suppose you can go. But you are to go straight there and back. Nowhere else. I expect you home in two hours."

It was a raw, ruthlessly chilly spring day with a bitter breeze. Nonetheless, I walked close to a mile to the Red Bush Café to meet Brian. Stepping into the café, I was greeted by the welcoming scents of warm cups of coffee and sugary desserts. With rosy cheeks and chattering teeth, I walked over to where Brian was sitting, his nose buried in a book.

"Hey, Brian," I said, sliding into the booth across from him.

"Hey, Sandy! What do you want to eat?" Brian asked. "Whatever you want, it's on me."

"I'll just have a hot chocolate." We quickly ordered and began to talk. I told him about the note and my evaluation of it.

"Like I said, I think that whoever left the notes probably snuck in. I really don't think they would have signed in."

"But maybe they did sign in. People who don't work at the school have to have a pass to be on campus," Brian said. "Maybe it was Mr. Stanton. He could know who we are."

"I guess it's possible," I admitted. "Possible, yet unlikely."

"Well, who do you think might've snuck in?"

"I don't know. I guess . . . I'm not sure. Maybe the writer of the notes works at the school. Like a teacher or administrator or something."

"Well I still think it's Mr. Stanton," said Brian. "Can you think of any teachers who would leave you that note?"

"Oh my gosh."

"What?"

"Mr. Phillips," I said. "He's nice to me. Maybe he left the 'Don't get involved in trouble' note to try and keep me safe at my next school."

"You think he cares about you enough to leave a note in your locker?"

"Maybe."

"Why would he have told me to stay away from you, though?" Brian asked.

"Maybe he thinks you're trouble? Maybe after hearing our conversation on your first day here, he thought we shouldn't be friends for some reason? Maybe he knows you encouraged me to skip class?"

"I don't know, Sandy. Why wouldn't he have just talked to you? Why would he have left notes?"

"Oh," I said, feeling defeated. "Yeah, you're right. Mr. Phillips also gave me a card, so why would he leave me a note as well? Still, I think it's more likely to be Mr. Phillips than Mr. Stanton."

"They are both reasonable suspects, as they were both there at the time the notes were dropped off. They both have access to records to find out which lockers are ours."

"But as far as we know, only Mr. Phillips might have a motive," I objected. "He is the one person who cares about me enough to do something like this."

"Hmmm . . ."

"We also don't know if the notes are a warning or a threat."

"We can't figure that out unless we know who wrote them," Brian said. "Wait—what if this has something to do with the stone? What if someone knows I have the stone and is trying to keep us apart? Maybe the note-writer wants to keep you away from me because I am 'trouble?'"

"Oh my gosh, you could be right."

"The thought of that terrifies me," Brian admitted. "I could go to jail . . . or worse."

I couldn't think of what would be worse, maybe he thought he'd be put to death, but I didn't have time to wonder.

Brian continued, "Now that I think about it, it does sound like someone is trying to keep you out of this. This whole thing, with the stone, it's . . . well, it's bigger than the two of us. So many people believe it's out there, dozens of countries are searching for it. They just don't know where to look." He put his head in his hands and rubbed his eyes.

"Hey," I leaned over the table. Brian looked up at me. "We'll figure this out."

"Thanks for the optimism, Sandy, really, I mean it, but it's not going to be that easy."

"I know, but I'm in this with you," I said. "Anyway, I was thinking, and I came up with an idea."

"And it is . . .?"

"I thought maybe . . . maybe the writer of the note wasn't the same person as the one who left it. Maybe the person who wrote the note got someone who can get on campus without signing in to deliver the notes."

"I definitely think that's a possibility," Brian agreed. "I'm going to sleep on it. I'll talk to you if I think of something else."

"How? I won't be at Mountain View anymore," I objected.

"I'll find a way. I always do."

"Okay. I trust you." There was silence between us for a while before Brian changed the subject.

"Are you hiding something? Is there more to your story than just not having a mom?"

I opened my mouth to respond, but then closed it just

as fast. Should I tell him? The clear answer was 'yes.' Brian had shared his biggest secret with me, a secret so big that by telling me he was risking his life. If he told me a secret like that, why shouldn't I be honest and tell him I was basically an orphan?

"Yes, there is more, something I didn't tell you yet," I said. My heart was picking up speed. "My parents . . . they disappeared when I was four. I don't know if they are alive or dead. I live with a woman named Ms. Evelyn Marsh, who is basically a temporary foster parent. I'm moving into an orphanage tomorrow, and like I told you, I'm switching schools too. I'll be going to Rolling Hills Middle School."

"I'm so sorry . . ." Brian murmured. And then his eyes widened. Maybe it had taken a few moments to let that information soak in. "Wait," his voice was low, "did you say Evelyn Marsh?"

"Yes, why?"

"Evelyn Marsh?" Brian repeated, his eyebrows almost disappearing into his hair.

"Yes, why?"

"I guess our lives are more intertwined than we thought," Brian said. He looked like he was still trying to grasp the concept. "Evelyn Marsh's sister . . ."

"Abigail? What about her?" I asked.

"She's my . . . biological mom," Brian said as if ashamed.

"Wait, your—"

"Yes, my biological mom. I didn't find out until somewhat recently that her name was Abigail Marsh. When I knew you in third grade, I wasn't able to make that connection—"

"Let me get this straight," I said. "Your biological mom is Abigail Marsh?"

"Yeah, she's my biological mom, but she's never been anything more. As soon as she gave birth to me, she relinquished her parental rights and put me into the foster care system. She probably didn't want the permanent responsibility."

I was appalled, gaping open-mouthed at Brian. "Then why on earth did she open an orphanage?"

"For the money," Brian muttered, "out of greed, maybe. I don't know."

"Can I ask you something?"

"Sure."

"Who do you live with now? And why isn't your last name Marsh?"

"Well, I live with a foster family," Brian replied. "At first, I was bouncing around from home to home, but I've been lucky enough to stay in this foster home for a few years now. They're nice. But honestly, I don't know why my last name is Moore. My foster parents' last name is McCormick, and my biological mom's last name is Marsh."

"What was your biological dad's last name?"

Brian sighed. "I never knew my biological dad. I don't even know his name."

"Brian, I'm sorry." At least I knew my dad, even if just for a brief time.

"It's okay," Brian shrugged. "You don't miss what you never had."

"Can I ask you something else?" I asked.

"Why so many questions?"

"I'm just interested, I guess."

"Alright, what's the question?"

"What really happened when you used the Stone of Discedo?"

Brian shifted in his chair. "I got stuck in time. For three months, I lived in the 1980s. It was a completely different place. When I got back to the present, three months had gone by, and I had missed so much . . .

"Were you still in Ohio when you were in the 80s?"

"Yes, I was still in Ohio. The only good thing that came of it was I got to see what the 80s were like. This building didn't even exist. This area was just an extension of the forest. None of these neighborhoods were around. It was just cornfields, forests, and a couple of streets," Brian told me. "In a way, it was cool to see. The cars were so weird, the phones were big, awkward, and hooked to the wall. The technology was totally different. Nobody had cell phones or laptops or tablets, and there wasn't Netflix or YouTube or things like that for people to watch videos on. Nobody had flat screen TVs or high definition television! Everyone survived without it. They did have movie theaters, though. In fact, I saw Back to the Future when it first came out. I know, I know, the irony. Oh, and the cars, no one used seatbelts, and nobody had electric cars. Oh, and the music . . . never mind, you probably don't care."

"That's not true!" I objected. "I think it's fascinating. When you were trapped in the 80's, where did you live?"

"For a while, the streets and for a while, an orphanage," he responded.

"Oh," I said, staring at the table. "Wait. Does that mean your foster parents know about this?"

"No. I just . . ." Brian fidgeted. "I had to lie. If I told them, I'd put them in danger, and I couldn't do that to them. I just told them I was being bullied, so I ran away. They switched my school too, you know, 'Keep me away from the bullies and give me a fresh start.' It worked out well because everyone at Valley Heights got suspicious and curious about what happened to me. I felt guilty for lying to my foster parents, but sometimes there is a higher priority than telling the truth."

"Like the Stone of Discedo," I said.

Sipping his drink, he nodded. "Exactly."

"Can you explain to me why you are so sure Mr. Stanton left the notes?" I asked after a minute of silence. "It doesn't really make any sense to me."

"Well, my foster parents had to go to the school board to get my school switched, so I met him briefly. I don't know if he remembers me or not, it's just a gut feeling that he has something to do with this. I don't know, Sandy, I really don't. I don't know any of the other people who signed into the school that day, and neither do you, and I . . ." his voice trailed off.

"That's why I think it's Mr. Phillips! It just makes sense! He has the motive, the means, and the opportunity—"

Brian's phone vibrated in his pocket. "I'm sorry, hold on a second." Brian pulled out his phone and read whatever was on the screen. "I've got to go," he muttered, jumping to his feet.

"Already?"

"I'm really sorry. Bye, Sandy." Brian threw some money down on the table, then waved goodbye and left the café. I watched him until he was swallowed up in the distance.

* * *

Sunday morning was another gray and rainy day. After pulling a brush through my hair, I hurried downstairs for breakfast. The night had been rough. I struggled with the concept that I might miss Mountain View Middle School.

Ms. Evelyn hadn't told me what time Ms. Abigail would be coming, so I waited out the day in anticipation.

That evening, I was busy mopping the floor when I heard a voice. "Open up!" a woman demanded from outside, banging relentlessly on the door.

"Sandy! Get the door!" Ms. Evelyn ordered from her bedroom. I opened the door, and a tall woman with bright red hair stepped into the room. The woman's face looked cakey with layers of makeup, her eyelashes unnaturally long and her cheeks impossibly pink. The woman looked down at me, her face showing thinly veiled signs of displeasure.

"Are you Sandy?" Ms. Abigail asked.

"Yes," I said, suddenly uneasy.

"C'mon, let's go. We haven't got all night." Ms. Abigail's face, though thickly covered in layers of makeup, showed discomfort. Why was she anxious around me? Well, maybe it wasn't me . . . maybe she was nervous being around her sister? But why?

"Don't you want to say hello to your sister first?" I inquired, slinging my faded drawstring bag onto my shoulder and wheeling my suitcase to the door.

"I don't have time," Ms. Abigail said. As if on cue, Ms. Evelyn came downstairs, and saw her sister.

"Abigail," she nodded formally.

"Evelyn," Ms. Abigail replied with a curt nod of the head. The sisters' blunt exchange was laughable. I stifled a giggle and brought my bags outside.

I wouldn't miss what I was about to leave behind: the chores, rules, discipline, and loneliness. Not at all. Or would I?

FOUR

I sat in the backseat of the car, rummaging through my drawstring bag. My suitcase was in the trunk, and I prayed I remembered to pack everything, not that I had much to pack. All my clothes were previously used, bought from thrift shops and Goodwills, just like everything I owned. My most valuable possession was my little doll, Jessie. My doll and my faded drawstring bag were the only things I had left from my parents.

Curiously, I peeked out the window. The moon offered little light, a slim silver crescent. The sky was starless, an empty black blanket. I was submerged in thought. Leaving Ms. Evelyn's house caused mixed feelings. I grew up hating it, hating her, but I recently realized that maybe it wasn't the house I hated. Maybe I hated not having parents. I wasn't sure why Ms. Evelyn opened her home to me. She bought me clothes and food and school supplies, the basic needs and nothing more, but still. She took care of me for eight years, and through all those years . . . I rarely said thank you.

As the car drove along, I pressed a hand to the cold window, wishing I could go back and say thank you. I never truly appreciated Ms. Evelyn or her house, but I should have. She made sacrifices for me, for eight years. A tear rolled down my cheek, and I didn't bother to wipe it away because more were soon to come.

• • •

It was late, and night was falling quickly upon South Toheeden. Ms. Abigail drove on, and the calming scents of pine and honeysuckle were replaced by an acrid aroma of stale beer. Trash cans lay on their sides, the contents spilling out of them, surrounded by hungry rats scampering around the garbage. Lampposts flickered feebly before going out, and the ones that were lit cast shadows across the dark alleys.

My mind wandered away, a happy daydream that kept me safe from the pain of reality. Yet somehow, my mind traveled back to the unanswered question I'd asked myself for years. Were my parents alive? Were they out there somewhere, unaware of how much danger their daughter might be in? Or were they dead, gone for good?

Hope for my parents' return was slowly draining from me. I felt I would never again know what it's like to be loved by my parents. I would never know the feeling of cuddling up with my mom to share a mug of hot cocoa on a winter's day. I would never know the feeling of taking out an old Monopoly game to play with my dad. I would never know what it's like to sit down at a table for a family dinner and talk about my day with people who cared. There were so many things that I would never be able to know, to feel, or to understand.

After a while of driving in silence, the only sound being the gentle hum of the engine, I was relieved to finally get out of the car. Ms. Abigail's orphanage was large and brick and sat back twenty feet from the road. The driveway was wide, and there were two vans parked side by side as well as a yellow school bus.

The orphanage was an old building, but there was something interesting about it. It was two stories high, complete with massive windows and a stone threshold that was curved into a braided design, embossed with curls, swirls, and spirals. The beauty of the doorframe was the one attractive thing about the place; the rest was dismal and screamed of neglect.

I grabbed my suitcase from the trunk, my drawstring bag hanging on my shoulder. Tentatively, I walked up the steep steps to the mahogany door. Anxiety thundered through my veins, and my hands began to sweat. My heart pounded, and I grew steadily more nervous. Ms. Abigail entered the orphanage and left the door open for me to follow. A petite Asian woman was standing in the foyer and waved at me when I entered. I assumed she worked here.

"Sixth-grade is upstairs, the last rooms. Girls are on the left, boys are on the right. I'll call Nick to help you with your bag," Ms. Abigail said in a cool voice. "Nick! Come down here!" she called. A skinny boy with unruly brown hair came running down the carpeted stairs. "Get her suitcase," Ms. Abigail ordered.

"Madam," Nick said, bowing to me.

"Nick," Ms. Abigail said through gritted teeth. Nick laughed and subserviently hoisted my suitcase into his arms and walked slowly back up the stairs. I followed, still trembling.

"Who was the woman downstairs?" I asked Nick. "Not Ms. Abigail, the other one."

"Oh, that's Jade," Nick explained. "She works here. Ms.

Abigail has a few assistants, but normally her assistants don't last very long, other than Jade. She's been here the longest." I followed him to the upstairs hallway. The hallway was long, and there were eight rooms on each side of the hallway. At the very end of the hallway was a fire exit. I followed Nick into the sixth-grade girls' bedroom. The sixth-grade girls' bedroom was the last bedroom on the left and had a pink number 6 on the wooden door.

Nick wheeled my suitcase beside my new bed. "This one is yours," he told me. Then he turned to face the group of kids hanging out in the room. "Guys!" he shouted. Nobody paid any attention, so he raised his voice a level and yelled, "Guys! Shut up! We have a new, um, friend." He turned to me. "What's your name?"

"Sandy," I answered softly. All the people in the room turned to look at me, their eyes filled with wonder and pity.

"Well, welcome, I guess, Sandy," Nick grinned. His mischievous green eyes looked me up and down. "What's your last name?"

I shifted my weight from foot to foot. I often did that when I was nervous. Should I tell them the truth? That my last name was the same as Ms. Abigail's? They'd find out sooner or later.

"Marsh," I murmured so quietly I wasn't sure if they could hear it.

"Marsh? Did she say Marsh?" One of the girls, the one with auburn hair, asked, looking at me with wide eyes.

"I think so," Nick said.

"Yes, my last name is Marsh," I confirmed.

"Are we missing something here?" the same girl asked.

"Well . . ." I began, "I used to live with Ms. Evelyn Marsh, Ms. Abigail's sister. Um, I don't know why my last name changed, because that wasn't the name on my birth certificate but . . . yeah," I finished awkwardly.

"So, you're not actually related to the Marshes?" Nick asked.

"Right," I nodded. I hoped they wouldn't think any less of me because of this.

It was awkwardly quiet for a while until Nick broke the silence. "I'm not exactly sure what to say. We haven't gotten a new permanent person in our grade since forever. I mean, we've had a few stay for a night or two. Most come and go." There was something about the word 'permanent' that sent a chill running down my spine. Nick said, "I guess in most scenarios it would be polite to say that we're glad to have you here, but it's probably not the right thing to say . . ."

"I can take over from here." A tall, intelligent-looking boy raised his head from a book and smiled at me. He looked identical to Nick. The only differences I could detect were the boy's studious brown eyes and glasses that gave him the look of a wise professor. The boy also had a few inches over Nick, who I assumed was closely related to him. "I'm Rick. Nick's older and more mature twin."

"Older by four minutes," Nick muttered.

"Yes, but still older," Rick smiled.

"I'll do all the introductions," said Nick. "I am perfectly calpable of doing it on my own."

"It's pronounced capable," Rick corrected as he returned to his novel.

"Now then," Nick continued. "This is Aaron. He's kind of the jokester in our group—"

"I can introduce myself, thank you very much, and I happen to find myself of quite the studious character." Aaron grinned devilishly at Nick, then turned his gaze to me. The boy, Aaron, had eyes the color of mud, a goofy, crooked smile, and untamed curly hair. Aaron was kind of scrawny, maybe due to a lack of decent food.

"Oh please," said Nick to Aaron. "*You* and *studious* don't even belong in the same sentence. Anyway, this is Rebecca." The taller girl jumped to her feet.

"Hi, Sandy. It's nice to meet you!" Rebecca had long, dark hair eased back into a ponytail. She smiled at me, enthusiastically shaking my hand.

"I'd love to show you around!" Rebecca offered.

"I'll help give a tour too," Aaron added. "Besides Rebecca, Nick, and Rick, I've been here the longest even though I'm the youngest. I'm still eleven."

"Oh, Sandy, by the way, I'm Tessa. I guess Nick forgot to introduce me," Tessa lowered her voice. "If you stay long enough, you'll know that him forgetting things isn't a surprise." She drew back and winked. Nick, unfortunately, overheard and his face became bright red with embarrassment.

I must've had a surprised look on my face, because Rebecca said, "Sandy, you should know that the five of us are close, we're like brothers and sisters. We joke around with each other, the boys pull pranks on us, and we tease them. It's how we are."

"Okay," I said, unsure if I should say anything else.

"We're close enough to be able to joke around and not offend one another," added Tessa. Her long auburn hair framed her face, effortlessly beautiful. She wore a white T-shirt and jeans.

"C'mon. This way," Rebecca beckoned to me, grinning slightly as she led me down the hall.

"Can I ask you guys something?"

"Sure, go ahead," Aaron nodded.

"Why is this place called an orphanage?"

"What do you mean?" Rebecca frowned at me.

"Aren't most places called group homes nowadays? I didn't think the term 'orphanage' was used anymore."

"Yeah, well some places are called group homes or children's homes, but everyone knows it's an orphanage," Rebecca explained. "And also, this place has been open for a long time."

"Oh," I said. "I guess that makes sense."

"Let's begin the tour, shall we?" Aaron grinned. He and Rebecca led me down the hallway. "Okay, that's the Beheading Room, and this one is where we keep all the mentally ill people. This is the room where we keep the knives and ninja gear, and finally, this room is the worst of all . . . the boys' bathroom." We all laughed.

"He's kidding," Rebecca promised. "Those are bedrooms. As you walk through the hallway, the older kids are at the front, the youngest at the back. The bedrooms on the left are girls, and the bedrooms on the right are boys."

"Wait it's split by gender and grade?" I asked.

"Yeah," said Rebecca. "But the five of us always hang out in the girls' room. Mostly because it's a lot neater."

"It's true," Aaron added. "Our room is a mess."

"What's the door at the end of the hallway?" I asked.

"It's a fire exit," Rebecca answered. "Ms. Abigail says if anyone tries to use it to get out, an alarm will go off, so avoid it."

Aaron paused, "Are you following so far?"

"I think so."

"Good." Rebecca nodded. "In both hallways, the bathrooms are in the middle. Boys' bathrooms are on the right, girls' bathrooms on the left. Still following?"

"Yeah."

"Here's a little disclaimer though: the bathrooms really do smell, even with Ms. Abigail's disgusting flower-scented air freshener. Use the bathroom at school if you can."

"Got it." I took a mental note to try and use the school bathrooms, even though those couldn't possibly be much better.

"We're so lucky, now that we are middle schoolers. We get to share a bathroom with the high schoolers here," Aaron added sarcastically. He and Rebecca led me to the first floor and pointed to a door across from the foot of the stairs. "This room . . . this room is what we call the Dream Room."

"The what?"

"The Dream Room," Rebecca repeated in a longing voice. "It's the Adoption Room."

I knew I wasn't ready to be adopted now, but maybe in the future, I could find a loving home with loving parents. I wanted more than anything for my parents to come back, but every second I remained an orphan drained a little hope from my heart. Part of me knew I'd never get them back, that there would always be a hole in my heart that no one else could fill. But maybe, now that I lived in the orphanage, I could someday be adopted and join a new family.

Rebecca continued, "The only problem is, it's the little kids they want. I've come to face the fact that I'll never be adopted. For a while I had my hopes up, hoping that someone would choose me to be their child—"

"Oh, come on, Rebecca, you're bumming her out," Aaron interrupted. "It's her first day. Give her time to take it all in and adjust."

"I know, but I don't want her to get her hopes up. I don't want her to make the same mistake I did," Rebecca's eyes met mine. "One thing you should know is . . . we are a family. The five of us."

"Six of us, now," Aaron corrected.

"Right. Thanks," Rebecca nodded. "The six of us, we are family. Despite what Nick may have led you to believe, it's not that bad here. The food may be a little . . . unappetizing, and the chores aren't fun, and Ms. Abigail—"

"Get to the point!" Aaron interrupted.

"I'm getting there! Like I was saying, you've joined the family now. All of us, we are here for you. It will take some time to adjust, but that's why we are here. To help you."

"Aww, Rebecca, that's sweet," I said, feeling close to tears. "I really appreciate that. Thank you."

"Anywaaay," Aaron said. "The older you are, the more kids in your grade there are," he explained, "because nobody wants us. Potential parents want the young kids."

"The cuter kids," Rebecca added with a painful grimace. "The ones they can help teach and shape. The kids that they can raise, the ones they can watch grow."

"Oh," I felt my heart sink, plummeting into my stomach. The blossom of hope that had persisted shriveled up and died, like a candle being blown out. I was never going to be adopted. I would never have parents again. But maybe . . . maybe it could be like Rebecca said. Maybe I would find a family in my new friends.

"There's one more thing," said Rebecca.

"Are we showing her the SE?"

"Yes, I think we should."

"What's the SE?" I asked, confused.

"You'll see," Aaron said with a smirk.

I followed the two of them into the lifeless yard behind the orphanage. It was mostly dirt, with a few splotches of dying grass. We were closed in by a high fence with barbed wire at the top. There was a rusted jungle gym that had clearly sat idle for years, and a rotting wooden treehouse that didn't look like it could hold any weight. In the left corner, there was an empty wooden shed covered in shadows from the large oak tree in the middle. Rebecca called me over to the shed.

"You want to show me a shed?" I asked.

Rebecca grinned and gestured for me to follow her. There was a large hole in the fence, just big enough for a person to get in or out.

"If we need to get out, we use the SE. It stands for Secret Exit," she explained, "and so far, Ms. Abigail hasn't noticed. Only the middle schoolers and high schoolers know about it. Once you graduate elementary school, the secret gets passed down to you."

"That's kinda cool," I said, even though I couldn't imagine a situation where I would need to escape.

Just then, it began to rain. The sudden downpour drenched my clothes as we sprinted back into the orphanage. The rain was cold and wet. Strangely, it felt good. It washed away my past, my fears, my worries. The rain gave me a new beginning. Hopefully, I wouldn't mess it up.

* * *

Once I got into bed, I grabbed my tattered little doll. I hugged Jessie every night. She renewed the hope my parents would someday return. Not knowing what happened to them was the worst part. Were they still out there trying to find me, or had they died? Did they know their daughter cried every night in her sleep, wishing and hoping to someday have her family back?

FIVE

That night I was restless. My mind buzzed, alive and full of thoughts and questions. The next morning, Monday, I awoke, my eyes underlined with purple bags.

"Here's the schedule for your new school, Rolling Hills. You start next Monday. Principal Higgins decided to give you a week to adjust before you start your new school. He said it would be a lot, probably too much, for you to start all these new things at once." Rick talked fast, and when he was done, he returned to his book.

Nick picked up where his twin left off, "Ms. Abigail insisted you start tomorrow, but the principal disagreed. Anyway, Principal Higgins assigned Tessa and Rebecca to show you around when your first day comes."

"School starts at 9:00, Ms. Abigail takes us on a bus, and we leave at 8:00. We eat the free breakfast at school. School ends at 4:15. In the afternoon we take the bus home, and we're back by 4:50. We do homework till 6:00 and for us, dinner runs from 6:00 to 6:45. The rest of the night is free time. Oh, and I'm sure you probably already knew this, but you'll have to get school lunch."

Those last two words drew up memories of a poem my parents had read me that made me laugh.

There once was a student,

Named Abigail Cleaton,

It's hard to believe what she tried,

Abigail Cleaton ate school food,

And Abigail Cleaton just died.

I wanted to smile, but at the same time, I wanted to gag. School cafeteria food was never anything better than barely edible.

"Get your taste buds ready to die," Aaron told me. "Mine already passed away."

"Aaron held a funeral for his taste buds on the second day of middle school," Tessa giggled.

"Point being, Rolling Hills's lunches are as bad as the other schools in the county," Rebecca laughed. Aaron mimed vomiting. Tessa handed me my schedule.

"It looks like you have at least one of us in each of your classes!" she said.

"How do you know their schedules?" I inquired.

"I guess I just have a good memory," Tessa replied with a shrug of her shoulders.

"Good? Are you kidding? Tessa could tell you precisely what she wore a year ago yesterday," Nick put in incredulously.

"A pale lavender T-shirt, denim blue jeans, white Adidas socks and my blue tennis shoes," Tessa recalled, smiling with mingled pride and pleasure.

"She has a photographic memory," Rebecca explained.

"An eidetic memory," Tessa corrected.

"Tomato, to-mah-toh," said Aaron from across the room.

"It's time to go," Rick said. "Let's head downstairs."

"Bye, Sandy! We'll see you later!" Rebecca said, waving good-bye.

About fifteen minutes after they left, the petite Asian woman I'd seen upon arrival, Jade, came up to the sixth-grade girls' bedroom

"I'm Jade, I don't think I ever actually introduced myself," she said. Jade handed me a bag of pre-packaged muffins. "Sorry, it's not something better. This was all I could get for you."

"Thanks, Jade," I said, taking the muffins. For lunch, she brought me a sandwich, which I ate in less than five minutes.

The day was long. I got lonely, not to mention bored. I ended up cracking open one of Rick's many library books. Finally, the others returned home but were buried in homework. Dinner was split into two shifts: first were pre-k and elementary school and second were the middle and high schoolers. When it was 6:00, time for the second shift, the six of us sprinted downstairs, hoping to be first in line.

About forty kids were living in the orphanage, mostly older kids, which made sense because the younger ones were the ones who got adopted. Even though it was split into two shifts, it was still chaotic. The dining hall had four tables. Rebecca, Nick, Rick, Tessa, Aaron, and I sat together at the one in the far corner.

"Hey, are you doing okay?" I heard a voice ask me. I looked up, and there was Jade.

"I'm okay, thank you," I said.

"It can be hard the first few days here," Jade said. "Let me know if you need anything."

"I will," I said, forcing a smile.

Once we finished our food—meatloaf and mashed potatoes— Rebecca suggested we go get some fresh air. It was unanimous. We all walked out into the backyard and sat under the oak tree.

I could hear the distant sounds of cars, the faint humming of birds—the town falling asleep. The soothing and refreshing spring night air smelled pleasantly of honeysuckle and pine trees. I let the arms of nature cradle me, surrounding me with all the beauty and pleasure they could offer.

After our brief time outside, the boys went up to their room, and we went to ours. I crawled into bed and curled up between the sheets which smelled of bleach. I pressed my head into the pillow, still contemplating all the things that had happened to me—*Brian, the Stone of Discedo, the mysterious messages, the move, and my new friends.*

I looked across the room, through the window, out at the night sky. Wispy clouds streaked the sky which was peppered with stars. The crescent moon sat silvery-white above the clusters of buildings, gleaming down upon the world.

Suddenly, a thought blossomed. Leave. Go for a walk. I needed fresh air; I needed some time outside, alone. I grabbed my jacket and drawstring bag. Silently, I tip-toed across the room, trying not to make even the slightest sound. I hoped that if Rebecca and Tessa happened to hear me, they would figure I was going to the bathroom.

As I moved towards the door, I considered going down the fire exit, but opening the door would set off an alarm, according to Rebecca. So instead, I slipped out the back of the orphanage and crawled through the hole in the fence. Once safely outside, the eerie silence and cool night air enveloped me. Slowly, I began to walk away. Just a little walk was sure to help me clear my mind and make me feel better.

I really was an orphan now. Yet somehow, I felt less alone. At least now, I had a family, as unusual as it might be. Tears began to brim in my eyes and fall onto my face, leaving glistening tracks in their wake. As I walked, I felt my mind calm down.

I walked about half a mile and was about to turn back when the rustle of a nearby bush caught my ear. I whirled around, but there was nothing there. I was probably imagining things. I turned around and bowed my head, so bewildered, so confused, so lost in my own mind. Suddenly, I walked into a man and looked up at him. My heart stopped, I couldn't think straight.

The man had dark balding hair streaked with gray. He wore dark green pants to match his shirt and a thick black belt, a deputy's uniform. He had a gun in one holster and a taser in the other. The deputy was slightly potbellied, and his head was sitting directly on his shoulders. I wondered if there was a neck in there somewhere.

"Where are you going? Where are your parents?" he asked in a gruff voice. When he talked, his toothbrush mustache quivered above his upper lip. He pulled his ID badge and showed it to me; not that I needed proof. I noticed his name was Deputy Brute. In any other situation, this name would be comical, but not here. Not now. "Did your parents drop you off somewhere at this time of night?" the deputy asked suspiciously. "Where are you headed?" I pursed my lips and searched my brain, desperate for a suitable answer.

"Uh," I mumbled. My heart began to race, faster and faster. I felt like I was going to pass out. I could hear my heart beat, louder than the chirping crickets or the hum of the police car waiting at the curb.

"You're not the talkative kind, are you?" Deputy Brute pulled a pen and paper from his chest pocket. "What's your name?"

"Sandy Marsh," I said, staring pointedly at my feet. I felt a surge of shame. The last name . . . it just wasn't mine. It didn't feel right. It didn't feel like it was my last name, my true last name. I wanted a last name that was mine. One that belonged to me, one that I could say with pride, knowing it was truly mine. Why didn't I get to keep the last name on my birth certificate? Why did it have to change? Even though I asked Ms. Marsh many times, she always flatly refused to give me any information about my name.

"Marsh? As in Evelyn or Abigail Marsh? Is one of them your mom?"

"No," I said.

"Where exactly are you coming from?"

"The . . . um . . ." I could feel my heart beat, like it was trying to escape my chest.

"The only place I can think of in that direction that you may be coming from is Ms. Abigail's orphanage. That's about a ten-minute walk from here." Ten minutes was about how long I'd been walking. "Well? Is that where you're from?" he demanded.

"Well, I—"

"I used to work at a middle school, Valley Heights. The kids there are tricky. I know the game—the spluttering, the playing dumb. Answer my question, Sandy. Is the orphanage where you came from or not?" I merely nodded, diverting my eyes from the deputy's stony glare. "A runaway, huh?"

"I needed some air," I said.

"And that's why you brought your bag?"

Why had I brought my bag? Maybe I felt less alone? The answer became clear. It provided a sense of security. Having my bag or Jessie with me was as close as I'd get to having my mom and dad with me.

"I don't know why I brought my bag."

"A likely story," Deputy Brute raised an eyebrow. "Get in the car. Now." Reluctant as I was, it didn't seem as if I had a choice. I shook my head and closed my eyes, clearing all the jumbled thoughts from my mind.

Soon I was on the front steps of the orphanage, Deputy Brute behind me. The door swung open, revealing Ms. Abigail. Her hair was in a messy bun, her eyes tired, and her face lacking all her usual make-up. She looked furious.

"Inside!" she shouted. "Get inside NOW!" I rushed inside and hurried upstairs. I could hear Ms. Abigail stopping to flirt with Deputy Brute, and part of me was tempted to stay and listen, but the other part knew I should give Ms. Abigail some space. Once I was back in the bedroom, everyone was already awake. Even the boys had come over into our room. I figured that maybe Rebecca and Tessa had gone to get them when they realized I was missing. The moment they saw me, I was immediately bombarded with questions.

"Where'd you go?"

"What happened?"

"Are you okay?"

"I . . . I needed some air. I'm fine, really," I assured them. "A deputy found me and—"

"A deputy?" Nick interrupted. "Cool!"

"It's not that cool, Nick," I said. "I was pretty scared."

"We're glad you're okay," Tessa said. "Aren't we, Nick?"

"What did the deputy say?" Nick asked, his eyes wide with interest.

"Nick!" Tessa elbowed him.

"Ow," Nick muttered.

"Sandy, we were so worried!" said Rebecca. "Tessa and I figured you went to the bathroom, but you never came back! We went to go find the boys and—"

Suddenly, our bedroom door burst open. Ms. Abigail stood there in her pink bathrobe, her face contorted into a furious expression.

"SANDY!" Ms. Abigail shouted. Everyone in the hallway, maybe even the whole orphanage, was awake by now. "I don't even . . . I can't even . . . You are in BIG trouble, missy! It's 11:30 at night! How could you . . . I don't . . . you'll get your punishment later!" With that, she stormed from the room.

"Wow," Rebecca whispered in shock.

"She lost the ability to speak in full sentences," said Aaron. "That happens when she is really angry."

Nick murmured, "She is really mad."

"We know that, Nick," Tessa snapped. "There's no need to state the obvious."

"Sandy, listen to me," Rebecca grabbed my hand and looked me in the eyes. I was slowly starting to cry. It was my first night at the orphanage, and I'd already gotten in trouble. "Don't tell Ms. Abigail how you got out. She can't find out about the Secret Exit, the SE. If she asks, tell her you snuck out the front."

"But that's impossible! She won't believe—"

"You'd be surprised," Nick said. "Ms. Abigail falls for a lot of crap," Aaron smirked at that. I'd bet money (if I had any) that Aaron had pranked Ms. Abigail more than a few times.

"Let's all go back to sleep," Rick suggested.

"Always the responsible one, aren't you?" Nick rolled his eyes.

"Always the irresponsible one, aren't you? Well, I'm exhausted. I think it's time to go to bed. Good night!"

"He's right. We should go back to sleep," Rebecca agreed. "We can talk more in the morning. Good night, guys!"

"Night," I whispered. I heard the boys leave for their bedroom and rolled over onto my side. My mind was buzzing with thoughts, dreams, questions, and visions. My body screamed for sleep, but my mind was too alive for that to happen. My eyelids begged me to let them close, but my brain forced them open. Too much, too many things to take in, to think about.

There I lay, wishing, dreaming, and thinking. Doing everything but sleeping.

SIX

It was another long night. Tuesday morning dawned with a light shower and cloudy skies. Nick, Rick, and Aaron, who were all ready for school, stopped by to say hi to me before leaving with Rebecca and Tessa for the bus.

"We'll see you later, Sandy!" Rebecca promised.

"Here's a word of advice. Stay up here as long as you can," Tessa advised. "Ms. Abigail is mad enough at you as it is. Give her space."

"Thanks for the tip." I forced a smile. My lips were tight, and the smile didn't reach my eyes, but I couldn't help it.

"I'll be right back," Tessa said, pulling Rebecca with her. Minutes later they re-appeared with a bowl of cereal and milk.

"I thought you ate school breakfast," I said, puzzled.

"This is Ms. Abigail's cereal," Tessa laughed. "We're not supposed to eat it, but nobody listens to her."

Rebecca handed me the bowl and a spoon. "She won't notice, anyway."

"Thanks, guys," I said, genuinely grateful.

"You're welcome, Sandy," Tessa said.

I waved and said, "See you later."

• • •

That afternoon, as reluctant as I was, I headed downstairs to the kitchen for lunch. Ms. Abigail was nowhere to be found— probably in her bedroom—and hadn't even thought about my lunch. I didn't see Jade either. I was on my own.

Looking around, I decided on a peanut butter and jelly sandwich. I quickly made a PB&J, rushed back upstairs, and ate in silence.

The doorbell rang as I finished my sandwich and I peeked out the window. Deputy Brute stood at the door. What did he want? Was I in trouble? Taking a walk didn't seem like a crime.

"SANDY!" Ms. Abigail shouted. I took a deep breath and rushed downstairs, my drawstring bag on my back. Something was reassuring about having my faded bag with me, a sense of security.

"The deputy wants to talk to you," Ms. Abigail told me. "Go with Deputy Brute— Deputy, may I call you Justin?"

"Uh, well—"

"Go with Justin," Ms. Abigail ordered. She winked at the deputy.

"Uh, Sandy, let's go," Deputy Brute rushed me out of the orphanage. "Ms. Marsh, we'll call you—"

"Please, call me Abigail."

"We'll call you if we need you to come to the station," said Deputy Brute.

The police car whizzed towards the police station. Every now and then, Deputy Brute looked back at me, as if expecting me to jump out of his car and run away. When he turned back to stare at the road, his stare left a sting.

I was sitting in the waiting room when I heard footsteps grow near. A deputy opened the door, but it wasn't Deputy Brute; it was another, taller, much slimmer deputy, Deputy Scordon. He, too, was balding, but he wore glasses that sat slightly askew on the bridge of his long, pointed nose.

"C'mon, we've got to ask you a few things in the interrogation room." I stood up nervously and followed the slender deputy across the the hall to the room where Deputy Brute sat, clutching a pencil, scribbling frantically on a notepad. A third man was present as well, and his silver nametag read Sheriff McKole. He was dark-skinned and had a tight buzz cut.

"Have a seat, Sandy," the sheriff said, making a brief gesture to the chair opposite him. Obediently, I crossed the room and sat down, my eyes trained on the table, a long, conference table of dark, polished oak. A harsh, bright light was suspended directly above the center of the table.

"We understand you ran away from the orphanage?" Sheriff McKole asked.

"No, I was only going for a walk. I never intended to leave the orphanage. Besides, I didn't even bring my stuff." Deputy Brute began to write.

"What time did you leave?"

"What time? I don't really—"

"Sandy, what time did you leave the orphanage?" Sheriff McKole repeated, his voice stony and his face impassive.

"About 10:50 maybe?" I said, not meeting his eyes as I shrugged my shoulders.

"Well, Sandy, we have to inform you that there was a burglary last night at about that time. It was at an electronics store, located right between the orphanage and where Deputy Brute found you around 11:15. There were several items stolen, and you're a suspect."

"What!" I exclaimed. "How could I? Why would I? I swear I didn't steal anything!" I jumped to my feet in disbelief. I couldn't believe I was being accused of such a crime. I couldn't even begin to imagine—

Sick to my stomach, I asked, "May I use the restroom? Please?"

"Go right ahead," Deputy Scordon nodded. "Do you know where it is?"

"Yeah, thanks," I said. Slowly, I got to my feet and walked into the bathroom. I cupped my hands under the steady stream of ice-cold water and splashed it on my face. I forced myself to look in the mirror at my reflection. The ocean blue eyes, the sand-colored hair, I looked the same as I always had. But I knew I was a different person than the person I was a few months ago. Here I was, involved in a mystery. A potentially dangerous mystery. Something the old me would have stayed far away from. Yet here I was, in the police station, handling myself as if I had a backbone. I took a deep breath in and let it out.

Even though no one was there to hear it, I said, "Bring it."

SEVEN

"Sandy, why were you walking at night?" Deputy Scordon asked.

I decided to stick with the truth. I hadn't stolen anything, so no harm could come by telling the deputies exactly what happened. I was still in shock that I was a suspect. I was only twelve years old. How could they even think I was responsible?

"I needed some fresh air. I needed to think," I answered.

"I see," said Deputy Brute, writing it down. The deputies asked me a few more questions after that, all of which I answered truthfully.

"Anything else you'd like to tell us?"

"Yes," I pulled myself together and straightened up. "I didn't steal anything. I'm barely capable of getting a B on a math test, so I'm not sure what makes you think I'm capable of robbing a store. I swear I didn't do this."

"Where were you at 10:45?" Deputy Brute inquired. His thick, black mustache quivered as he spoke, his chestnut brown eyes shrewd and inquisitive.

I answered, "In bed." I knew I had left the orphanage at about 10:50.

"Asleep?"

"Not really, no," I replied vaguely.

"What exactly do you mean by 'not really'?" Sheriff McKole asked.

"I was, like, not fully awake—really tired—but still aware." Out of the corner of my eye, I saw Deputy Brute writing.

"Sandy, I'm going to tell you something," Sheriff McKole said.

"Okay."

"I don't think you did it. None of us think you were responsible for the crime, but, as law enforcement, we must follow leads and evidence, not our hearts. And right now, as much as I hate to say it, the evidence points in your direction."

"And what evidence is that?"

"Not much," Sheriff McKole admitted. "Just the fact that you were found 25 minutes after the alarm was disabled, right near the store that was robbed. And the fact you had a backpack with you that clearly wasn't empty. If Deputy Brute had thought to look in it, then we might not be here today. The problem is you took the backpack to the orphanage, and if you stole the electronics, they could be anywhere by now."

"But—"

Deputy Brute interrupted, "While this may not be strict evidence, orphans are prone to—"

"I am not an orphan!" I shouted before I could even register what I was saying. My mouth seemed to have a mind of its own.

Deputy Scordon looked sympathetic. "Sandy, I understand it's hard to adjust to this, but—"

"Thanks for understanding, but please just finish telling me what the evidence is," I said. It hurt to even think about it.

"I hate to say this, but sometimes kids dealing with—"

"I didn't do it! I didn't commit a crime! I never would even think of doing it! I—"

Deputy Brute held up a hand for me to stop and began scribbling on his notepad. Then he set the pad down on the table. He, the sheriff, and Deputy Scordon left the room to speak in private. I stood up and looked at Deputy Brute's notepad. There was something familiar about his handwriting, the way his "y" curled into a loop that stretched down a line or two. He was also writing in a dark blue pen. Dark blue was the same color as the notes. Not that it mattered, lots of people had dark blue pens, but it got me thinking. The dark blue ink and curly letter y's had sparked a train of thought, and that train was speeding towards the station.

Everything fell into place. Could Deputy Brute have left the notes? After all, he was a deputy, and his job was to keep people safe. Maybe he thought that Brian was a suspicious character. That made sense. Brian told me he disappeared for three months when he was at his old school, Valley Heights. That would certainly attract attention. At that precise moment, a vivid memory popped into my mind. Deputy Brute said he was once a deputy at Brian's old school, Valley Heights. It all began to make sense.

Even though I felt confident I had solved the mystery, I still had an uneasy feeling that someone was out there, waiting and watching. My mind returned to the notes. Could the same person who stole the electronics also be writing the notes? Were the notes, after all, a threat rather than a caution? I speculated that the three were linked. The notes, the burglary, the Stone of Discedo ... it all had to be connected somehow. Maybe I was what connected it. I didn't know, but I was going to find out.

The sheriff and the deputies re-entered the room.

"We'll do our best to find the culprit, Sandy. I promise." Sheriff McKole closed his notebook, snapping me back to reality. "For now, you can go back to the waiting room. Ms. Abigail and the other kids in your grade will come after school."

"Why are my friends coming?" I asked.

"We are going to question them."

"Why?" I interrupted.

"Sandy, please understand we are trying to find the person responsible," Deputy Scordon explained. "Let us do our job."

I went back to the waiting room. My heart ached, and my head pounded. I wished my parents were here. Where were they? Were they alive? Would I ever know?

• • •

I was sitting in the waiting room, staring at the ceiling, when the lights began to flicker. On and off, on and off. I jumped to my feet, rattled. Peeking through the rectangle of glass in the door, I noticed the lights were flickering in the hallways and the other rooms too. The receptionist's footsteps were receding, maybe she was going to check the circuit breaker. My heart was racing, not because I was afraid of the dark, but because of the ominousness of the flickering lights. I sat back down, trying to control my breathing, *deep breath in, deep breath out.* Just then, the lights went out. The waiting room was flooded with darkness. It was raining outside, and not much light came from the window. Chills sprinted down my spine. Deep breath in, deep breath out . . .

A silhouette appeared in the glass window of the door. A man. It's probably one of the deputies, no reason to freak out . . . The door eased open. The man was not wearing a deputy's outfit, and his face was masked by shadows. I inched into the corner, gripped by fear. I gulped, panic spreading to every inch of my body. My breaths were short and shallow.

The man whispered, "Sandy—" But then he was cut off. He stopped moving towards me and froze. I closed my eyes, praying for him to disappear. A moment later, I opened my eyes, and the man was gone. I looked around the room, but he was nowhere to be found. The lights flickered back on. My heart was still racing. I sat in my seat, staring out the window at the rain falling outside. Who was that man? What did he want? And how did he know my name?

A few minutes later, the door opened, but this time it was Ms. Abigail and my friends. Ms. Abigail sat on the opposite side of the room, and my friends came to sit by me.

"Sandy, are you okay?" Rebecca asked, looking at me with concern. "You look a little rattled."

"I'm fine," I lied as Ms. Abigail's phone began ringing.

"I have to take this," she told us. "Behave yourselves." With that, Ms. Abigail stepped out into the hallway.

"Okay, I'm really not fine," I corrected once the door closed.

"Sandy, we may have just met you two days ago, but you should know you can always confide in us," Tessa assured me.

"Yeah, Sandy," Nick added, "you can tell us anything."

Aaron chuckled and said, "Except the really personal stuff like—"

"Bro, shut up," Nick nudged Aaron.

I told them about the man during the power outage. "—and then he disappeared," I finished.

"The man you saw was probably a janitor or something," Aaron assured me.

"But the man . . . he said my name," I objected.

"Yeah, so maybe he works here," said Aaron with a shrug.

"It was so weird. I closed my eyes for a moment, and when I opened them, the man was gone," I shook my head, trying to clear my brain. So many thoughts were rushing around.

"I know this seems like an obvious question," Rick began, "but is it possible he walked out?"

"I don't know," I admitted. "Maybe." I could've sworn he disappeared into thin air.

"Look, Sandy, I don't think it's anything to worry about," Rebecca assured me. "Power outages are perfectly normal—"

"That's not the part that scared me," I interrupted. "It was that man . . ."

We didn't get to finish our conversation because right then Ms. Abigail re-entered the waiting room. I was aware my face had been washed of all color, and all I could do was think about what just happened. Tessa held out her hand, and I took it.

"Sandy, we are here for you. We all have at least one thing in common, none of us have parents. But the six of us, we're our own little family. We take care of each other. You'll be okay."

"Thanks," I whispered. I searched for more words, but unable to find them, I turned and looked outside. A thick veil of spring rain blanketed the town. The rain cascaded off roofs and pooled at the foot of nearby buildings, forming small puddles along the sidewalk.

• • •

Deputy Scordon took my fingerprints and sent me back to the waiting room. He then brought Ms. Abigail in for questioning. I sat in silence with Tessa and Rebecca flanking me. The three boys sat next to Rebecca.

I sucked in a deep breath and told my friends everything the sheriff had said, including the part about me having a backpack, and that because they hadn't looked in it, it was evidence against me.

"Sheriff McKole told me that the alarm was disabled at 10:50," I shared.

"That was the time you left, I would know, I was awake. I heard you. I mean, I thought you were going to the bathroom, but anyway, it's proof! You couldn't possibly have made it to the electronics store and robbed it all at the same time," said Tessa.

"But I see where they are coming from," I said. "They found me, an . . . orphan, near the site of the burglary with a backpack at 11:15, twenty-five minutes after the alarm was disabled. There's really no proof other than our testimonies, and I don't know if that's enough."

"But how could you have done it anyway?" asked Tessa. "If they don't know who did it, the person must have disabled the security cameras and alarms. No offense, but you're not clever enough for that, let alone tall enough to reach them."

"Or strong enough to carry a ladder," Nick added semi-jokingly.

The door opened, and Ms. Abigail and Deputy Scordon entered the room.

"Rebecca Taylor, please come with me," Deputy Scordon said. Rebecca jumped to her feet and went with him.

My stomach was still turning over and over even though I was confident I'd eventually be found innocent. It was sickening to think that someone was out there who was responsible for the burglary, maybe the same person who was leaving the notes, and maybe even the same person who planted the Stone of Discedo. But who?

· · ·

"They can't possibly still suspect you after they get more evidence. Give them time, and they'll figure out who really did it," Rick stated. "We all just need to stick to exactly what happened."

"Will it all be okay?" I asked, seeking reassurance.

"Yes," Tessa said.

"Promise?"

"Promise."

I already felt as if we were our own little family, Rebecca, Tessa, Nick, Rick, Aaron, and me. I couldn't recall ever feeling a connection like this before. The love and care, the friendship, the feeling that, even as an orphan, I had friends who were still there to look out for me.

I looked outside. The sky was serenely blue, streaked by a few wispy clouds. The storm that had swallowed South Toheeden was over, though abundant puddles and pools of rainwater lingered in the storm's wake. Now the sunshine was soft and golden; the calm after the storm. As soon as Rebecca came back from being questioned, she told us precisely what they asked and the answers she gave.

"They asked me when the last time I saw you was and I told them the truth. It was about 10:45 as I was falling asleep. They also asked me whether you would be the type to steal, whether you were capable of doing something like that, and a bunch of other stupid things." It was a relief to know that the facts were on my side. Most of them, at least.

"I have to take another call," Ms. Abigail announced. "Behave yourselves." She left the room, pressing her phone to her ear.

I heard Deputy Scordon call, "Rick, please come in."

Rick set his book on the chair behind him and left the room, not showing any sign of anxiety or nerves. He strode eagerly from the room, radiating confidence. Nick watched his brother leave and then, after ensuring his brother was behind closed doors, picked up the book and examined the cover. It was a different book than the one he'd been reading when I first arrived at the orphanage. The title, etched in thick, black letters, read **Ohio Criminal Evidence**.

"He's reading this for you, you know," Nick told me. "Rick normally reads nonfiction, but never law. He's going to outsmart them. Just watch. He will pull out a fact from his warehouse of usually useless information and put them on the spot like he always does to me," Nick sighed, grinning. "It'll be nice to see him correct someone else for a change," he added, setting the book back on Rick's empty seat.

"There's only one way to find out if you're right," Aaron said, crossing the room and pressing his ear to the door. One by one, the remaining four of us pushed our ears up against the oak door.

"—last see her?" Deputy Scordon was saying.

"About 10:45, I left the room," Rick replied. "But that's not to say she wasn't there after that. And as you said, the burglary occurred at 10:50. Sandy had no way to steal anything if she was elsewhere five minutes before the burglary occurred. Again, that's not to say she didn't remain in her room after I left. Furthermore, how would a kid break into a store with high-tech security? How would a kid disable the alarms? I consider myself highly intelligent, and even I would never be able to do the things necessary to pull off this burglary. Just think for a moment. You are accusing an innocent child of stealing thousands of dollars in electronics when she was at the orphanage in bed." None of the deputies spoke. Rick pressed on, "I mean, consider what you're doing here, and how nervous you're making poor Sandy feel!" Silence.

Finally, after a minute, Sheriff McKole spoke. "I understand what you're saying, but you have to understand that we found an orphan near the site of a burglary 25 minutes after the crime began."

"But Sandy left at 10:50! The same time the alarms were disabled!"

"Rick, you may go back to the waiting room," said the sheriff. Hearing Rick's footsteps, we rushed back to our seats and sat down. Rick opened the door and walked in, leaving the door open.

"How'd it go?" Nick asked his twin as if we didn't already know.

"I think it went okay," Rick shrugged and sat down.

Rebecca's eyes were narrowed, and she was staring at the floor.

Nick cocked an eyebrow, "What?"

"Shhh!" Rebecca hissed. She was listening for something.

"—store footage?" Sheriff McKole was asking.

"Nope," Deputy Scordon replied. "Whoever this criminal is took care of everything. The cameras were broken, and the security system was deactivated. The only thing we were able to figure out was that it was deactivated around 10:50 by whoever broke in, but you already knew that from talking to the security company. If whoever did this is experienced, which I'll bet they are, then Deputies London and Sphinx will come back empty-handed."

"What time did the store close, and who closed it?"

"It was closed at 10:00 by the manager's son," Deputy Scordon was saying. "And the manager told us his son always activates the security system before leaving. The security company confirmed the alarm was turned on at 10:00 sharp."

My ears rang with the sound of a squad car engine as it pulled up to the station. I heard the squeak of the front door, followed by a "Hello, boys" from Sheriff McKole, who I assumed greeted them at the door.

One of the deputies began speaking instantly, "Sheriff, there wasn't any—"

"Go back," Sheriff McKole interrupted. "I want you to go back. I want Sandy cleared. She didn't do it."

"With all due respect, sir, how can you be sure?" the other deputy asked. This one had a much deeper voice. I felt a surge of dislike blossom in my chest.

"My two best investigators couldn't find a single bit of damn evidence, that's how I'm sure!" Sheriff McKole bellowed. "This was not the work of a twelve-year-old, TJ! Besides, if she is telling the truth about leaving at 10:50, she couldn't possibly be responsible. But we need solid evidence. You should've figured that out by now."

"Sorry, sir," the deputy with the deep voice said.

I could hear the other one ask, "Sheriff?"

"Hmm?"

"Can I ask the girl a few questions?"

"Sure, Deputy London, she's right in there," Sheriff McKole said. "While you and Sphinx question Sandy, I want Deputies Scordon and Brute to go to the store. And Daniel, I don't want you to come back until you've found something." At this point, the South Toheeden police force seemed desperate and unsure of what to do next. These officers were nothing like the ones I'd seen several times on television shows like CSI.

"Yes, sir," Deputy Scordon said, pulling me from my thoughts. We could hear his shoes on the linoleum floor as he went to find Deputy Brute. Suddenly, Deputies London and Sphinx were standing on the threshold.

"Sandy, come with us, we have a few questions we'd like to ask you," Deputy London said. He had pale skin and salt and pepper hair. Deputy Sphinx was much younger than his partner and looked buff. His jawline was strong and set, which only added to how intimidated I felt. I obeyed, not without trepidation, and took a seat at the table back in the interrogation room. Goosebumps rose on my arms, all my hairs standing on end. A chill ran down my spine as Deputy London clicked the tape recorder on. Deputy Sphinx slipped into the room, followed by the sheriff.

"Sandy, I need you to tell me the truth. All of it, okay?"

"Yes sir." I nodded.

"I know you recently moved into the orphanage, which was probably difficult for you. Maybe even a little stressful. Sometimes stress can cause us to do things we normally wouldn't. Would you say you've been feeling stressed lately?"

"Maybe a little," I said. That was an understatement.

"Would you say you've been nervous about anything?"

"Yes," I said before I could even think about it.

"What about?" Deputy London asked. Oh no. Should I keep my mouth shut and keep my promise to Brian about not saying anything, or should I spill? There was no doubt in my mind that the mysterious notes and the stone were somehow connected, and both qualified as a source of nervousness. I was unsure of what to do or say.

"Um, school," I said. "School has been making me nervous."

"I understand that," Deputy London said. "You're starting a new school, you have every right to feel a little nervous. Would you say anything strange has happened?"

Oh no. I looked for loopholes, but couldn't find them. If I spilled, then Brian could be hunted down and thrown in jail, but if I didn't say anything, then I would be lying to a deputy.

"Whatever it is, you can tell us," Deputy London hinted. "We want to help you."

I knew I was a terrible liar. My heart was racing, pounding loud enough for me to hear it. My breathing was fast and choppy, uneven and anxious. I knew they would realize this, and piece together I was hiding something. My hands shook as I placed them out on the table in front of me. I couldn't control this, any of this. I was nervous, and there was no hiding it.

"Sandy, are you hiding something?" Deputy London asked. He and the other deputies probably already knew the answer.

"Sandy, tell us what you're hiding," Deputy Sphinx demanded. It wasn't a question. "We are trying to help you."

"No, nothing strange has recently happened to me," I answered in a measured, careful voice.

"Nothing?" Deputy Sphinx raised an eyebrow.

"Nothing," I shook my head.

"Then why do you look so nervous?"

"I'm only twelve years old, and I'm being questioned by deputies."

"Are you done now, boys?" Sheriff McKole asked.

"I guess so," Deputy Sphinx shrugged. Deputy London merely nodded and escorted me back to the room where Ms. Abigail and my friends waited.

"Sandy, our best investigators are on the case. We'll try and figure this out as soon as possible," the sheriff assured me. "If anything new or strange happens, you come back here and let us know, okay?"

"Yes sir," I nodded my head. I hoped I would receive another note, something that could clear up whether the notes were from someone who meant to harm me or a warning from someone who cared about me. It was hard to imagine either.

"Keep your eyes open, Sandy," Deputy London cautioned.

"Okay," I said, ready to leave.

Out of the corner of my eye, I saw Sheriff McKole throw away a piece of paper with a cell phone number on it. I stifled a giggle and followed my friends and Ms. Abigail out of the station.

"So, Ms. Abigail," Aaron said as we walked to the bus, "did you get his number?"

"That's it!" Ms. Abigail shouted. "Extra hour of chores tonight, Aaron."

In a low voice so Ms. Abigail couldn't hear, Nick said, "Rick, what you did back there was amazing. You should be a lawyer when you're older."

"How did you hear what I said?" Rick asked, looking confused. "Wait, let me guess . . . eavesdropping was Aaron's idea?"

"Well of course," said Aaron, grinning from ear to ear.

"You really should be a lawyer when you're older, Rick," I agreed.

Rick pushed his glasses up and blushed, "I'd like to be a doctor or a lawyer. Maybe even an author." He was clutching his book close to his chest as we piled into Ms. Abigail's bus. It was awkwardly silent. Ms. Abigail was ticked off, and none of us felt like talking around her.

"Sandy, don't think you're going to get away without punishment," Ms. Abigail broke the silence. "Extra chores and community service. Nobody leaves the orphanage without telling me." I stifled a groan.

"I guess I should tell you I'm going to a bar with some friends tonight," Aaron joked.

"What was that?"

"Oh, nothing," Aaron said.

"Sandy, for a month, you have laundry duty plus community service every Friday after school at Mountain View Middle School. I arranged with Mr. Ross Phillips for you to file his papers and help clean his classroom." I felt a bit of relief. At least it was with my old teacher, Mr. Phillips. "A city bus will take you from Rolling Hills to Mountain View, and on his way home, Mr. Phillips will drop you off back here at. You'll start next Friday."

"But—"

"It'll teach you not to leave without my permission. Those deputies let you go free, but at my orphanage there is discipline. Your actions have consequences." We drove the rest of the way in silence.

"Go inside and get to work," Ms. Abigail's sharp voice broke the silence as we pulled into the orphanage driveway. "Nick and Rick, you can clean the floors. Rebecca and Aaron, clean the showers. And Tessa and Sandy, you two can do the laundry."

Once we got to our bedroom, Tessa stared at the floor looking disappointed. "By laundry, she means we wash all of her clothes."

"Well, it can't be that bad. I mean how many clothes could she possibly have?" I whispered in return.

"You'd be surprised," Tessa muttered in response. "But it's not nearly as bad as shower duty."

"You're telling me," Aaron interjected. "You have to go into all the showers and clean them."

"How bad could that be?" I asked, trying to remain optimistic.

"Are you kidding me?" Nick exclaimed.

"You have no idea," Aaron shook his head. "Those showers are disgusting."

Nick added, "It's the worst chore there is! Shower duty even makes floor duty look good."

"And floor duty is?"

"Mopping and sweeping all the floors," Rebecca explained.

Tessa grabbed my hand and said, "Sandy, come with me, I'll show you how Ms. Abigail likes her laundry done." I sighed but followed, not that I really had a choice.

• • •

On Wednesday, I watched the others leave for school, gazing out of the bedroom window as they clambered into the bus. Principal Higgins insisted I wait until Monday to start school, so in the meantime, I sat idly by.

The pleasant scent of blooming spring flowers wafted through the open window, carried by a cool morning breeze. As I inhaled, I felt a sense of calm soar through me. I closed my eyes as I inhaled, knowing that another round of chores lay around the corner. I sat there contemplating anything and everything when the bedroom door swung open. There stood Ms. Abigail, her face covered in thick layers of makeup.

"Downstairs. Now."

I followed Ms. Abigail to the dining hall where Jade was cleaning up plates and bowls left on tables. "Help Jade with this," Ms. Abigail demanded. "You might as well be useful while you're here." Then she turned and walked into her bedroom, slamming the door in her wake. Jade winked at me.

"How long have you worked here?" I asked Jade.

"Seven years," Jade replied. "And I lived here for three."

"Wait, you lived here?" I asked. Jade had been one of us.

"Yes. When I was 15, I was pulled out of my home. I didn't know it then, but my parents were drug dealers. I was taken here. For some reason, Ms. Abigail took a special interest in me and got me a counselor to help with the trauma. I finished high school with straight A's and got a partial scholarship to Ohio State. I went there, got my degree in accounting, got a job at a local business, but it never felt . . . right." Jade stopped picking up plates and sat down in a chair. "So, I came back here, and Ms. Abigail put me to work. I spend a lot of time with the younger kids, helping them with whatever they need. I wanted to help kids the same way my counselor did for me so many years ago."

"That's amazing," I said.

"It was only right for me to pay it forward," Jade told me. "So here I am." And then she continued to clean the tables.

•   •   •

I spent the entire day mopping, sweeping, ironing, and finishing Tessa's and my share of the laundry. Ms. Abigail had handed me three immense hampers worth of dirty clothes and demanded they be washed, dried, pressed, and folded by tomorrow, Thursday morning. It was rumored that a pair of potential parents were stopping by tomorrow, looking for three kids to adopt.

I stood in her bedroom ironing an ugly chartreuse blouse. "Why don't we just clean and iron what you're wearing tomorrow, instead of all your clothes?" I asked in exasperation.

"Oh, I don't know what I'm wearing tomorrow!" Ms. Abigail said prissily. "I like to have options." I heard the doorbell ring and Ms. Abigail shouted, "JADE! Get the door!"

The others were still at school, and I was here, ironing all of Ms. Abigail's outfits. I wished she would spend a bit less money on her attire and more on decent food. As I folded her clothes, Ms. Abigail sat in front of a vanity mirror fixing her hair.

"Sandy, pass me that catalog," she said, placing a bobby pin in her hair. Ms. Abigail was glancing down at her phone which rested on a stand on the bureau. I rolled my eyes but nevertheless, I retrieved the catalog and handed it to Ms. Abigail, who snatched it out of my hands. "You can leave."

Without hesitation, I left the room and headed back upstairs to our bedroom. I picked up Jessie from the foot of my bed where she sat on my crimson bag, hugged her, and cried. I cried because I was now stuck with Ms. Abigail. It seemed the others had come to terms with living here, with not having parents. I always knew there was a difference between knowing and accepting, and not having a family was something I knew to be true, but struggled to accept.

• • •

With an exhausted sigh, I removed my shoes and flopped on my bed. The moment I laid down, I heard a crinkling sound. Perplexed, I sat up and pulled out a piece of paper that was wedged between the sheets. A third note. It read:

EIGHT

I sat on the edge of my bed, staring blankly at the note until my friends came home from school.

"What's that?" Tessa asked.

"Oh, it's—it's nothing," I stammered, trying to hide the note under my leg.

"Well it's not nothing," Tessa said. She walked over to me, a hand on her hip. For the first time, I found her a little intimidating.

"Tess, it's none of our business," said Rebecca.

"Yeah, you're right," Tessa shrugged and went over to her own bed.

"I'm sorry, but I can't tell you."

"That's okay," Tessa said. "I guess I shouldn't have asked in the first place."

"I'll be right back, I have to go to the bathroom," I said. I needed to splash some water on my face. Maybe this was all a dream, maybe I'd wake up and be in Ms. Evelyn's house on Spring Break.

The cold water from the sink felt good on my skin. Refreshing, awakening. However, I shivered, not just from the icy water. There was something about that note that scared me much more than the other ones. It felt like a threat. It felt like someone was watching me and my every move and had been in my bedroom.

Slowly, I walked back and found Tessa, Aaron, and Nick sitting on my bed. Nick was holding the note. Oh no, I thought, I forgot to take the note with me.

Tessa sprang to her feet. "Sandy, I'm sorry, we didn't mean to be nosy, but you left this on your bed, and Nick saw it and—"

"Stop," I interrupted her. I felt like the universe was spiraling out of control.

"We told them not to look at it," Rick said on his and Rebecca's behalf. "But they did it anyway."

"Sandy . . ." Tessa said, her voice small. "What's going on?" I shook my head. I couldn't tell them. I promised Brian I'd keep his secret.

Rebecca began, "Sandy, what—" Tessa held up the note, and Rebecca read it. Her mouth fell open, and her eyes widened.

"Sandy, are you in trouble? Should we call the police?" Rick asked upon seeing the note himself. Again, I shook my head.

"Sit down, take a deep breath," Rebecca suggested.

"And then tell us what is going on," Tessa added.

I couldn't . . . Could I?

"I'm going to go call the police," Rick said, getting to his feet.

"Don't," I objected. "Please don't."

"Sandy, tell us what's going on," Tessa said. "We want to help you—"

"I can't," I interrupted. I squeezed my eyes closed and shook my head. "I just can't."

"Why not?" Aaron questioned.

"It's not my secret to tell."

"Please, Sandy," Rebecca said, and in that moment, I forgot myself. I couldn't resist. I told them everything—*the notes, the Stone of Discedo, Brian being Ms. Abigail's son, how the stone was left in his locker.*

"So, Ms. Abigail has a son," Aaron said. "Is he a moron too?"

"Far from it," I said.

"Is he greedy? Dumb? Mean?"

"No!" I said. "Brian is none of those things."

The others still had expressions of mingled surprise, awe, and confusion. Eyes were wide, mouths were dropped.

"Of all the things Sandy told us, that is the first thing you wanted to ask?" Tessa said to Aaron. He shrugged.

"So, there have been more notes?" Rick asked.

"Two before this one," I answered. "Brian got the first note. It said, 'Stay away from the girl.' We both agreed that I am 'the girl.' We think it means someone wants to keep Brian and me apart. I got the second note on the same day, and it said, 'Don't get involved in trouble.'"

"And then this one?" Tessa asked, holding up the 'Watch your back' note.

"Yes," I nodded. "You have to promise to keep all of this a secret. Nobody can know."

"Your secret is safe with us," Rebecca promised.

"Do you think the notes are related to the stolen items?"

Tessa wondered aloud.

Rebecca shared, "I don't think it's a coincidence. Everything—and I mean everything—has to be connected."

"Well, mysterious things do happen to orphans," Aaron said. "In the movies, at least."

"I used to watch these detective shows," Tessa shared, "and with almost no clues, detectives still managed to solve mysteries."

"Yeah, but this is real life, Tess," Nick said.

Twisting her hair, Rebecca said, "Let's try to think through this logically. The person who left the notes may or may not be the same person who committed the robbery. We can't use the break-in to figure out who left the notes. Let's stick with what we know. Whoever left the notes somehow got into Mountain View."

"And now the orphanage," Rick added.

Tessa said, "Obviously, they're meant as a threat, and not just a warning."

"Tess, the notes may be a warning," said Rebecca. "We can't be sure they are a threat. Sandy, can you think of anyone who would write those notes to you as a threat? Anyone who hates you?"

"No," I hesitated.

"How about anyone who cares about you enough to leave the notes as a warning?"

"Brian and I did discuss Mr. Phillips as a possible suspect."

"Mr. Phillips? The guy you have community service with?" asked Tessa.

"The very same," I said. "Mr. Phillips really liked me, and I thought maybe he left the notes to try and keep me safe. I thought maybe he would want me to stay out of trouble at my next school. But then we realized that Mr. Phillips had no reason to leave the notes if he could talk to me in person. Plus, he already gave me a card. And now it seems even more unlikely because he couldn't have left school during the day to bring a note over here."

"Maybe we should ask Ms. Abigail if she let anyone into the orphanage," Rebecca suggested.

"Nah," Tessa said. "Whoever wrote the notes is probably sneaky. I doubt they would have just knocked on the door. Plus, even if they did, what are the odds Ms. Abigail would let them in?"

"She would if he was a good-looking guy," Nick corrected.

"There are deliveries and visitors in and out of here all day, every day," Rick said.

"We should ask just in case," Rebecca insisted.

"I'll bet she's painting her nails right now," said Nick.

"You're probably right," Rebecca agreed. "C'mon."

"I don't get why women paint their nails anyway," muttered Nick. Standing in her doorway, we discovered Ms. Abigail was indeed painting her toenails an awful shade of bubblegum pink. She sat on the edge of her bed near the door.

Rebecca smiled, artificially sweet, "Ms. Abigail, did you let anyone in here today?"

"Why do you want to know?" she inquired, not lifting her eyes from her feet.

Nick said, "We . . . um . . ."

"Forget it. Get out of my sight," Ms. Abigail ordered harshly, and she reached over and slammed her bedroom door in our faces.

"That went well," Aaron said.

"Not much else we can do now," Rebecca stated once we were back in our room.

Outside, the sun began to set, slipping slowly below the horizon, bathing the sky in an ombre of pink, orange, and yellow. I could see the shadows lengthening as the sun sank. I watched it while the others finished their homework. The guys had come over to the girls' room, and it seemed like it was part of their normal routine.

"School was so boring today," Aaron moaned, reclining on Rebecca's bed. "Katie and Allison are so lucky."

"How so?" Rebecca asked.

"They pretended to be sick today, so they didn't go to school."

Tessa jumped to her feet. "They did? Maybe one of them saw something! Aaron, why didn't you mention that earlier? Let's go ask!"

"You guys go without me," Rebecca said, staring at the ground. Not wanting to participate seemed out of character for Rebecca.

"Why don't you come?" I asked.

"Katie is my sister," Rebecca said, "and we don't get along."

"Oh," I said, surprised. I didn't know Rebecca had a sister.

The rest of us raced down the hallway to the eleventh-grade girls' bedroom. A tall, very pretty girl opened the door. The girl looked almost exactly like Rebecca, she had the same slender body, dark hair, bright eyes, and long lashes. The only difference was her hair was shoulder-length.

Katie was leaning casually against the doorjamb with a

hand her hip. "What?" When she saw who we were, she added, "Where's Rebecca? Usually, you guys are inseparable."

"Well, she, um—"

"She didn't want to come, did she?" Katie rolled her eyes. "That's my sister for you."

None of us said anything to that. Tessa stepped into Rebecca's empty role of spokesperson. "Katie, did anyone come to the orphanage today? Anyone . . . suspicious?"

Katie frowned in thought, "There was a delivery guy."

"Can you describe him?" Tessa asked.

"He was tall with black hair and a scruffy beard," Katie recalled. "He had a big box of something. Oh, and there was also Principal Higgins from Rolling Hills. He came and dropped off someone's school books and supplies."

"Probably mine," I muttered. "I start there on Monday."

"Yeah, I bet they are yours," Katie agreed, nodding. "Good luck with that. Let's see—well, I think a deputy came by."

"Was he kind of fat? With no neck?"

"That's an awfully weird question, but yeah, I'd say so."

"Deputy Brute," I whispered.

"Excuse me?" Katie frowned.

"Oh, nothing. Was there anyone else?"

"Well, today was another busy day. There was a lady who came to tutor, I think her name was Ms. Isabel or something. There was also a school board member who came by to talk to Ms. Abigail—"

"By any chance, was it the head of the school board? Mr. Stanton?" I inquired.

"I don't know the name, I just remember seeing him."

Tessa gave a quizzical look, "Him? So, it was a man?"

"Yes," Katie said, narrowing her eyes. "Why do you ask?"

"Just wondering," Tessa replied.

"Have you been watching more of those silly detective movies?" Katie questioned.

"No," Aaron said. "Nobody watches those cheesy shows anyway." Tessa rolled her eyes.

Katie shrugged, "I guess you're right."

"C'mon Katie, we're about to start!" a voice called from inside the bedroom.

"I've gotta go," Katie told us. "I can tell something is going on. If you decide to tell me, I could be of help. You know where to find me." Katie winked and closed the door, and we hurried back to the privacy of our bedroom without another word.

"Sandy, if there were so many people that came to the orphanage today, how come you didn't see any of them?" Tessa asked.

"I spent the entire day in our bedroom, Ms. Abigail's bedroom, or the laundry room."

"Right," said Tessa. "I'm not surprised." She told Rebecca everything Katie had told us.

"Hmmm," Rebecca was pensive.

"It has got to be Mr. Stanton," Aaron stated. "The signs are all pointing to him."

"But I don't know him, and more importantly, he doesn't know me!"

"Just because you don't know him doesn't mean he doesn't

know you," Rick stated as if echoing Brian. "Still, I'm not sure. That doesn't seem right."

"I think it was Stanton," Nick said. "He came to Mountain View on the day you guys got the first and second notes, and he came to the orphanage the same day you got the third note. It all makes sense! I think Mr. Stanton has to be the one leaving the notes."

"That's what I think," Aaron nodded, "and great minds think alike."

"Great minds," Tessa rolled her eyes. "Right."

"I have to disagree," Rebecca said. "I don't think it was Stanton."

"Neither do I," Tessa said.

"Same," I added. "Katie said a deputy came by. I think it could be Deputy Brute who left the notes."

"What makes you think that?" Rick queried.

"Well for one, he's a deputy, and it's his job to keep people safe. Maybe he thinks the Stone of Discedo is dangerous."

"How would he know that Brian has the stone?" Rick frowned.

"He used to be the school deputy at Valley Heights. That was Brian's school before he came to Mountain View. When Brian disappeared for three months, maybe Deputy Brute figured it out."

"You know . . . that actually makes sense!" Rebecca said.

"Deputy Brute was here at the orphanage when the note was dropped off," I continued. "I really think it's him."

"I agree," Tessa and Rebecca said in unison.

Despite our argument that Mr. Stanton was not the writer of the notes, the boys remained adamant about their suspect choice. There was nothing we could say or do to convince Nick and Aaron otherwise.

Rick, however, remained undecided. "Well, I can sort of see both sides of the argument. Sandy, Rebecca, and Tessa make a good point in that Mr. Stanton doesn't know her, so it would be unlikely that he is the person to leave the notes. On the other hand, Mr. Stanton was there the day the notes were left at Mountain View, and he was here today when you got the third note. It's hard to believe that's a coincidence. I also understand why you would think it could be Deputy Brute because he worked at Brian's old school and might've noticed his disappearance. Deputy Brute could be suspicious of Brian and trying to keep you safe. On the other hand, he's a deputy, and if he found out that Brian has the Stone of Discedo, I think he would do a little more than leave Sandy notes."

"Like what?" Nick argued.

"Like start an investigation or something," Rick answered. "And it could also be the tutor that Katie mentioned, Ms. Isabel. She could probably get into the orphanage any time she wanted and might even have access to schools."

"Well, Rick? What do you think? Pick a side," Nick demanded.

"I pick my own side," Rick replied curtly.

"And what side is that?" Nick demanded, folding his arms across his chest.

"Undecided," Rick answered.

Tessa reasoned, "I mean, Sandy doesn't know Stanton, and I doubt he knows you. However, Deputy Brute does know both of you."

"I think maybe it is someone with access to the school, like maybe someone who works there. Somehow they knew which locker was yours and which one was Ryan's." Rebecca said.

"Brian's locker, his name is Brian," I corrected. "I agree with Rick."

"I still think that it's Stanton," Nick insisted, earning an enthusiastic nod from Aaron.

"Hold on a second," Rebecca whispered, quietly moving to the door and opening it. In fell Katie and Allison giggling, "Why are you pressing your ears to the door?" Rebecca glared.

"Isn't it obvious? We want to hear what's going on," said Allison.

"It was her idea," Katie said, receiving a doubtful look from her sister.

"True," Allison admitted. "Katie told me how you guys wanted information about who came here today. We want to know what's going on. And we want to help."

"If you wanted to help, you could have knocked and asked," Rebecca stated.

"Yeah, but we still would have said no," Aaron added, grinning.

Rebecca looked at her sister. "Sorry Katie, I know you want to know what is going on, but this is between the six of us."

"Fine," Allison said, helping Katie to her feet. The two girls departed, conversing in hushed whispers.

"That was a bad idea," Katie was saying. "Note to self, don't let Ally talk me into something ever again."

"Whatever," said Allison. "I still want to know what they're up to."

"Shush! Keep your voice down!" Katie hissed. "Knowing my little sister, she'll be listening to us."

"This place has no privacy," Aaron commented. "We should probably have, like, look-outs or something."

Rebecca rolled her eyes. "They'll be back. Let's drop the subject until tomorrow."

"No," Aaron disagreed, making it obvious that he was already scheming. "We'll return the favor."

"And how exactly do we go about doing that?" Tessa asked.

Aaron lowered his voice, "I say once we're sure they are back, we stage a conversation in which we mention a fake plan to throw Katie a surprise party. That will teach them not to eavesdrop."

"I like where this is going," Rebecca said. "Finally. A chance to get back at Katie. Her birthday is coming up." Two sets of footsteps could suddenly be heard, coming closer and closer. Aaron winked at us, and mouthed the words 'Follow my lead.' "So, Nick, you've started on the invitations?"

"Oh, yes. They're perfect!" Nick winked, simultaneously suppressing a laugh.

"And Sandy, you ordered the banner?" Aaron was grinning devilishly.

"The 'Happy Sweet Sixteen, Katie!' banner?" I asked. I felt a smile break across my face.

"Yes, that one," Aaron said.

"Yep!" To this, there was a distinct shuffling and whispers behind the door.

Rebecca grinned and said, "Yeah, I booked the Dolph Building for next month." More muttering from outside the door. Katie and Allison were falling for it.

"Great. The party is going to be incredible," Aaron said with a smirk. "I'm going to get some juice." I heard two sets of footsteps scurrying away. Aaron smiled, satisfied, as he opened the door. He headed downstairs to get a cup of orange juice. Nick added a quick "me too" and followed Aaron out of the room.

"He can be pretty clever, you know," Rebecca smiled.

"Not really what I'd call school smart, but he can be street smart sometimes," Tessa agreed.

Rebecca sighed, "We should probably get to bed. It's getting late."

"Good night," Tessa said as she switched off the light. I opened my mouth to say something, but my eyes closed, and I was soon immersed in a blissfully dreamless sleep.

• • •

I awoke to the sound of a girl's scream. The others were wide-awake too, though as I glanced outside, I realized morning had not yet dawned. I glanced at the clock. It was just after midnight. I heard another scream from the hallway. The girl's terrified shriek rang in my ears. My heart began to race.

"What's going on?" I asked. Rebecca, Tessa, and I raced into the hallway where the scream had come from.

"SKYLER!" Rebecca screamed. A girl was lying on the floor with blood seeping from a gash in her stomach. A bloody knife lay beside her as she yelled and moaned in agony.

Kneeling down by Skyler, Rebecca yelled, "Sandy! Get help!"

I had to call 9-1-1, but the only working phone in the building was Ms. Abigail's cell phone. I ran down the stairs to Ms. Abigail's room and found her bed empty. She was nowhere to be found. Wherever she'd gone, she'd taken her phone with her because the phone wasn't on her vanity or in any of her drawers.

Running back upstairs, I could hear Skyler's strained moaning. Her face was pale and gray, and her breathing was raspy. Rebecca was pressing a T-shirt to the wound, but it didn't seem to help.

"Skyler! Skyler, can you hear me? Skyler!" Rebecca cried. "Wake up! Skyler, talk to me!" Skyler didn't move.

"Ms. Abigail isn't here!" I shouted.

"Tess, go to the front of the orphanage. To the right of the door is the alarm panel. Press the two buttons on the bottom left. Those will call the police and the paramedics," Rebecca said, tears covering her face. Nick went with Tessa, and the two of them sprinted downstairs.

"What if whoever did this is still here?" Allison asked nervously, her hands shaking as she ran them through her hair. A few terrible minutes later, I heard the front door bang open. The sheriff and deputies, as well as paramedics, had arrived. The paramedics began to attend to Skyler. Deputies Brute, London, Sphinx, and Scordon, in addition to Sheriff McKole appeared at the foot of the stairs.

"Everyone downstairs! NOW!" Sheriff McKole bellowed. My heart was pounding, and my brain seemed to be trapped in denial.

Was this really happening?

The rest of the kids were funneled downstairs to the dining hall while I stayed back to be with Rebecca. A medic was pulling her away from Skyler.

"No!" Rebecca sobbed. "Skyler needs me! I can't leave her!"

The medics continued to work on Skyler, and I pulled Rebecca away. She put up a fight, begging to stay with Skyler, but eventually, I hauled her towards the stairs. Rebecca's face was soaked with tears.

"She's in good hands, Rebecca," I assured her. My words sounded as false as they felt.

"She . . . she's my friend," Rebecca sobbed.

"Take a deep breath," I told her. I gave Rebecca a hug and rubbed her soothingly on the back. "Let's go downstairs." I let Rebecca walk in front of me. I turned around and looked at Skyler. It was then that Skyler sucked in her last breath . . . And suddenly, it was too late.

• • •

All the kids congregated in the dining hall where some of the deputies stayed with us. Jade was there, consoling five kindergarteners at once, whispering in their ears, holding them close. I wished I could be over there, being hugged and consoled, but I was an older kid, and I had to be strong and hold myself together.

We sat in silence for a few minutes until Sheriff McKole appeared at the foot of the stairs. He was wearing two beige latex gloves and holding an evidence bag containing the blood-stained knife. The sheriff turned to his deputies and told them, "I want at least one of you here at all times." Then he turned to face us and said, "Everyone must remain downstairs, away from the crime scene. Anyone who thinks they might know anything about this needs to come forward now."

Nobody moved. It was deadly silent. So quiet, in fact, you could've heard a pin drop. I spotted Ms. Abigail in the corner of the dining hall. Her face was white, and her hair was disheveled. Her eyes were wide and flitted back and forth.

* * *

The deputies held a formal inquiry, asking each of us questions about Skyler's murder. It took hours. Every officer from the station had come to the orphanage to ask questions. The detectives were upstairs examining anything and everything they could find. Every child was rattled to the bone. Nobody felt safe anymore. I saw people looking over their shoulders, people sticking in pairs. I saw Ms. Abigail, Jade, and other assistants scrambling around trying to keep things in order.

Everyone, from the kids barely old enough for kindergarten to the high schoolers about to graduate, felt scared. It was as though a blanket of fear had wrapped itself around the orphanage and wasn't about to let go.

Once the formal inquiry was over, Sheriff McKole announced that from now until the case was solved, a deputy would stay at the orphanage for protection. Ms. Abigail didn't mind, of course, because the deputies and sheriff were in her words "easy on the eyes."

By the time the blood was cleaned up, and we were sent back to bed, it was about 3:30 in the morning. Ms. Abigail told us that we could sleep in, and everyone would go to school for a half day. Even though we were eventually sent back to bed, I don't think anyone slept a wink.

Thursday morning, my mind still raced with questions. Who killed Skyler? Who, and why? Rebecca, who had gotten out of bed a few minutes after I did, flopped onto my bed.

"I still can't believe she's dead," she said. With her words came tears.

"Me neither," I whispered.

"You didn't get to meet her," Rebecca sobbed. "Skyler was amazing. Even though she was in seventh grade, we were still friends. Hold on, I want to show you something." She crossed the room to her bed, and from underneath it, she pulled out a small purple box. Rebecca pulled a small stack of photos out of it, and from the stack, a square piece of paper. On it, was a picture of her and Skyler. With a sickening jolt, I realized that Skyler looked just like me. She had a small, button nose, hair the color of wet sand, and countless freckles peppering her pale cheeks.

A horrible thought came to mind, making me sick to my stomach. What if the murderer meant to kill me and thought Skyler was me? What if she died because of me?

NINE

The worst part about not yet attending school was that I couldn't stop thinking about Skyler. In addition, Ms. Abigail acted like nothing had happened and assigned me chore after chore. Thursday was a sad and tedious day. Ms. Abigail expected me to polish the hardwood floor, clean and fold the laundry, make all the beds, clean and dry the dishes, and take out the garbage.

Finally, because she could not come up with more chores for me, Ms. Abigail said sourly, "You may go up to your room." I tried and failed to repress my look of relief as I bolted up the stairs two at a time. I threw myself back onto my bed and propped myself up on my pillows. Gazing absently out of the window, I ran over everything that had happened to me—the notes, the stone, the stolen goods, Skyler. All those things couldn't be a mere coincidence. It was more than that.

I walked downstairs and then outside into the yard. The trees, with their green leaves, were whispering in the raw spring breeze. I needed a quiet space to brood over the unusual events, mysterious notes, my new friends, and most of all, Skyler's murder. Had someone been willing to kill to get the stone? Was that what all of this was about, someone wanting the Stone of Discedo for themselves? And Skyler had gotten caught in the middle of it. I never had the chance to get to know Skyler, but she was a friend of Rebecca's. It wasn't fair for her to die.

The late afternoon sun hid behind a cloud as it shifted in the sky. I watched it for a while. Despite my desire to remain in the yard forever, I headed back into the orphanage. Ms. Abigail greeted me with a duster and a pair of gloves.

"Go dust all the baseboards, the tops of the doors, and the dressers," she ordered. Grudgingly, I took the duster, put on the gloves, and started with the downstairs rooms.

Then I trudged upstairs and worked my way to the end of the hallway. The last door I had to dust was the fire exit. Above the door was a sign that read: EMERGENCY EXIT ONLY-SECURITY ALARM WILL SOUND IF OPENED.

I stood on my tip-toes, placing one hand on the door handle to keep my balance. I reached up and ran the duster along the top of the door frame when I accidentally pushed the door open. I closed my eyes and waited for an alarm to go off, but nothing happened. I let the door fall closed and continued to dust. Suddenly, a small, gold key clattered to the ground.

Now knowing that there was no alarm, I opened the fire exit door again, stood on the landing, and peeked outside. Narrow rusted metal stairs were leading down to the alley and a giant green dumpster. Before going back inside, I tried the key in the lock on the door, and it was a perfect fit. I closed the door, happy to have found another way to get out of the orphanage if needed. It made sense to me that Ms. Abigail wanted the kids to believe there would be an alarm. But now that I knew the truth and had a key to the outside door, it would be a whole lot easier to get in and out.

I knew Ms. Abigail had a key of her own, so I slipped the key into my pocket. Having access to this could come in handy, in case I ever needed to sneak into the orphanage. I smiled. Maybe this was a sign. Maybe living here wouldn't be all bad.

• • •

Friday evening, at dinner, Jade and Ms. Abigail told us Skyler would be buried privately. We would have a memorial service for her, and everyone would be able to share memories. This was Ms. Abigail's only acknowledgment of Skyler's death. Probably her way of coping, I thought to myself, trying to see the good in her. But Ms. Abigail made this even harder when she handed me a mop and a bucket.

• • •

The weekend was slow and uneventful. Rebecca, Tessa, and I played a bunch of board games, Rick read his book, and Aaron and Nick fooled around and played ball. My new usual.

On Monday morning—my first day at Rolling Hills—I was filled with anxiety. Rebecca tried to soothe my nerves, but I heard little of what she said.

"Rolling Hills is a great school," Rebecca assured me.

"As far as middle schools go, she means," Nick added, earning an elbow from Tessa.

"Don't worry. At least one of us is in all your classes," Tessa said. "The day will be over before you know it."

"Okay," I said, unsure if I believed her or not. "I hope you're right."

Principal Higgins permitted Tessa, Rebecca, Aaron, and me to enter the school early so they could show me around and introduce me to my teachers. We grabbed a quick breakfast from the cafeteria and began my tour of the school.

"This is your homeroom," Rebecca told me. The two girls continued leading me through the hallway, showing me my classrooms in order as Aaron gave a running commentary about which teachers had unusual habits, which ones had odd features like weird moles or tattoos, and which ones tended to give mountains of homework.

It was difficult for me to focus and act like everything was normal. However, I knew school would help me get my mind off my fear and the insanity of the events surrounding me.

Tessa read my schedule. "Third-period science, Ms. Reyna. You have that class with Aaron and me."

"Too bad," Rebecca said. "I have Mrs. Pointer. She's one of the best teachers I've ever had."

"Ever?"

"Ever. Mrs. Pointer left a great job to come teach middle schoolers to love science the way she does. That's the sign of an amazing teacher."

Aaron looked over Tessa's shoulder to see my schedule. "Let's see, PE fifth period. Oh, we just got a new teacher, Coach Simpson. He's nice, not very strict . . . Too bad you don't have him. You have Coach Edwards."

"Where did Coach Simpson teach before coming here?" I asked.

Aaron frowned, "I don't know. He didn't say."

"He didn't tell us much about himself," Tessa added.

Aaron continued, "Sixth period reading . . . Oh, Mr. Levers, he's got a nasty mole the size of a—"

"Shut up, Aaron," Tessa interrupted. "It's her first day."

"Just giving her a fair warning," Aaron sighed, earning an impatient elbow from Tessa.

Tessa said, "Anyway, I don't really like Mr. Levers, but that's just a matter of opinion."

"I get in too much trouble in that class," Aaron added.

Rebecca shot him a glare. "I like Mr. Levers."

"That's because you're a good student," Tessa said.

"So are you," said Rebecca, "and you don't like him."

"The only reason I do well in that class is because I have an eidetic memory," Tessa said. "But it doesn't help me in every subject."

"The real reason you like him, Rebecca," Aaron said, "is because you're the teacher's pet."

"Am not!"

"Are too!"

"So, how's my seventh-period teacher?" I asked, changing the subject.

"Ms. Lopez is the best band director ever," Tessa assured me. "You'll love her."

"How come band is on my schedule?" I asked. "I didn't take band when I was at Mountain View."

"Maybe that was the only elective left," Rebecca speculated.

I looked at my schedule. "And what about eighth period? Is

Ms. Chambers nice?"

"She's certainly eccentric," Aaron put in, "but she's the best math teacher."

"You only like her because she gives out candy and plays old records," Rebecca accused.

"Not true! I also like her because she doesn't yell at us when we fool around."

"Ms. Chambers is also the coach of the basketball team and runs the school crochet club."

"You have a crochet club here?" I asked. There weren't very many clubs at my old school.

"Yep! We also have chess club, drama, student government, honor societies, et cetera," Rebecca said. "I'm in most of them, except chess."

"Rebecca's understating it," Tessa said, rolling her eyes. "Rebecca isn't just in the clubs, she's the president of them."

"Well, it's not that—"

"Don't be modest, be proud!" Tessa interrupted Rebecca.

The three of them led me out to the lush courtyard. The sky was smoky gray, and the sun was obscured by opaque, ominous looking clouds.

Nick and Rick walked into the courtyard, laughing and talking. I was surprised to see them getting along so well. The two of them sat down on a bench, and Rick cracked open the book about Abe Lincoln he was holding.

"Rick, are you ready for the math test today?" asked Aaron. "I totally forgot to study."

"I'm sorry, what was that?" Rick asked, looking up from his book.

"Put the book down for a sec," Aaron told him.

"Your ignorance is one of your most annoying qualities," Rick said, laughing a bit, as he placed a bookmark in his book. "Abraham Lincoln had an enormous influence on our country, and the Civil War is an important unit in the curriculum. It's not just for background knowledge, but also for our final exams in June. A lot of people are ignorant regarding the Civil War. They don't realize what a crucial factor it was in American history. Lincoln was especially significant—"

"You know what would be helpful?" Aaron interrupted. "If you stop using big words."

"Just because you and Nick can't understand them doesn't mean I shouldn't use them."

Right then, the bell rang to start the day. Tessa walked with Rick and me to my first-period class. Ms. Watson, the old, wizened history teacher whose face had cobweb-like wrinkles, opened the door. Tessa waved goodbye and departed for her class. I turned to face the classroom full of unfamiliar faces. "This might be a long day," I muttered.

TEN

Rebecca and Nick were in my language arts class, but the two didn't make eye contact. Rebecca seemed overly interested in the Tinker Bell memorabilia on Mrs. Reed's desk, and Nick seemed to be strangely intrigued by the artwork on the walls.

A few minutes into class, it came time for a group project on punctuation. I was paired with Rebecca, Nick, and a girl named Maria, and our group was assigned the Oxford comma. Rebecca, as usual, took the leadership role.

"Okay, so here's what I was thinking—now, we don't have to use this, it's just an idea—maybe we have the definition right here in purple since purple pops on white. The example can be below it in blue. We can write the words 'Oxford comma' in black on the top like this," she ran a finger around the top of the poster, "in block letters. What do you guys think?"

"Sounds good to me," I nodded my approval.

"Ditto," Nick grinned. Rebecca delegated different tasks to each of us. I had a feeling that, with Rebecca in charge, this would be an easy 'A.'

Third-period science was taught by Ms. Reyna, a mouse-like

woman who was squat, strict, and critical. Her lecture was sleep-inducing, and concentration proved to be unattainable. My eyelids begged me to let them close, and as hard as I tried, I couldn't focus. I needed to get up and move a bit, so I raised my hand.

"Can I go to the bathroom, please?" I asked once I was called on.

"It's 'May I,'" Ms. Reyna corrected.

"May I go to the bathroom?" I asked.

"I suppose so," Ms. Reyna said.

I got to my feet, grabbed the hall pass, and left the classroom.

When I got back to class, I finished my worksheet. The bell rang, and I leaped to my feet, eager to go to lunch. It was one of the highlights of my day and the only time I was with all my new friends.

I dropped my books off in my locker and headed to the lunchroom. Lunch was strangely awkward. Nick, for once, didn't say anything. Tessa and I filled the uncomfortable silence with off-topic banter about the upcoming spring break. Keeping my mind off Skyler's death was hard. Sadness consumed me, alongside fear and anger. I couldn't understand why all this had to happen.

"I still can't believe Skyler is dead," I whispered.

"I would rather not talk about it," Rebecca admitted.

"Why do you think she was murdered?" Rick asked.

"I don't know," I replied a little too quickly.

"Yes, you do," said Rick, cocking an eyebrow. "What do you think?"

"Well, I . . ."

"Sandy, just tell us," Tessa pleaded. "C'mon."

"Fine. I think . . . I think Skyler was killed by mistake."

"By mistake?" Rebecca asked.

"I think whoever was responsible for the murder was trying to kill me, and because Skyler looked like me, I think the murderer messed up."

"Interesting theory, Sandy," Rick nodded. "I have to say that makes sense, now that I think about it. She looked a lot like you—same build, same hair, same freckles." He pushed his glasses higher on the bridge of his nose, closed his book, and slipped it into his backpack, which was practically busting at the seams with all the things carried in it.

"I think it might even be because someone wants the Stone of Discedo. Maybe Skyler's murderer intended to threaten me until I told them how to get it. Maybe they intended to kill me to scare Brian. But either way, I think Skyler was in the wrong place at the wrong time, and the murderer thought she was me."

"Sandy, do you realize what this could mean?" Rebecca asked me.

"What?"

"You could still be in danger. If whoever it was figures out they didn't kill you, then they may come back."

• • •

I was in a daze. Everything seemed insignificant in comparison to Skyler's murder. Rebecca's point about me still being in danger made my head spin. Every little thing frightened me, a door closing, kids shouting . . . I was on hyper alert. Considering the possibility that someone might want me dead made me sick to my stomach. What if the murderer had messed up and realized it? What if they came back? I needed to get my mind off things. I needed a serious distraction.

Fifth period, I had PE with Tessa and Nick. The class was in the middle of a flag football tournament. Coach Edwards told me to join whichever team I pleased. So naturally, I chose the team with both Tessa and Nick.

The game began right after attendance was taken and started off smoothly. Nick sprinted in and out down the field to the end zone with the football clutched close to his chest. His agile footwork allowed him to juke around defenders and score a touchdown.

Tessa lingered on the sideline, waiting and watching. I couldn't tell who specifically, but she was watching someone carefully and closely. Suddenly, I realized who Tessa was watching. A boy I'd met in language arts, named Derek, was doing something to his flags.

"Stop!" Tessa shouted across the field. Everyone froze. "Derek, I see what you're doing!" She was yelling so everyone could hear her. "Watch this." Tessa strode up to Derek, whose face had turned bright red. Tessa yanked at his flags, but they didn't come out, "I saw you putting something on your flags. You put sticky-tac on them," she told him. Everyone on the field was frozen, watching the scene unfold. Derek's face was still bright red, beyond embarrassment. The gym coaches spoke to Derek as the rest of us headed back to our respective locker rooms.

Right before the bell rang, a girl named Purva came up to Tessa. "That was awesome what you did back there. Nobody ever stands up to Derek."

"Well, it was time someone did," Tessa shrugged, "and anyway, he deserved that humiliation."

"Totally," Purva agreed. With that, she walked away.

"Does Derek always do stuff like that?" I asked her.

"Yeah. He's a cheat, and a bully and—"

"I get it," I interrupted, not eager to see Derek again.

"Tessa, can I speak to you?" Coach Simpson called to her as we left the locker room.

"See you later, Sandy," Tessa smiled, and we parted ways.

I had sixth period reading with Rebecca, Nick, and Aaron, so I had slightly higher expectations. The tardy bell rang as Nick sprinted into the classroom. Mr. Levers gave him a stern warning and let him off the hook, but it was a close call.

"Who knows what a connotation is?" Mr. Levers asked the class. When nobody raised their hand, he said, "Nick, do you know?"

Nick, who was bent over his notebook, doodling in the margins, abruptly looked up, "What?"

"I asked you what a connotation is," Mr. Levers repeated frustrated.

"A connotation is . . . um," Nick stumbled. "It's . . . I don't know."

"That's because you weren't paying attention," Mr. Levers chided. "Rebecca, do you know?"

"A connotation is a feeling or idea that is related to something else. For example, a dove's connotation is peace."

"Very well done, Rebecca!" Mr. Levers congratulated. "Class, I want you to copy down exactly what she said." Aaron, whose goofy grin spread to his ears, mouthed "told you so" to me and looked back down at his paper to finish writing. Aaron had been right. Rebecca was the teacher's pet. Not that that was a bad thing.

When I got to seventh-period band, I introduced myself to Ms. Lopez. Her face was full of joy that matched her brightly-colored floral dress.

"It's nice to meet you, Sandy," Ms. Lopez beamed at me. "Welcome to my class! Did you take band back at your old school?"

"Yes. For three weeks in the elective wheel."

"And what instrument did you play?"

"Flute," I answered.

"Let's get you situated with a flute, then," Ms. Lopez said with undeniable enthusiasm. "I'll go see which flutes aren't being used. Sit tight." She left to go check the cabinets, and I took a seat by her desk, my eyes fixed on Ms. Lopez's massive Potato Head collection.

While I was waiting for her to return, my mind wandered. I thought about what Tessa said to Derek, how she stood up for what she believed in. The sound of Ms. Lopez snapping her fingers brought me back to reality.

At the end of the day, we boarded the bus which drove us back to the orphanage. Deputy Scordon was sitting in the kitchen.

"You guys go upstairs, I'll be up soon," I told them. They shrugged and left.

"Oh, hi," Deputy Scordon smiled at me. "How was your day, Sandy?"

"Can I tell you something?" I asked.

"Shoot."

"I think I know why Skyler was killed."

"And why is that?"

"I think it was a mistake. I think the killer meant to kill me, not her. We look an awful lot alike."

Deputy Scordon took a second to think that over and then nodded, "Thank you, Sandy. I'll make sure we look into this. Now go upstairs." I felt his gaze digging into my back as I climbed the stairs. Back in our room, Rick was already working on his homework, unlike his twin, who didn't even have a book out. Neither did Aaron.

"Are you guys going to do your homework?" Rick questioned at last. Nick and Aaron stopped playing catch with a foam ball and looked at him.

"It can wait, bro," Nick shrugged. "I'm not too worried about homework."

Rick shook his head, speechless, "When you decide you actually care about your education, let me know."

"That was a very Tessa-ish thing to say," Nick said dryly. Tessa seemed to be indifferent, but Rick inhaled deeply, shook his head, and continued his work. Aaron chuckled and continued to pass the ball around with Nick. The whole time, Rebecca had been sitting on her bed, her homework laid out in front of her, but her mind seemed to be elsewhere.

"What are you thinking about?" Tessa asked before I could.

"Everything, Skyler, especially."

"We have to do our best to move on," Tessa said, sliding over to Rebecca's bed and sitting down on the end.

"It's hard to move on," Rebecca's eyes were filling with tears. This was a softer side of her, a fearless leader turned emotionally tender. My heart took control of my feet, and I found myself walking over to Rebecca to give her a hug.

"Thanks, Sandy," Rebecca said. I wiped the tears from her face and looked her in the eyes.

"It'll all be okay. The Sheriff's department will figure this out, and make sure justice is served."

Rebecca gave a small nod, "I hope you're right."

* * *

Everyone at the orphanage was on edge because of the murder. The deputies were using the dining hall to question each of us again, so we were allowed to eat dinner in our rooms. Everybody got a tray and a plate, took their share of food, and hurried back upstairs.

"That greedy old witch!" Tessa hissed once we were out of Ms. Abigail's earshot. "She should be spending less on herself and more on better food." She speared a chunk of mystery meat on her fork, and glared at it with repulsion, "This is gross." Tessa plugged her nose and ate it, wincing as it met her tongue. Aaron mimed vomiting into his plate of cold, soggy mashed potatoes.

The stormy sky blackened as the sun slipped below the horizon. The evening was tediously quiet, the absence of Aaron's usual uplifting jokes was more than noticeable. Rebecca sat at the foot of her bed, doing homework on cell division and homeostasis. Rick helped her on the harder questions, simultaneously reading his book in between.

"We should probably get ours done too," Tessa said, eyeing

her homework with reluctance. "Ms. Reyna gave us a lot of science problems."

"Yeah," I agreed. I bent down to retrieve my book from my backpack when I saw a slip of paper wedged in the pages. Perplexed, I grabbed the paper and began reading.

> ○ DON'T UNDERESTIMATE THE
> ○ POWER OF A SMALL OBJECT.

I nudged Tessa and thrust the note into her hand. "A fourth note! This confirms it. It's talking about the Stone of Discedo! It all makes sense! The stone is really small but really powerful! Whoever is writing these notes knows about the Stone of Discedo and is trying to protect me, not threaten me! Brian said if the stone were found in our possession, we'd spend the rest of our lives in jail. That could explain the first note: 'Stay away from the girl.' Maybe the writer didn't want me to be involved with Brian or the stone because of the danger involved. That ties in the second note: 'Don't get involved in trouble.'"

"Sandy, I think you're onto something," Nick confirmed. "The 'Watch your back' note . . . maybe they were talking about . . . maybe they knew something about Skyler's murder?"

"Or maybe it was referring to starting at Rolling Hills?" I paused for a moment to consider my own idea. "I think that makes sense. Whoever it is knows about my switch because they managed to get into my third-period classroom or break into my locker."

I paused again, "Did anyone come in during class while I was in the bathroom?"

"No."

"Okay," I said, a little disappointed. "Then it was someone who could get into my locker. Which teachers have master keys to the lockers?"

"I know some of them: Mrs. Reed, Ms. Reyna, Mrs. Pointer, the PE coaches, Ms. Chambers, and the assistant principals," Tessa said.

"Did you say Ms. Reyna? Maybe she put the note in my book," I suggested.

"In the detective movies, they talk about how the criminal has to have a motive, but you just met her, so I don't see why she would have left the note." Tessa reasoned.

"All her teachers are new to her. Why would any of them be responsible?" Rick asked pointedly.

"I have to call Brian," I said, breaking the tense silence. "He should know about this."

"You're right," Rick agreed. "But there are two problems with that. One, you don't have his number, and two, none of us have a phone."

"We could use the orphanage phone," I suggested.

"It's broken," Nick said. "Ms. Abigail wouldn't let us near it anyway."

"She wouldn't mind if we used her personal phone if she didn't know about it," Aaron corrected, a scheming glint in his brown eyes. "I've got a plan."

"We need his number first," Tessa protested.

"I have it," I said, remembering the slip of paper he gave me with his number on it. "It's in my bag." I rummaged around in my backpack, and at last, I found the piece of paper and placed it on my nightstand. "Let's deal with this tomorrow after school. I need to get some sleep."

. . .

Tuesday dawned with a beautiful sunrise and the harmonic chirps of birds in the distance. At breakfast, I noticed there was a group of adults I'd never seen before. Jade saw me looking at them.

"They're counselors," she explained. "For the kids who need help processing the trauma of Skyler's death." Then she froze. "Mr. Dylan," she whispered.

"Who is Mr. Dylan?" I asked. Jade pointed at one of the men in the group of counselors. What was left of his gray hair was neatly combed. He had a wrinkled face with a warm smile.

"Jade?" he asked. "Is that you?" I pieced together that Mr. Dylan was the counselor Jade had mentioned, the one who helped her when she first came to the orphanage.

"Yes!" Jade exclaimed, beaming. She ran towards him and pulled him into a big hug. This caught the attention of some of the surrounding kids, who watched with interest.

"What are you doing here?" Mr. Dylan asked her once they stopped hugging.

"I work here," Jade responded with a sense of pride.

"I thought you got a degree in accounting," Mr. Dylan said, looking a little puzzled.

"I did, but it didn't feel right," Jade explained. "I wanted to help kids, make a difference. You inspired me."

"Are you happy?"

"Absolutely."

Mr. Dylan smiled, "Well that's all that matters."

• • •

At school, the moment I arrived at language arts class, Rebecca pulled me aside. "Who was that man Jade was hugging this morning?" she asked. I told Rebecca Jade's story.

"That's incredible. I never knew."

"Alright, get into your groups and finish your posters," Mrs. Reed interrupted. "We'll present them in ten minutes."

When it was time for our presentation, both Maria and I were reluctant to speak, so Rebecca took the lead. Every once in a while, Nick decided to cut in, finishing his sentences with "or something like that" or "I don't really know."

In third period science, which I had with Tessa and Aaron, Ms. Reyna passed back our tests. Tessa picked up her paper eagerly, only to look disappointed.

"Eighty-six," she sighed, "It's okay. I'll do better next time. Science and math are the two classes my eidetic memory gets me nowhere."

Ms. Reyna passed back Aaron's test next, and even though he was at another table, he mouthed 'seventy-eight' at us. He seemed pleased with himself. When Ms. Reyna passed back my test, my eyes were immediately drawn to the large '80' in the top left corner. Tessa discreetly peeked over my shoulder.

"An eighty isn't that bad," she said. I said nothing. To me, an eighty was average. Subjects like math and science had never come easy to me.

When the time came for fifth-period gym, Derek looked

annoyed. He was on the sidelines, watching bitterly because he was suspended from playing flag football. The game was back and forth, for a while we were losing, then tied, then winning, then losing again. Eventually, Nick managed to score and lead our team to victory. On the way back to the locker rooms, Derek stomped over to Tessa and me.

"Snitch," he muttered.

"I wouldn't have said anything if you weren't doing anything," Tessa answered.

Glowering, Derek said, "This isn't over."

"I think it is," Tessa said, striding into the girls' locker room without another word. Most of the girls in the class surrounded her, some complimenting, some admiring, and some even thanking her for standing up to Derek.

The whole P.E. drama was the most eventful thing happening. The rest of the day was a bore, and unfortunately, the workload was heavy. When the final bell rang, I felt a surge of relief which was quickly doused by anxiety. Would Aaron's plan to use Ms. Abigail's phone work, or would it somehow get us into deeper trouble? I could not push the thought from my mind.

Once the bus dropped the six of us off, Rebecca opened the large mahogany doors and led the way to our bedroom. The room was unusually clean. The floor sparkled, the beds were made with military precision, the drapes were parted, and the bed frames were washed.

"What is going on?" I narrowed my eyebrows, confused.

"This happens twice a year when the state comes by for their inspection," Rebecca informed me. "It's the only time she ever hires a cleaning service."

Tessa said, "Anyway, Aaron is going to tell us the plan now. You better get out the paper with Brian's phone number on it." Nodding, I crossed the room to my nightstand.

"Um, guys?" I said.

"What?" Tessa asked. "Is something wrong?"

"The paper with Brian's phone number isn't here," I whispered. "It's gone!"

ELEVEN

The others looked at me, their eyes wide.

"The paper has to be here. It was here yesterday," I said. "Where could it have gone?"

"There are two possibilities," said Rick. "The first is that someone took it, which is highly unlikely unless they heard us talking. The second possibility is that whoever was cleaning in here today mistook it as scrap paper and threw it away."

"I bet someone trashed it," Aaron said.

Tessa's mouth dropped open, "Um, guys . . . the garbage truck comes this afternoon. It comes every Tuesday."

"Darn it!" Nick muttered.

"We've got to get down there!" I said.

Aaron consulted his watch, "We only have an hour or so to find that paper before the garbage truck comes."

"Not to be rude or anything, but why is it so important that we find Brian's phone number?" Nick asked.

"Because, Nick," Tessa began, "whoever is leaving the notes might know he has the Stone of Discedo. If the person who killed

Skyler really meant to kill Sandy, then both Sandy and Brian are in danger. There's someone out there willing to kill for the stone. And we know the authorities are looking for it. If Brian is caught, he could go to jail!"

"Exactly why would he go to jail?"

"The Stone of Discedo was stolen from a lab in Germany—from the German government. It has an unimaginable amount of power. Anyone found with it in his or her possession is in major trouble," I explained. "We have to warn him! We have to find his phone number, fast."

"That's like trying to find a needle in a haystack, though," Nick objected. Hastily, he added, "It's not that I'm not going to help, but we better start now."

"Agreed."

"I have an idea how we can get out of the orphanage," Rebecca said. "We can use the fire exit now that we know there isn't an alarm."

"Good thinking!" said Tessa.

We followed Rebecca out of our bedroom. I eased open the fire exit door, and the six of us stepped outside and crept down the metal stairs to where the dumpster sat. It was filled with heavy duty garbage bags that had been thrown pell-mell into the massive bin. Dozens of flies buzzed around the dumpster's rim.

Tessa tore open the first black bag and rummaged around in it, finding nothing but empty nail polish bottles, tubes of lipstick, and stained cotton balls blotched with nail polish. Rebecca fished through a second bag filled with empty tuna cans, sandwich bags, and used tissues, much to her disgust. Rick discovered empty soda cans, paper plates, plastic utensils, bits of rope, and other miscellaneous objects. There was no slip of paper to be found. Aaron was fishing through a garbage bag when he came across a small rectangular black box.

"Hey guys, come here for a second," said Aaron.

"What's that? What's inside?" Nick asked.

"Does it look like he knows what's in it yet?" Tessa said.

Aaron's hand was shaking as he opened the slender black jewelry box. Inside were a set of six rings, unblemished in mint condition. Each ring had a colored stone: one red, one orange, one yellow, one green, one blue, and one purple.

I held one of the rings up in the air; its polished red stone glittered in the afternoon sunlight. "I wonder why Ms. Abigail threw these away." Tessa said.

"Maybe they weren't nice enough for her," Nick said. "Either way, they could be worth something." Rick nodded in agreement.

"Can I have a ring?" Aaron asked. "They're very macho."

"Ha ha," said Nick. "You won't be making fun of them if we get money for them."

Rebecca kept the purple ring and passed the others out. Tessa got the red one, Aaron the orange, Nick the green, and Rick the blue, leaving the yellow one for me.

We spent a little time trying to figure out why Ms. Abigail threw them away, but we kept going around in a circle, each idea a dead end. With no idea why the rings, in all their beauty, had been thrown away. We continued to search through the bags of trash.

I found a soiled newspaper with an article about a missing person, a cruddy watch that no longer functioned properly, a weathered notebook, and a bunch of other trash. The moment I tore open one of the last garbage bags, my eyes were drawn to a sealed white envelope. What was a perfect envelope doing in a filthy dumpster? I bent over to retrieve it, opened it, and pulled out the piece of paper. It read:

> SANDY,
>
> I KNOW ABOUT THE STONE. WATCH OUT FOR YOURSELF. THERE ARE SOME PEOPLE IN THIS WORLD WHO WILL TRY TO RUIN YOUR LIFE. DON'T GET YOURSELF INTO TROUBLE, WHATEVER YOU DO.
>
> STAY SAFE.

A feeling of shock ran through my body. My hands shook as I turned it over. The fifth note was in the same handwriting, written by the same person who left all the other notes. There was no longer any doubt in my mind that all the notes had been warnings. Someone was trying to keep me safe. But why? Who really cared that much? And why was the note in the dumpster?

"Guys! Guys look!" Tessa took the note out of my hand and read it. "Sandy found another note!"

"We need to figure out who is writing these notes," Rebecca said to unanimous agreement, "and we also need to figure out why."

"Was it signed?" Nick asked.

Tessa glared at Nick. "If they had signed it, wouldn't we know who wrote it? Hmmm, do you think it was put in the dumpster on purpose? Maybe whoever wrote it trashed it. Or maybe Ms. Abigail threw it away."

"Oh yes, that makes lots of sense," Aaron rolled his eyes. "Someone wrote a note to Sandy and then thought, 'Oh, never mind, I'll just put it in the trash and hope she goes dumpster diving and maybe finds it!'"

"Someone probably threw it away by accident," Nick said.

Rebecca pulled Tessa out of the dumpster, "Let's ask Jade who cleaned the orphanage today. The rest of you keep looking for Brian's phone number."

"Rebecca's right. It has to be in here somewhere."

"Wait, how are you two going to get back in?" asked Rick.

"We can use the SE," said Rebecca. She and Tessa took off towards the backyard.

"Um, Sandy?" Nick asked, once the other two were gone.

"Yeah?"

"Um, well, if the notes are a caution and not a threat, is Brian still in danger?"

"The writer seems to think so," I said.

For the next five minutes, the four of us worked in silence. Aaron occasionally paused to complain about the abundance of empty make-up containers and beauty products.

"Oh my gosh, all this rotten food stinks!" Nick plugged his nose, looking repulsed.

Rick nodded. "I've never had the misfortune to smell such a rancid odor."

"Really?" Nick said. "Why can't you talk like kids your age?" Rick opened his mouth to reply, but second-guessed himself, shrugged, and continued to search without another word. After a few minutes, Tessa and Rebecca came back outside, except they came from the front of the orphanage.

"How did you get out the front without Ms. Abigail seeing you?" Nick asked.

"She was busy." Rebecca shrugged. "And neither Jade nor Deputy Sphinx saw us come outside."

"Deputy Sphinx kind of just sits in the dining hall, so he can't see the front door anyway," Tessa added. "We can all go back in the front."

"Well, Tessa?" I asked. "What did Jade say?"

"She said Ms. Abigail hired a new company, *Julianne's Cleaning Services*. She got them from a business card left in the mailbox with a flyer offering a special price for the first cleaning."

"Julianne is probably the owner of the company," Aaron said.

"Duh," Tessa said.

"Hold on, guys, we can't jump to conclusions like that," said Rick. "We need to—"

"Guys, I found it! I've got his number!" Nick triumphantly brandished the paper.

"Yes!" I said as the four of us scrambled out of the dumpster.

Tessa suggested, "I think whoever wrote the notes somehow got into the orphanage to leave the note and trashed the number. But why?"

"Maybe so Sandy couldn't contact Brian," Rick said. "The first note, 'stay away from the girl,' says the person obviously wants you and Brian to have nothing to do with each other."

"But if this person wants to keep Sandy separated from Brian, leaving her notes only makes her want to contact him," Nick said.

"The person may not know that," Rick argued.

"So, let's say it is someone trying to keep Sandy away from Brian," said Nick. "Why?"

"Maybe he or she believes that Brian and the Stone of Discedo are dangerous, and is trying to keep Sandy safe," Rebecca said.

"I don't know who could care about me that much. Other than maybe Mr. Phillips, but we kind of already ruled him out. He had no reason to leave the notes since he could have talked to me. Plus, he couldn't have left school to leave the more recent notes anyway," I said. "Wait, someone probably posed as a cleaner to—"

Aaron said, "Someone is super mysterious, and like, they need a disguise so why not a cleaner? Cleaners are so cool and mysterious."

"Actually, it makes perfect sense," Rebecca said. Aaron looked like he wanted to eat his words.

"I don't know," Nick said. "Whoever cleaned the rooms did a pretty good job. I mean, what if it was a real cleaning service and they threw it away thinking it was scrap paper?"

"But then what about the note in the envelope?" asked Rebecca. "Maybe the person didn't want Sandy to contact Brian, so they threw away his number and left the envelope to warn her?"

"Then why was the envelope in the trash?" Nick asked.

"We can talk later," Aaron interrupted. "We've got Brady's number."

"Brian," Tessa corrected him before I could say anything.

"Right," Aaron said, "we've got Brian's number now, so we

need to get moving. Commence Operation Use-The-Phone!"

Tessa giggled, "I like the name."

"Thanks!" Aaron grinned.

Rebecca explained the plan to us, "Are we ready?" A chorus of "ready" rose from our group.

"Let's do this."

• • •

Rebecca and I walked side-by-side into Ms. Abigail's bedroom. Rebecca was doing all the talking.

"Ms. Abigail?" she asked in an artificially sweet voice.

"What is it, you disrespectful child?" she demanded.

"There is a man here to see you," Rebecca lied in a surprisingly convincing voice.

"Oh really, now?" Ms. Abigail asked. Her eyes lit up as she suddenly turned to look at us.

"Yep," Rebecca nodded and offered a small smile. "He's outside right now. Says he can't wait long."

"Well then," Ms. Abigail draped a hideous, flowered shawl delicately across her shoulders, sprayed a bit of perfume, and applied a fresh layer of lipstick. The results were anything but effective.

"And where is he?" she asked, tightening the strap on her high, scarlet heels, and smoothing her hair.

"He wants to meet you in private. He's in that building over there. I think he wants to buy it," Rebecca said, indicating the old brick building to the left of the orphanage.

"Oooo. I like a rich man with a little mystery." Ms. Abigail cackled and trotted off to join the invisible man. We heard the front door close, and our friends rushed over to Ms. Abigail's bedroom.

"I know she's stupid, but I can't believe you got her to fall for that!" Nick said. Rebecca blushed.

Aggravated, Tessa said, "I don't know why we didn't just wait until she hung up to use her phone."

"Because she's always on that thing, and if she's not, it's within reach," Rebecca said. "We caught her by surprise, so she didn't even think to take her phone with her."

"True, true," Aaron agreed. "Phase 1: Old Hag Extraction is complete. Commence Phase 2: Call Mystery Kid."

"Brian is not a mystery," I objected.

"He is to the rest of us," Aaron said.

"Tess, Rick, let's go wait closer to the front of the orphanage," said Rebecca. "Remember, Nick, Aaron, Sandy, when you hear our bird-call signal, Ms. Abigail is coming back in."

Aaron nodded and gave a double thumbs-up. Rebecca, Tessa, and Rick ran off.

The remaining three of us looked for Ms. Abigail's cell phone. I grabbed her phone as soon as I saw it on her vanity.

"Ugh. What's the password?" I asked.

Aaron remained completely calm. "Try 1025."

"Of all the numbers in the world, why 1025?" Nick asked

"It's her birthday. I've used her phone once or twice," Aaron said. "But that was a while ago, she might have changed it since then. Well? Did it work?"

"I can't believe it," I said as I typed in Brian's phone number. I pressed the phone to my ear. It rang. And rang. And rang. Finally, he answered.

"Hey Brian, it's me, Sandy."

"Sandy?! What are you doing? Where are you calling me from? Is something wrong?"

Instantly, I dove into telling him everything that had happened since I left Mountain View, including that I was using Ms. Abigail's phone and only had a brief time to talk.

"Whoa," Brian said. "A murder? An anonymous letter? I can't believe it. I'll try and figure this out. I'm sorry I got you involved in this."

"Don't apologize," I said. "I was the one who asked to know in the first place."

"Okay then," Brian said, but he didn't seem convinced. "Listen, before you hang up, clear the recent calls. If she checks the list and sees that there was a call she didn't make, she'll get suspicious."

"Oh, right. Thanks. I would've forgotten."

"No problem. Now go before she comes back."

"Bye." I hung up the phone and cleared the call from Ms. Abigail's lengthy list of recent calls. Suddenly, I heard a rather loud, unnatural cawing noise from outside, and I realized with an unpleasant jolt it wasn't a bird. It was the signal our friends had created. Ms. Abigail was headed back in the orphanage.

"Hide!" Aaron hissed. Nick yanked open the door of Ms. Abigail's walk-in closet which was filled with heaps of clothing, beaded jewelry, and lavish dresses. The three of us rushed in. Nick closed the door in our wake just in time. The distinct clicking of

Ms. Abigail's heels could be heard entering the room.

"Those lying little brats!" she hissed. "Extra chores tonight." Ms. Abigail paused, "Why just tonight? Why not extra chores all week?" She let out a shrill cackle. My heart began to pound, faster and faster. My breath became uneven and choppy. We were trapped.

TWELVE

There, in her colossal closet, enveloped in darkness, apprehension, and anxiety, Nick, Aaron, and I sat crouched against the wall. The darkness was suffocating, and it seemed like the walls were slowly closing in. We heard Ms. Abigail's footsteps right outside. It sounded like she was talking on her phone.

Suddenly, a long beam of light swept the closet, its point of origin from the ceiling. I looked up. The light was coming from the large air vent. A hand pushed the vent open. The vent's hinges squeaked. I prayed Ms. Abigail hadn't heard. Rebecca was there, beaming with pride and holding a flashlight. She smiled and gestured us towards her. Rebecca extended a hand, and I grabbed it, using the shelf to support myself as I climbed into the surprisingly roomy vent. Ms. Abigail's orphanage was an old building, and there were several things, such as the fire exit and large vents, that made it seem even more so. Hastily, Rebecca helped the other two up into the vent and then replaced the cover.

"One moment, Luana, I need my shawl," Ms. Abigail said. I assumed she was on her phone. She opened the closet door and flicked on the light switch, flooding the closet with light.

"Luana, remind me to call the air conditioning guys. There's a weird noise coming from the vent." Then she left her closet, plunging it back into darkness. The only light in the vent was that of Rebecca's flashlight. We were army-crawling along, spread far apart so there wasn't too much weight in a certain area at once. Rebecca wasn't sure how much the air vents could hold because she'd only used them twice before when she was a lot younger. Dust coated the walls of the vents, causing Rebecca to sneeze. We followed her directions to the next vent.

Upon opening it, she announced, "This is the laundry room." One by one, we climbed out of the vent and onto the dryer.

"Ugh, I feel like when I was in 3rd grade and couldn't stop sneezing because of our class bunny," said Rebecca. "I'll have to take some allergy medicine." As if on cue, she sneezed again, and Nick laughed. Cautiously, we left the laundry room, crept upstairs, and made it back to our bedroom. Rick was sitting cross-legged on a wooden chair in the corner, his glasses perched on the edge of his nose and his eyes transfixed on a book.

"Brilliant plan," I said.

"Rebecca's idea," Tessa said.

"We came up with it together," Rebecca corrected. "It was both of us."

"Not really, but thanks," Tessa said.

"I guess we can call this mission successful." Aaron grinned his proud, mischievous smile.

"Yeah, yeah, this is great, but we need to focus on Julianne's Cleaning Services. Maybe someone posed as a cleaning person to dispose of the number and plant the envelope in the bedroom,"

Rick said. Then he frowned, "But then why would the envelope be in the trash?"

"I know this is a long shot," said Nick, "but maybe the writer of the notes trashed Brian's number so you couldn't contact him, then planted the envelope somewhere in this room—"

"But we already talked about that," Tessa said. "What we don't know is why the envelope with the note to Sandy was in the trash."

"I wasn't finished!" Nick said. "What if the writer of the notes was working with actual cleaning people who threw the envelope away by accident?"

"You're right," Aaron said. He waited a second then added, "That is a long shot."

"Then how else did the envelope make it into the trash?" Nick said. We all thought for a moment.

"I don't know," Rick admitted.

"We should try to figure out whether the paper with Brian's number was thrown away on purpose or by accident," said Rebecca. "Then maybe we can figure out the envelope."

"Purpose," Rick said at the same time as Nick said, "Accident."

"It was just a scrap piece of paper with a few numbers on it," Nick reasoned. "It could easily be mistaken for trash."

"A real cleaner would have checked to see what was on the paper before throwing it away," Rick said. "Besides, it's clear someone wants to keep Sandy away from Brian and the stone, therefore, away from trouble. Rebecca and I can do some research on Julianne's Cleaning Services. Maybe we can figure out when they opened. If it was in the past two weeks we know, that most likely, it was made up as a ruse for whoever wrote the notes."

"Sounds like a good idea," Rebecca agreed.

"There's one problem," said Rick. "We'll need to use the internet. That means we need Katie's tablet."

"Oh," Rebecca said. "Well, I don't know . . ."

"Come on, Becca," said Tessa. "Can't you put aside your differences with your sister for a few minutes? This is much bigger than the two of you."

"Well, I guess you're right. I'll see if I can borrow Katie's tablet."

"Is there even Wi-fi here?" I asked.

"We use the Wi-fi from the building next door," said Rebecca.

"How do you know the password?"

"Aaron figured it out," she said. "I'm not sure how, but he did."

"It's guest1234," said Aaron. "Nothing too difficult."

"We need to get back on track," said Rebecca. "I'll try to get the tablet and Tessa can go downstairs and look for the company's business card." Tessa gave her a nod, and the two of them left the room.

The rest of us waited in silence, left to our own thoughts. My mind danced around school and chores, but then took a turn and thought of all the people I'd probably never see again. I started crying, every tear that fell was a part of my life I would never get back—*Ida, Amanda, Olivia, and worst of all, my parents.*

• • •

Tessa came back first, holding the company business card in one hand and clutching Ms. Abigail's cell phone in the other.

"You got her phone too?" I said in disbelief.

Rick jumped to his feet, "How?"

"Easy," Tessa said. "She was in the kitchen helping Chef Jamie cook dinner. Well actually, she was overseeing dinner being made, she would never offer her help. Anyway, she was busy, so I took it from her couch. Simple."

"We should have done that earlier," Nick said. "That would have been so much easier."

"We didn't have time to wait for her to start helping make dinner," I said. "Besides, there was no way of knowing if she was going to help or not."

Rick said, "We've got to call quickly before she notices it's gone."

Tessa nodded, "What's the password?"

"It's 1025," Aaron said.

"How do you know?"

"It's her birthday," Aaron said.

"Shhh," Tessa nervously dialed the number as silence blanketed the five of us.

"Hello?" Tessa said into the speaker. "Yes, this is Abigail Marsh. I would like to ask your owner a question. Yes, I'll hold." Tessa paused for a moment. "Yes, hello again . . . yes, this is Abigail Marsh. Okay, I'm uhhhh . . . I'm filling out a form for the State, and I need to know how long your company has been in business? Hello? Hello?" Tessa pulled the phone away from her ear and frowned at it. "They hung up," she said. "They avoided the question. That means they probably aren't a real company. If they were genuine, they wouldn't have any problem answering that question."

Rebecca walked in holding Katie's tablet. "They didn't answer your question when you asked?"

"No, they just hung up," Tessa said.

"Let's look them up online." She typed 'Julianne's Cleaning Services' into the search bar. Nothing came up. "There's nothing."

"So they're not real," said Tessa.

"Just because they don't have a website doesn't make them fake," said Aaron.

"In this day and age?" Tessa said. "Yeah, it does."

"Tess, on the phone was it a woman or a man?" asked Rebecca.

"A man," Tessa replied as she pocketed the company card. "I'll keep this just in case."

Silence soon descended upon us, and I fell prey to my thoughts. This was all so confusing. There were too many possibilities.

Rick broke the silence. "Now that we know the cleaning company is a facade—"

"Hang on," Rebecca said. "We can't be sure just yet."

"What do you suggest we do?" Rick asked.

"Why don't we call and ask them to come to a random location tomorrow? They'll likely decline, and then we'll know."

"What if they say yes?" I asked.

"If they agree to come, then we'll wait five minutes, call again, and cancel," Rebecca said. "But I doubt that'll happen."

"You never know," I said. I didn't know what to believe anymore. I once doubted magic, but in the past few weeks, I discovered that the impossible was in fact real. My whole world had been turned upside down.

Rick said, "Rebecca and I will do some research later and try to find out more. Maybe 'Julianne's' isn't the name of the owner. Maybe Julianne is someone the owner knows or something . . ."

Tessa left to return Ms. Abigail's phone before she noticed it was gone. I looked out the window. The afternoon slowly faded. Tuesday was leaving fast as the sun was slipping below the horizon.

* * *

Still adjusting to Rolling Hills and the orphanage made the days pass quickly. On Wednesday night, while we were eating big, steaming bowls of chili, Nick suggested that we go outside.

"Ms. Abigail doesn't want us outside after dark," Rick said. "The sun is setting."

"To hell with Ms. Abigail's stupid rules!" Nick said. "We're old enough to stay out after dark!"

"Nick, chill," Rick said.

"It's the backyard. It's literally right outside the orphanage. Ms. Abigail doesn't care about us. She cares about the paperwork she'll have to fill out if something happens to us!" Nick said.

"She's a witch," Tessa agreed.

"I'd use a slightly different version of that word," Nick grumbled.

"Let's stay inside," I said. "It's not worth it."

"Nick, all of what you say is true, but be quiet. Someone may hear you," Rebecca said.

"Can we please go outside? I think better when I'm outdoors," Nick said.

"Fine," said Rebecca.

"I guess so," I said with a shrug. The six of us slipped out of the noisy dining hall and into the quiet calm of the backyard. With loathing in his emerald eyes, Nick looked back at Ms. Abigail, who was in the dining hall having dessert. "She's a bi—"

"Nick, take a deep breath. We get it," I said.

"Right," Nick said his eyes still fixed on Ms. Abigail. "Sorry about that. I . . . I've been here at the orphanage for so long, and you know . . . my dad . . . Never mind." His voice instantly died.

"No, bro, you can tell us," said Aaron. "We're friends, we can trust each other."

"Yeah, Nick. C'mon, please?" Rebecca said. Nick looked sideways at his twin, who nodded.

"Fine," Nick agreed. "My dad, Tyler, well, he used to drink and do drugs. He would whip Rick and me. Yell at us. Curse at us. And when our mother tried to stop him, my dad hurt her. Finally, she'd had enough and left. Six months later, there was an article in the newspaper about a Cheryl Powel who committed suicide by jumping off a bridge. That was our mom." Nick sniffled but didn't cry. "There was a funeral service for our mom, but our dad wouldn't take us. Not too long after, our dad was drinking and driving and crashed, killing himself. Fortunately, neither of us was in the car. It was the police who came to our house to tell us he was dead. When they arrived, they realized that Rick and I were all alone. They asked about contacting our grandparents.

We didn't have any, so the state social workers picked us up and dropped us here. There wasn't a funeral. He didn't have any friends."

"Wow," I whispered. "Rick, Nick, I'm so sorry."

"I'm over it now. But I still don't really like talking about it," Nick said.

"Same," Rick agreed. "It's a difficult subject, but it's also all that I can remember. I don't remember much of living with our parents. Being orphans is kind of normal to me, I guess."

"I understand," Rebecca said. "Sorry for prying. We didn't mean to make you feel uncomfortable."

"It's okay," Nick said. "Aaron, can you tell us your story? Like you said, we're friends."

"Using my words against me," Aaron sighed and added, "Fine. I guess since you told your story, it's only fair I share mine."

"I was four years old when my parents died. At the time, I was at my friend's house. My father was using the oven but accidentally left it on, and it caught fire. The house burned, and both my parents were killed. Our dog, Smokey, was taken home by a fireman and I was taken here."

"Aaron, how sad," I whispered. Even though he wasn't crying, I felt sympathy tears well up in my eyes.

"It's okay. I barely remember them. I've been here for seven years."

"Sorry, bro," Nick said.

"Here's a big moment of cheesy wisdom; it makes me who I am. If my parents hadn't died, I wouldn't have the world's greatest friends."

"Thanks, bro," Nick said, slinging his right arm across Aaron's skinny shoulders.

"I didn't mean you, I meant the girls," Aaron said. For a second, Nick looked hurt. "Relax, it was a joke." Nick laughed and kept his arm around Aaron.

"You know, I've never been one for that touchy-feely stuff," Aaron grimaced and pushed Nick's arm away.

"Oh, heh, yeah, me neither."

"Sandy, it's your turn. What happened to your parents?" Nick asked. I shook my head.

"We told our stories, now you tell yours," Nick said.

"I don't really know," I said.

"What do you mean you don't know?" Rick frowned.

"Well, my parents dropped me at a friend's house when I was four years old because they claimed they had to go on a trip for a few days. But they disappeared. My parents just mysteriously vanished. They were never found. The worst part is, I don't really know if I'm an orphan. I don't know if they are alive or dead."

"Wow," Aaron said.

"This is just making me sad," said Nick at last.

"It's hard being an orphan, but I can't imagine how much harder it would be not knowing what happened to my parents," said Rebecca. "Sandy, I'm so sorry."

"Thanks," I said. "I just wish I knew."

"I don't blame you," said Tessa. "That's terrible."

"I'll be right back. I want to show you guys something," I said with my doll Jessie in mind.

"If you go back in there, Ms. Abigail will make you do

chores," Nick said. "You can't go back in right now."

"Yes, I can. I'll go out through the SE, go around the side of the orphanage, and go up through the fire exit."

"That door is locked," Rick said.

"I was dusting and knocked the key off the top of the door frame by accident," I explained. "It's still in my pocket."

"Well that's fortunate," said Rebecca.

"I'll be back in a minute." I looked through the screened door. Ms. Abigail had left the dining hall probably to go to her bedroom, so I walked towards the shed. Gingerly, I slid in between the back of the shed and the fence and went through the SE one foot at a time. Then, I snuck around to the side of the orphanage. The large green dumpster sat at the foot of the metal stairs leading up to the door.

I climbed the stairs two at a time and knelt on the cold metal surface that was the platform. The door was open a few inches. Someone had been here. In case the person was still nearby, I slowly crept back down the stairs—my heart racing faster than ever—and made my way back to the others.

Nick frowned, "What—"

I pressed a finger to my lips, "The door is slightly open. I think someone is in there." I was beyond scared, my heart pounding almost loud enough for the others to hear. Fear thundered through my veins, freezing me to the spot.

"Rebecca, what do we do?" Nick asked.

"Is Deputy Sphinx still here?"

"Yes, I think so," Tessa answered.

"We need to go tell him, then," Rebecca said as we started

running to the door. When we got inside, Ms. Abigail was coming out of her room.

The moment she laid eyes on us, our ears were pierced by her sharp, venomous voice. "You were outside after dark! Extra chores for a month!" I would've bet anything that she saw us out there but didn't say anything so she could punish us later.

"Like we don't already have that," Aaron muttered.

"Where is Deputy Sphinx?" Rebecca said.

"He just left. His shift ended."

"Then where is Deputy London?" Rebecca asked.

"On his way, I assume. What's it to you, anyway?"

"Tessa, go call 9-1-1," Rebecca said. Tessa nodded and sprinted into Ms. Abigail's bedroom.

"You are not allowed in there! Come out right now!"

"Ms. Abigail, someone broke into the orphanage," Rebecca said. "The fire exit door was open and—"

"That door is always kept locked from the outside."

"Well, someone must have picked it," Nick said, avoiding the truth, which would surely get me into even more trouble.

Tessa ran out into the foyer where we stood waiting. "Deputy London is almost here.

"Whoever it is probably left by now," said Nick.

"They may have left evidence," I said as Deputy London came dashing in.

"Where was the break-in?" I noticed his hand was on his holster.

"The upstairs hallway," Rebecca said. Deputy London rushed

up the stairs, and despite my instinct to follow him, I didn't. On the off-chance they were still here, it would be better to stay downstairs until Deputy London called the coast clear. In about fifteen minutes, Deputy London shouted, "He's gone!"

"Or she," Tessa muttered. Our group dashed upstairs, Ms. Abigail in our wake. I was still shaken and terrified, but I didn't let that stop me.

"Did any of you see anything?" the deputy asked us. Everyone said no. Except for me.

"I found the door open," I said.

"And that's it?" Deputy London asked.

"Yes."

"Ms. Abigail, do you keep the door locked from the outside?"

"Yes," she said. "At all times."

"And you have the key?"

"Yes, there is a key on my key ring, although I never use it," Ms. Abigail answered. I felt only slightly relieved by that answer. Maybe she had forgotten there was a second key. A second key that was normally on top of the door but now resided in my pocket.

"Is it possible that one of the kids opened it from the inside?" asked the deputy.

"No, all the middle and high schoolers were in the dining hall at dinner anyway," said Ms. Abigail. She whispered something in the deputy's ear. I imagined she was telling him she'd led all of us to believe an alarm would go off, so none of us would try to open the door.

"I'll still check for fingerprints," said Deputy London. My

heart began to race, and I felt dizzy until I remembered I had been wearing gloves while doing my chores. My fingerprints wouldn't be on the door. Relief rushed through me, calming my heart rate and soothing my fear.

After a while, Deputy London came back. "There were no fingerprints on the inside of the door. That means someone came in from the outside. Did you say the door is always locked from the outside?"

"Yes," said Ms. Abigail.

"If the person who got in didn't use the key to get in, and the door is always locked from the outside . . . then we have to see if it looks like the lock was picked." Deputy London said to himself. "I will call on some detectives to come and inspect everything. I'll be here all night. Come downstairs if you find anything or, you know, if something happens." Ms. Abigail followed Deputy London downstairs.

"Is there a new note?" Rebecca asked, as we walked to our bedroom. I crossed the room to my suitcase, and looked in it, expecting a note. I checked my bed, but there was no note to be found.

"No, I don't see any," I answered.

My heart rate slowly returned to normal, and I closed my eyes running over everything in my mind. Maybe it was the wind. Maybe nobody broke in; maybe it was just my wild imagination. But the door hadn't been open before . . .

Rick was sitting on the chair in the corner of our bedroom reading his book, while Nick and Aaron passed a foam ball back and forth. Rebecca and Tessa worked on their homework.

"Nick, you have homework too. You should work on it," Tessa said.

"You're not my mom," Nick snapped.

"I'm aware. But I do have your best interests at heart."

"Well, what I'm interested in," Nick said, "is playing catch with Aaron."

"Whatever. I tried."

I figured it would be smart if I finished my work too so I could sleep with a little peace of mind. My mind was elsewhere, but nevertheless, I finished all my homework, feeling that I may have managed decent grades.

That night, I was restless, and even though I was beyond exhausted, sleep seemed to be just beyond my grasp. At last, I managed to fall asleep around midnight, but just as I did, the nightmare began.

In the nightmare, I watched as a masked figure stabbed Skyler. I heard her screams echo in the dark hallway. I watched as tears soaked her face, and blood soaked her clothes. It was as though I was reliving the whole thing, although it was much, much worse seeing every little detail.

* * *

Thursday, my twelfth day at the orphanage, dawned with gray skies and a light drizzle. I changed out of my t-shirt and sweatpants and went over to the boys' room. To my surprise, Aaron was already awake. He was scanning pieces of lined paper that were stapled together.

I whispered, "What's that?"

Aaron passed the paper to me, and it didn't take long to figure it out. It was a list of the best pranks he'd pulled over the years.

*June 2nd – Covered the toilet with saran wrap

*August 5th – Replaced parmesan cheese with powdered sugar

*August 15th – Drew a mustache with permanent marker on Ms. Abigail while she slept

*September 25th – Put ketchup in Ms. Abigails red nail polish bottle

*January 16th – Prank called Ms. Abigail and convinced her she had to fly to Canada for a Best-Painted-Toenails contest

*August 13th – Put a fake tarantula in Ms. Abigails car

*September 1st – Convinced Ms. Abigail that the orphanage was haunted

*October 6th – Purchased a box full of foam balls using Ms. Abigails credit card

*November 20th – Snuck a fake snake into her bed

*March 19th – Poured prune juice into the grape juice

*June 15th – Placed a bucket of ice water over her door

*August 1st – Painted her soap bar in clear nail polish so she couldn't use it

*October 16th – Covered her toothbrush with green food dye and colored her whole mouth green

*May 29th – Poured itching powder in her bed

*April 5th – Texted her boyfriend from her phone to break up with him

*September 12th – Pulled her deodorant stick out of its container and replaced it with cream cheese

*October 2nd – Put bleach in her shampoo bottle and Ms. Abigails hair turned lime green

*October 14th – Slipped laxatives into a batch of brownies and left them for her to eat

The list went on, but I got the gist. Aaron was grinning with pride as I passed the list back to him.

"I'm planning my next prank," he said. "Want to help me with it?"

"Who are you pranking? Ms. Abigail?"

"Of course. I was thinking something along the lines of replacing her nail polish with colored super glue. Want to help?

"No, I'm good, thanks," I said. I didn't want to get in trouble.

"Are Tessa and Rebecca still asleep?" Rick asked me, changing the subject.

"Yeah. I came to hang out with you guys because I don't want to wake them."

Nick began to talk about sports and Aaron began to crack jokes, and for the first time in a while, I felt at home.

THIRTEEN

The others were awake by now, and it was almost time to go to school. I started to pack my backpack when I saw it. Peeking out of the front pocket was a small piece of paper the size of a sticky note. I gulped and slid it out. With shaking fingers, I unrolled it and read.

> ○ THEATER, SHIP, AND
> ○ PARADISE IN HISTORY

"Guys, I found another note." Even though part of me expected one, I was still shocked. Rebecca slid off her bed and crossed the room to come sit by me.

"'Theater, ship, and paradise in history?'" Rebecca looked confused as she read the sixth note. Aaron and the twins entered the room, their hair wet from the shower.

"Is that another note?" I nodded and handed Rick the note. He read it, then narrowed his eyes. "Now we know someone really was in here last night when we were all at dinner."

"That's the weirdest one yet," Nick said.

I shook my head, "This is getting too strange. We're calling Brian. Maybe he can figure this out. Or maybe he found something new."

"We called him yesterday," Nick said, "I doubt he has found anything else since then."

"Even if he hasn't, we should tell him about the note we found. Maybe he can figure out what it means," Tessa said.

"I agree," Rebecca said, "but there is no way we can get Ms. Abigail's phone again, nobody here has a phone, and the orphanage landline is broken. We'll have to use someone else's phone or something."

"So now, we have two calls to make, one to Brian, and one to Julianne's Cleaning Services," I said.

"We should do that after school, though. It's time to go," Rick said.

First-period history was dominated by Rick, as usual, who answered every question directed at the class. In second period, I found myself daydreaming about the note, *'Theater, ship, and paradise in history.'* I didn't even know what to make of it, or where to start. The bell rang, and it took me a moment to register it was time to leave class.

After lunch, I walked with Tessa to fifth-period gym. Once we got there, I changed quickly and rushed outside. The sky was clear. The sun's misty afternoon rays of light shone down upon the fields. The air was warm and humid, the grass damp and slippery beneath my sneakers. A sporadic breeze whispered in the trees, the sound broken by the waves of banter coming from the crowd near the locker room. Derek glared at Tessa and sat down on the sidelines to watch us play flag football. For most of the game, my mind was elsewhere. On the way back to the locker room, I spotted Derek talking to a girl named Kyra, who I recognized from science class.

"You're black. You shouldn't be allowed to go here," he was saying. "What makes you think you can represent our school?" Kyra stood there, frozen. People began to form a crowd around them to listen to the argument. Even Tessa stopped walking to listen. "You don't belong here," Derek continued.

"Kyra is just like any of us," Tessa shouted, "and to say that she isn't, is racist."

"It's not racist. It's a fact."

"Kyra is allowed to be here, and has the same rights to a free public education as anybody else," Tessa added. "It doesn't matter what her skin color is, we're all the same inside," she paused for a moment, "except the people like you, who are mean on the inside. You are the one who shouldn't be wearing our school shirt, Derek, because you are a bully."

Derek looked infuriated, "Blacks are—"

"Come on, Kyra," I put my arm around her and walked with her and Tessa into the locker room.

"Thank you, Tessa," Kyra said softly, "and you too, Sandy."

"No problem," Tessa smiled at her. "It's bullies like Derek who are the problem, not you."

Kyra smiled and said, "Thanks."

"We better get changed," I suggested. "Class is about to end." I gave Kyra another hug, changed, and took a swig of water from my water right before the bell rang. The moment the bell sounded, the girl's locker room and boy's locker room doors opened, and the whole class blended together.

At the end of the day, the final bell rang, and the six of us met at the bench near the bus lane. Waves of other students passed, boarding their own buses or stopping to gossip with friends. Aaron was the last to arrive, and together we got on our bus. Soon enough, we were back at the bleak orphanage.

"This place is so happy-looking," Aaron said as he jumped from the second step onto the gravel. "It always makes me smile."

"Totally," Nick laughed.

"Alright. Well now that we've all established we're at the happiest place in South Toheeden, let's talk about my plan to get the phone we need. Ms. Abigail won't part with her cell phone anymore, but I have a plan to get the phone we need to call Julianne's Cleaning Services and Brian," Rebecca began. "So—"

"How come one of us can't make the plan every once in awhile?" Nick complained.

"We don't have time for that," Tessa said. "Besides, Nick, do you even have one? Oh wait, let me guess, steal from Ms. Abigail?"

"No. I've got a good plan, and it will work."

"We came up with it together," Aaron said. "Right now, I'm two for two, and by the time we go to bed, I'll be three for three."

"Right," Tessa said, "and I bet you forgot to plan how we are going to get wherever it is we're going. There isn't a phone we can use here."

"As a matter of fact, I didn't forget," Nick said. "I just didn't make a plan for that."

"I figured as much," said Tessa.

Aaron rolled his eyes, "You're jealous because our plans work out and yours don't."

"No way! You are jealous of me because I have an eidetic memory," she paused for a moment, "and good grades." As I watched them go back and forth, I remembered what Rebecca had said about them squabbling like siblings.

"Guys!" Rick said. "Please, let's keep the peace."

"Right," Tessa said. "Sorry."

"It's okay, Tessa," Nick intervened. "Sorry, Rebecca. Continue." Rebecca looked between Nick and Tessa before proceeding.

"First, who could we ask to use their phone?" Rebecca said.

"Doesn't Jade have a phone we could use?" I asked.

"No. Ms. Abigail pays her next to nothing. She lives here for free and has no family," answered Aaron. "Before the landline broke, I saw her using it on rare occasions. I guess she never had a reason to get a cellphone."

"We can try to use Ms. Abigail's phone again," Aaron suggested. "Nick and I can watch in case she puts it down."

"That's good, but we need a backup," said Rebecca. "Does anyone have a person they can ask to use their phone?"

I thought about it for a moment, "There is one person I could ask."

"Who?" Rebecca asked.

"Remember how Ms. Marsh set up that Friday volunteer thing where I have to go help a teacher? The teacher, Mr. Phillips, really liked me when I was his student. I'm sure he'd be happy to help."

"Sounds good to me!" Tessa said.

"If Aaron and I can't get Ms. Abigail's phone, then you can ask Mr. Phillips for his," Nick said.

"I guess I'll have to ask him when I see him tomorrow," I said, "but I'll be by myself. You guys won't be there with me."

"We will in spirit!" Nick said.

"You'll be fine, you're perfectly capable," Rebecca said. We entered the orphanage and were greeted by Deputy London.

"How was school today, kids?" he asked.

"Regular, boring, awful school," Aaron said. Deputy London laughed as we headed upstairs to our rooms. I dropped my backpack onto the floor by my nightstand and threw myself onto the mattress. I found I was already anxious about tomorrow.

• • •

The next morning, Friday, a spring storm was rolling in. I heard the crackle of lightning and the booming of unruly thunder. Nick and Aaron had failed to get ahold of Ms. Abigail's cell phone, leaving the responsibility of getting a phone to me. The six of us hurried downstairs to the coat room to grab our jackets, just in time to hear Ms. Abigail arguing.

"You're breaking up with me?!" Ms. Abigail was screaming into her phone. Tessa giggled, stifling it with her hand. Ms. Abigail's voice lowered and was now incoherent, muffled by the oak bedroom door between us. Rebecca rushed to the kitchen and grabbed four of Ms. Abigail's personal glasses, passing them to Aaron, Tessa, and me. We pressed them gently up against the door, instantly able to hear bits of her conversation.

"But we just got together!" Ms. Abigail protested. Silence.

"How dare you! I will not be treated like this!" I heard her groan. Then we heard footsteps coming towards the door. Rebecca grabbed the glasses and rushed back into the kitchen, stuffing them into the cabinet. The rest of us hurried toward the front as Ms. Abigail opened her door. Unfortunately, she saw Rick and me, who were the slowest of the group.

"You brats! You were listening to my conversation!" Ms. Abigail's face was bright red. "How stupid do I look?"

"Very," Aaron said. He and Nick began to laugh.

"EXTRA CHORES FOR A MONTH!"

"Have a good day at school, kids," said Deputy London as we ran outside to board the bus. Once we were on, Aaron and Nick began to laugh again.

"What's so funny?" I asked.

"It's like the fourth time she's given us extra chores for the month, but we already got extra chores the first time, so it's just an empty threat," Aaron whispered. We all laughed.

First and second period dragged on, and third period was even worse. Ms. Reyna was grumpier than usual. Aaron was laughing with his friend, Kyle, in the back of the room. Kyle was a big kid with spiked bleached blond hair, who made Aaron look even scrawnier in comparison. Ms. Reyna's beady, hawk-like eyes were trained on them like a predator eyeing its prey.

"You boys continue to goof-off. It doesn't seem like you've learned your lesson! Three conduct cuts each!" When Kyle began to doodle in his notebook, she added, "Kyle, I'm up here. Pay attention."

I spent all day thinking about having to go back to Mountain

View. Ms. Abigail had signed me up for "community service," and my service was helping Mr. Phillips there. This was my punishment for my night walk. I wasn't sure if she knew what community service really was, but I wasn't about to say anything.

When the final bell rang, and I was about to get on the city bus to Mountain View, Tessa passed me an envelope with Julianne's Cleaning phone number, as well as Brian's number. Rebecca reminded me that I needed to type *67 before dialing so the call to Julianne's Cleaning Services would be anonymous. The others wished me luck, and I waved goodbye as they boarded their bus. I climbed hesitantly into mine, using the bus pass Ms. Abigail had given me.

Why was I nervous? Mr. Phillips wouldn't care if I used his phone. I inhaled and exhaled slowly, but it didn't help. I closed my eyes, feeling the vibrations of the engine against the cold metal beneath the window. I kept my eyes closed, and waited for those vibrations to stop.

Once I arrived, I crossed the pristine office to Miss McLaughlin's desk. I noticed she had added some Charlie Brown and Snoopy paraphernalia to her collection, but otherwise, everything looked the same.

"Hi, Miss McLaughlin," I said.

"Hello, Sandy! How are you doing?"

"Great," I lied. "How are you?"

"I'm doing well, thanks!" she said. "I assume you're here to help Mr. Phillips?"

"Yes, ma'am."

"Let me call his room and tell him you're here," Miss

McLaughlin said. She dialed a few digits and pressed the phone to her ear. The envelope with the phone numbers began to feel heavy in my back pocket.

"Hmm, he's not answering," Miss McLaughlin frowned. "Hold on a second." She dialed a few more numbers and waited, "Hi, Mr. Bluecrest, could you check next door and see if Ross is there? Yes, I'll wait." Silence. "Oh, he's not there. Do you know where he might be?" More silence. "Okay. Thank you, John," Miss McLaughlin hung up the phone. "Sandy, dear, Mr. Phillips must've left. He's not answering his phone, and his room is dark."

"Do you have his cell phone number?"

"I'm afraid not," she sighed. "But I know who might. Try the band teacher, Ms. June."

"Thank you." I forced a smile and walked to the music suite and opened the door to the band room. Ms. June, who was standing near the door with her back to me, turned around, immediately spread her arms wide, and beamed at me. She wore a cotton dress with lavish designs including swirls and flowers.

"Ahhh, Sandy! It's great to see you! How are you?"

I tried shouting back, but my voice was drowned out by the sound of the band practicing.

"I'm doing fine, thanks," I answered. "I'm here to see if you have Mr. Phillips's phone number."

"As a matter of fact, I do. Why do you ask?"

"I'm supposed to help him this afternoon, but he's not here."

"Would you like to call him on my phone?"

"Yes, please," I replied.

"Here." Ms. June handed me her phone, which I took a little

too eagerly.

"Could I maybe go outside?" I asked. "It's pretty loud in here."

"Sure," Ms. June agreed, "but be careful."

I realized that Ms. June would be able to check the recent calls, and if she didn't see Mr. Phillips's name, she might get suspicious. I tapped the search button and typed: Ross Phillips. I hit call and pressed the phone to my ear. After two rings, a voice answered.

"Hello? Veronica?"

"No, this is Sandy Marsh. Hi, Mr. Phillips."

"Sandy? Why are you calling on Veronica's—I mean Ms. June's—phone?"

"Long story. Sorry to bother you, Mr. Phillips, but I was wondering where you are."

"Someone in the front office should've told you." He sounded confused. "There was a district meeting that ran late. I'm on my way back now. I'll see you in about ten minutes."

"Okay, thanks, Mr. Phillips. I'll see you soon."

My mind evaluated all my options. I trashed my original plan to use Mr. Phillips's phone. I had a cell phone, right here in my hand. I pulled out the business card for Julianne's Cleaning Service, and typed *67 into the phone, followed by the number. My hands were shaking as I held it to my ear and read Rebecca's step-by-step instructions on the back of the card.

"Hello?" A man's voice said. "Who is this?"

"Um . . . San—" Then I remembered I shouldn't use my real name. "Sandra Hopkins."

"What can I help you with?"

"I know it's short notice, but we were wondering if you could come by tonight."

"Tonight? We're um . . . busy."

"Tomorrow, then?"

"Busy. Where did you get this number?"

"From a friend. Can you come in two days?" I awaited the confirmation of our theory.

"Booked. Goodbye."

"Don't hang up. I need your name because . . ." I racked my brain for a reason, ". . . I have to nominate you for the best customer service award."

"I'd, uh, rather not be nominated. Goodbye."

"No don't—" The man had already hung up. Even though I hadn't gotten the name of the man who worked there, our theories were confirmed that it was likely a fake company. I quickly deleted the call from her recent calls list.

"Sandy, dear?" Ms. June had come outside. "Did you call Mr. Phillips?"

"Yes, ma'am."

"Okay, can I have my phone back?"

"Uhhhh," I still had to call Brian.

"Sandy, I need to use my phone."

"Sure." Reluctantly, I handed her phone back. What was I going to do? I still had to call Brian somehow . . . And then it hit me. 'I have band practice after school most days,' I remembered Brian saying. What if he was in there? What if I could talk to him right now and in person?

"Sandy, I'm sure Mr. Phillips won't mind if you wait for him

185

in his classroom," Ms. June said.

Needing to get back into the band room, I faked a sneeze into my elbow. "Achoo!" Can I get a tissue please?"

"Of course," Ms. June said. "They're on my desk." Ms. June typed a number in on her phone and pressed it to her ear. I went inside, leaving her just outside the door. I took this opportunity to search for Brian. My eyes were first drawn to Ida. Her red hair was the brightest thing in the room.

"Sandy? You're back!" Ida began.

"Ida!" I beamed at her and pulled her into a hug.

"What are you doing here?" she asked once we pulled apart.

"I need to talk to Brian. Do you know where he is?" I asked.

"Over there, in the French horn section," Ida pointed. "Why do you need to talk to him?"

"Long story," I said and ran over to Brian.

"Sandy?" Brian's eyes widened. "What are you doing here?"

"Brian, you need to come with me," I said.

"Is everything okay?"

"It is about . . . you-know-what."

"What is you-know-what?" Ida had come over and listened to our conversation.

"I'm sorry, but I can't tell you."

"Sandy, you suddenly turn up at Mountain View, asking Brian to skip band practice and run off with you. Can you at least tell me why?"

"Ida, I'm sorry, but I don't have time—"

"Sandy—"

"Ida, I don't have to tell you everything!" I snapped. Then I took a deep breath and regained control of myself. Her eyes locked on mine. I felt as if she was burning a hole right through me. And then all her pent-up anger and bottled-up emotions came rushing out.

"You know I thought that if you ever came back, you'd be excited to see me and we could talk or something. You never trusted us, your closest friends, with any secrets, even though we confided in you with all of ours," Ida said. Our argument had gained the attention of some students nearby. The teacher, however, had yet to notice. "You never trusted us," she finished. "I thought we were best friends."

"Best friends understand when someone has to keep a secret, and some secrets are just too big to share."

"Like what?"

"You wouldn't believe me even if I told you," I responded in a calm and measured voice.

"Whatever," she said walking back to the trumpet section.

My heart ached at the sight of seeing her leave, possibly forever. As much as I hated it, this secret was bigger and more important than my friendship with Ida.

I sighed deeply, turned to Brian, and continued, "Please, Brian this is important."

Brian leaned in and whispered into my ear, "Leave the band room and wait outside. I'll be out soon."

"But—"

"Trust me," he whispered. I did trust him. I left the band room without another word. I was waiting by the courtyard when

I heard the band room door creak open. There Brian stood with a bathroom pass in his hand.

"Clever," I said.

"What's going on? What do you need to tell me?"

In a whisper, I told Brian everything, including our suspicion Julianne's Cleaning Services was a ruse to leave the notes, and our theories about who could've left them. Most important of all, I told Brian about the latest note, that said 'Theater, ship, and paradise in history.' He looked shocked.

"I can't believe it either," I said in response to the shocked look on his face.

"We need to all sit down and talk," Brian said. "By 'we,' I mean you, your friends, and me. This needs to be figured out somewhere more private."

"How about you come to the orphanage?" I suggested.

"That's not private enough, not with one of the deputies there. It would be impossible to talk in secret, especially because I have the you-know-what. And besides, I'm not too keen on seeing her."

"Oh, yeah, it has to be really weird knowing Ms. Abigail's your mom. Where else can we meet besides the orphanage?"

"The Red Bush Café, maybe."

"But that's really crowded and noisy."

"Exactly. If it's noisy, nobody will hear what we're saying."

"Okay, that makes sense. How will we get there? I guess we could ask Mr. Phillips to take the two of us to the café. But how will the others get there?"

"I'll take care of that," Brian said.

Moments later, we spotted Mr. Phillips walking in.

"Hi, kids!" Mr. Phillips greeted us.

"Mr. Phillips, we need to ask you a huge favor," Brian began. "We need a ride."

"Where to?"

"Well, we kind of need to meet some friends at the Red Bush Café," I said.

"Why?"

"We need to . . . talk," I said.

"I guess so, sure," Mr. Phillips said. "I occasionally stop by there after work anyway. Sandy, you do still have to do your community service. We can go afterward."

"Okay."

"And you'll have to check with Ms. Abigail," Mr. Phillips added.

My heart sank. What was I going to do?

"I'll take care of that," said Brian. Mr. Phillips looked confused, but then shrugged and started walking to his classroom.

"I'll meet you back here when band is over," Brian said as he texted his foster parents on his way back to band.

I followed Mr. Phillips to his classroom, waved at Mr. Bluecrest, and set to work filing papers. The time crept by, but at last Mr. Phillips told me it was time to go. Brian was there waiting for us, and we headed outside towards Mr. Phillips's car.

"If you don't mind my asking, why do you have to meet some friends at the Red Bush Café?" Mr. Phillips asked. Brian shook his head at me, a silent motion not to tell him the truth.

"It's . . . We're, um . . . We're meeting with some of my friends from the orphanage," I said. I saw Brian out of the corner of my eye shaking his head. "We are doing a project."

"Oh, for what?"

"It's on . . . being in the foster care system and being an orphan," I answered at last. That actually made sense.

"Well that's interesting!" said Mr. Phillips. "And Ms. Abigail is okay with you getting home late?"

"Yeah, she said it's fine," Brian said.

I didn't know what was going on. Had Brian called Ms. Abigail or was he just pretending?

Mr. Phillips pulled into the parking lot of the Red Bush Café and asked, "Brian, your parents are coming to pick you up here, right?"

"Yes sir. And thanks for the ride Mr. Phillips," Brian said.

"I'll be right over there," said Mr. Phillips. "Let me know when you're ready to go, Sandy."

I nodded as Brian and I headed to the secluded corner booth while Mr. Phillips took a seat by the window.

A waitress came by to ask if we wanted anything. "Uh, I don't have any money," I said.

"That's okay, I'll pay!" Brian ordered two lemonades.

"How are Rebecca and the others going to get here?" I asked.

"I called Ms. Abigail," he said. "I had her number from when you used her phone to call me."

"What did you say?"

"I pretended to be Mr. Phillips and told Ms. Abigail that you have to work late. I also convinced her to let me talk to Rebecca. I told Rebecca everything, and she promised to figure out a way to get here," Brian told me. I sighed with relief. The problem was in capable hands. Our waitress brought our lemonades as we waited.

I knew my friends would eventually come, but when? What if Rebecca couldn't figure out a way to get here? Five minutes after that thought crossed my mind, the door to the Red Bush Café opened, Rebecca, Aaron, Nick, and Tessa rushed into the crowded restaurant holding textbooks, notebooks, and pencil pouches. I noticed that Rick wasn't with them.

"Where's Rick?" I asked. "And how did you get here?" Tessa slid into the booth next to me, smiling widely.

"I told Deputy London we had a study session here and that we wouldn't be able to go, so he offered to bring us when his shift ended," Rebecca explained. That answered the question of why they had books and supplies, but before I could object that we couldn't talk with police around, she added, "Deputy London said he'd wait outside in the car. Unfortunately, there were only four seats, so one of us had to stay behind, and Rick volunteered."

"That was nice of him," I said.

"I don't think I ever got to formally introduce myself," Brian said. "I'm Brian. Nice to meet you." He extended a hand, and the others shook it and introduced themselves. The same waitress came by and asked if Rebecca, Tessa, Nick, or Aaron wanted drinks.

They ordered sodas and lemonades, and I wondered how they were planning on paying. A minute later, Rebecca brandished a twenty-dollar bill and set it on the table.

"No, I'll pay," Brian shook his head and made Rebecca put away her money.

"Are you sure?" Rebecca asked.

"Absolutely. It's only about eight dollars anyway."

"Thank you, Brian."

"Rebecca, how did you get that?" I asked. I didn't think any of us had any money.

"Deputy London gave it to me," Rebecca said. "It was really sweet of him. I think he feels bad for us."

"Wow, that was really thoughtful," I said.

Tessa nodded in agreement.

"Anyway, we need to figure everything out," Rebecca said. "Katie let me bring her tablet with me. I'm going to do some more research on Julianne's Cleaning Services and the Stone of Discedo."

"I'll help," Brian offered.

"Get out the stone, I want to see it," Nick said.

"Not here. Anybody could see it," Brian said. The waitress came back with the drinks and passed them out. Nick took his soda and began to sip it.

"Oh, come on, nobody is looking, and so what if they see you holding a big green rock?"

"There are pictures in the news, Nick, and I would prefer not to spend time in jail, so no, I am not taking it out. I brought it with me today because we're getting our house cleaned and I didn't want it to be found."

"Whatever," Nick said. "It's just a rock."

"It is not just a rock, Nick. It is the most amazing discovery in the history of science. With this stone, you could change any mistake you ever made. That is if you use it correctly. I lived in the

80's for three whole months until I figured out how to get back."

"Wait a second," Tessa said. "That means your foster parents must know about the stone."

"Nope. I convinced them I ran off because kids were bullying me, so when I came back, they let me switch schools."

"I'm impressed," Aaron said.

"Thank you."

"Let's get started," I said. "We have to figure out who is writing these notes. They could be meant as a threat or a warning. We don't know. But we do know that someone wants to keep me away from Brian and away from trouble."

"Or maybe someone wants the stone for themselves!" Nick said.

"No, that doesn't make sense," said Brian. "I think if someone knew I had the stone and wanted to get it, they would've done something already."

"Then what's the point of leaving the notes?" asked Tessa.

"To try to keep Sandy safe!" Aaron said.

"That's one of the reasons it could be Deputy Brute. It is his job to protect people, and his handwriting is similar to the one on the note with his curly y's. Plus, he was at the orphanage the day you got the third note that said, 'Watch your back.' He wouldn't have to sign into a school to get on campus, he could just walk in. It all makes sense!" Tessa said.

"Why would he go to all that trouble though?" Aaron asked. "He's a deputy, if he knows Brian has the stone, he would've said or done something more serious by now."

"Aaron's right. It's got to be Mr. Stanton," Nick said. "He was there the day the first two notes were delivered, and he was also there the day the third note was left at the orphanage. He also wouldn't need to sign into the school to get onto the campus, and he has access to records. It would be a cinch for him to find out which locker belonged to you and which one belonged to Brian."

"Exactly," said Brian. "And Mr. Stanton might know who you are. He knows I transferred schools because my parents and I had to go to the school board. He knows about my disappearance."

"But you said you told the board you ran away," I argued. "Mr. Stanton has no reason to believe you were trapped in time."

"Guys," Rebecca whispered, her eyes stuck on the screen of Katie's tablet.

"What?"

"There might be a second stone, the Stone of Moraetas."

"The Stone of what?" Nick asked.

"The Stone of More-ay-ah-tus," Rebecca said, pronouncing each syllable for him. "Apparently, it's very similar to the Stone of Discedo."

"No way, there are two time-traveling stones?!" exclaimed Nick.

"We can't be sure. The thing is, the Stone of Moraetas hasn't been seen in the centuries. Nobody knows if it even exists," said Rebecca.

"And you think all of this is connected to the notes?" Nick asked. "And the person leaving them?"

"I don't think it can all be a coincidence," said Rebecca.

"Who do you think could be leaving the notes?" Tessa wondered.

"I don't have any idea," Rebecca admitted.

"What I want to know is how come I'm the one with the stone, but you are the one getting the notes." He met my eyes. I searched for words but couldn't find them.

"I hate not knowing things," Rebecca said, "but we can't just sit here and wait until we figure it out. We should use the stone."

Then we all started talking at once.

"You're kidding."

"No way."

"You can't be serious."

"Are you crazy?" Brian asked. "I don't want to get stuck in the 1980s again, or anywhere for that matter. There is no way we can do this!"

"Why not?" asked Rebecca.

"To fix something in your lifetime, you first must fix three horrible events in history," Brian said.

"What if we fix two, but not the third?" I asked.

"Once you make changes, the changes are permanent. However, if you fix two events instead of three, you can't fix something about your own life. You have to fix all three catastrophic events to fix something on your own timeline."

"Sounds dangerous," I muttered.

Tessa agreed, "It's possible Skyler was murdered by mistake, and if the murderer knows that, Sandy could be in danger. Someone is out to get her."

"I don't know . . . If we got lost . . ." Brian said.

"We won't," Tessa said.

"If we get stuck . . ."

"We won't," she repeated.

"There is no guarantee. Time can be a tricky thing . . ."

"Brian, please?" Tessa said.

"Guys, I don't think you understand how dangerous this *really* is."

"I do!" said Tessa. "We all do. This is important. If Sandy's parents never left, then she wouldn't have gotten notes, and Skyler wouldn't have been killed."

"We can't—"

"Please, Brian," Rebecca begged. I could feel the argument was losing strength.

"By going back in time, we put all our lives on the line," Brian said. "If you get lost, you don't come back. If you mess something up, you can't change it. If you get killed, nobody will remember you. Time is unpredictable."

"I understand that," I said at last. "But Brian, someone is leaving me mysterious notes, breaking into the orphanage— someone was even murdered because of this. Who is to say one of us isn't next? I'm in danger, and that might mean you and the others are too."

"Sandy, we don't even know for sure Skyler was murdered by accident, you might not even be in any danger. But going back in time . . . would put you in real danger," Brian said.

"He's got a point," said Aaron softly.

"C'mon, dude, where's your sense of adventure?" Nick said. "Don't you think it would be cool to time travel?"

"True," said Aaron.

"Like I said, we have to fix three horrible events in history before we can do anything in our own timelines. So, if we want to stop Sandy's parents from disappearing, first we have to go to three places where something went terribly wrong."

"Okay," I said.

"But still, I don't even know if we can use the stone. I'm not sure how I activated it the first time, and I don't know if I can do it again."

"Didn't you say that a note was found in Simon Moreno's hideout that said, 'by one with a pure heart and even purer intentions?'" I asked.

"Yes," Brian said.

"I think the stone can be activated as long as the people trying to use it have pure hearts and pure intentions."

"That makes sense," Brian said.

"I wonder if going back in time to stop your parents from leaving is considered good intentions?" Rebecca asked.

"If they died, we'd be saving their lives," I said.

"But what if they didn't?" Tessa asked.

"We'd still be saving Skyler's life," I said. Then added, "I mean, if I never came to the orphanage, Skyler might not have been killed."

"Guys, I don't think—"

"Please, Brian. We could save thousands of lives, and maybe my parents and Skyler, too."

Brian considered this for a second, then sighed deeply and said, "If you're willing to take the risk, then so am I."

FOURTEEN

Rebecca said, "I think we should go back in time before Sandy's parents left and warn them. Tell them not to go, and then, if they never leave, they will never disappear. Then you wouldn't be in danger." My heart skipped a beat. Would my new friends really do all this for me? It had been less than two weeks I'd lived in the orphanage, less than two weeks I'd known my friends, and yet they were willing to take such a big risk.

"Are you sure??" I asked.

"Sandy," Rebecca's eyes met my mine, and her hands gently held my hands, "you're in danger. Skyler was killed because of this, whatever this is."

"As much as I hate to say this, if the murderer meant to kill you and realizes he didn't, he might come back," said Tessa.

Rebecca added, "You and those around you could be in danger, and there is only one way to stop it. We have to make sure your parents never leave, and you never get into the situation in the first place."

I shook my head adamantly, "Rebecca, I can't let you—"

"It's decided," Rebecca told me, straightening up. "We have to do this now."

"Rebecca's right. Sometimes you only have one chance, so you must take it when you can," Brian said.

"You'd all be willing to do this for me?"

"Heck yeah!" Nick said. "It'll be fun! Going back in time will be an adventure."

"It's certainly an adventure, but calling it fun might be a stretch," said Brian.

"And Sandy, keep in mind, we might be saving our own butts too," Aaron said. "It's like you're attracting danger."

My body relaxed a little bit. Aaron was right. Skyler died because of me and who was to say one of my other friends wouldn't be next? Who was to say I wouldn't be next?

Brian opened his messenger bag and pulled out the most recent note. "I'm trying to figure out what this last message means . . . 'Theater, ship, and paradise, in history.' What do those three things have in common?"

"History," Aaron said.

Brian jumped to his feet. "That's it!"

"Wait, Aaron got something right?" Nick laughed, and Aaron elbowed him in the ribs.

"Well . . . kind of. The 'Theater, ship, and paradise' part is the places we have to travel back in time to."

"What?" Nick's eyebrows narrowed, creasing his forehead.

"We have to fix three horrible events in history to fix what we want."

"Why?" Rebecca asked.

"I don't know. The legend states that is the way the stone's power works. Maybe it's so the user only changes time when it's important. If not, everyone would use the stone if they had it, even for simpler things like a football game or the lottery. The rule makes it so whoever intends to use the stone must consider how important changing an event in their life is. They have to be committed, and willing to risk everything," Brian explained.

"I'm confused," Nick said.

"You should be used to it by now," Aaron laughed.

"Shut up."

"Shutting."

"It's about time," Tessa muttered to Nick and me. They really do argue like siblings, I thought to myself.

"Why would someone leave the note implying we go back in time?" Rebecca questioned.

"And why would they want us to?" I wondered aloud. "This last note doesn't seem like a threat or a warning like the others do. This last one seems more like a clue."

"Okay, so let's say, hypothetically speaking of course, that the first five notes were a warning. Then was the murder a warning? The murderer was just trying to keep you safe?" Tessa argued. "This makes no sense. Someone tried to kill you. They'd have to have multiple personalities disorder if they were trying to kill you, and then turn around to warn you. I think the first five notes were a threat."

I began to think. "It could—no, that's stupid. Never mind."

"What?" Nick asked. "What is it?"

"It's stupid. Forget it."

"No," Nick said.

"I thought that maybe . . . maybe it was two different people, one trying to save me, and one trying to, you know . . ." My voice trailed off into silence as I realized how stupid it sounded aloud. Rebecca frowned, thinking hard.

"It's not a stupid idea," Nick said, "it would explain a lot."

"Okay, let's say it is two different people. One person is leaving notes to protect you from the other person who is trying to kill you . . . why would the first person suggest you time travel? Time travel is dangerous . . . why would they try so hard to protect you and then suggest you risk your life?" Brian wondered.

"I don't know."

"The best we can do is guess," said Rebecca.

"Guys, you don't have to do this for me," I objected. "You're putting yourselves in danger."

"Drop it, Sandy, we're doing this," Tessa said.

"Like I said, we might be saving our own butts," Aaron said. Tessa elbowed him in the ribs. Aaron looked disgruntled but nevertheless excited.

A shiver ran down my spine, raising goosebumps on my arms. Someone was watching me. I could feel it. Someone was out there in the shadows, waiting. I shuddered at the thought. Could it be there were two different people? One trying to save me from the other? Was I truly in danger? Enough danger that someone had to keep a careful eye on me?

"Guys, focus. We have to find a place where nobody will see us disappear," Brian said.

"How about the bathroom?" Aaron suggested.

"Nah. First of all, it's too small, and second, wouldn't it

be weird to see a bunch of girls and boys going into the same bathroom?"

"True," Aaron said. "I wouldn't go in the girl's bathroom anyway, and if they came in the boy's bathroom, they'd—"

"Thank you, Aaron," Tessa interrupted, "but we really don't want to know."

"We can use the abandoned building near the orphanage," Rebecca said.

"Excellent idea," Brian agreed.

Rebecca strategized, "Let's ask Deputy London to take Nick, Tessa, Aaron, and me back to the orphanage. Sandy and Brian can go with Mr. Phillips. We'll go up to our room so Ms. Abigail thinks that's where we are, then sneak down the fire exit, and go to the abandoned building."

"Hey Brian, when we come back, what time will it be?" Aaron asked.

"It should be the same time as when we left," Brian answered.

"Then why'd you say when you got stuck in the 1980s you disappeared for three months?" Nick asked.

"There's a difference between getting lost in time and traveling through it. If you are somewhere for more than a day, regular time will continue without you. Basically, real time is on pause while you travel, but once you stay somewhere for 24 hours, time will resume because you're 'lost.'"

"Oh."

"The four of us," Rebecca gestured to herself, Nick, Aaron, and Tessa, "will tell Deputy London that our study group ended early or something like that. We'll meet you in that abandoned building by the orphanage when we all get back."

"Okay," I agreed. "Brian, what are you going to—?"

"I'll figure something out, don't worry," he shrugged, "my foster parents won't be mad or anything." The other four left the crowded restaurant and headed out into the parking lot where Deputy London sat in his car. Brian and I went over to the booth where Mr. Phillips was finishing the last bites of his dinner.

"Thank you so much for the ride here, Mr. Phillips," I said. "Would you mind giving Brian and me a ride to the orphanage?"

"It'd be my pleasure," Mr. Phillips agreed. "But I thought Brian was getting picked up here?"

"Change of plans," I told him. That was true.

Without another word, we walked out into the fading afternoon sunshine of the parking lot and clambered into his car. Mr. Phillips pulled out of the parking lot heading toward the orphanage.

I thought to myself—*What if we get lost or stuck in time? What if we lose the stone? What if we get stuck in the 19th or 20th century?*

Brian whispered, "We won't get lost in time. And we won't lose the stone either."

"How did you know what I was thinking?"

"I got lucky I guess."

I shook my head, confused, and pressed my face to the cool glass of the window. Soon, we arrived at the orphanage.

"Thanks, Mr. Phillips!"

"No problem. I'm happy to help," said Mr. Phillips with a smile. "I love helping kids, that's why I became a teacher. In fact, I kind of wish I had kids of my own." A bubble of hope blossomed in my mind. Could Mr. Phillips adopt me? That bubble of hope was soon shattered by the needle of reality. Things like that only happened in movies. Brian and I got out of Mr. Phillips's car, which soon disappeared into the distance. Daylight was fading slowly.

"C'mon," I led the way into the orphanage, Brian at my heels.

"I can't come with you in there," he whispered.

"Why not?"

"It'll be suspicious," he said. "And besides, I don't want to see *her*. I'll wait for you in the abandoned building. I have to call my foster parents anyway."

"Okay," I nodded and hurried into the orphanage running into Ms. Abigail.

"You're late!" She said looking up from the dining room table where she was unpacking a large cardboard box full of cosmetics.

"Mr. Phillips had me do extra work," I lied.

"So I was told," she said. "Serves you right." Ms. Abigail muttered something under her breath, then returned to what she was doing. I headed upstairs to where the others were waiting. Deputy London had dropped them off just before Brian and I arrived.

"Ready?" Rebecca asked.

"Ready." I nodded.

"Wait a second," Nick objected. "Where's Rick?"

"I don't know," Aaron answered.

"He was here when we left," Rebecca added, frowning.

Nick said, "Well, we can't go without him!"

"I guess we'll have to tell Brian we can't go today," Rebecca said. "We can't go without Rick."

"Let's go tell Brian," Nick said. "We'll have to go tomorrow or some other time." I felt disappointed. Where was Rick? Part of me wanted to blame him for us not being able to go now, but I knew it wasn't his fault. Rick didn't know what we were planning. The five of us slipped out the fire exit and across the alley to the abandoned building. We left the door ajar for when we came back. It was a matter of when, not if. Besides, it wouldn't take long to tell Brian we couldn't use the stone today.

The door to the abandoned building creaked open, and I saw almost everything was draped in cobwebs. Apparently, Ms. Abigail owned the building but hadn't stepped foot in it for years. The structure had long since been left behind to wallow in neglect. Ancient chandeliers dangled from the ceiling, adorned by more cobwebs. Empty picture frames sat atop a once-handsome mantel that overshadowed a cold, empty fireplace. A hearth rug lay frayed and tattered at the foot of the fireplace, the fringe around it uneven and coated in charcoal-colored soot. A wooden staircase led upstairs and gave way to a sheet of darkness.

Brian gingerly set his bag on a three-legged, lopsided table and carefully removed the magical Stone of Discedo. There it sat. No bigger than a tennis ball, but more powerful than anything in the world. And here it was— in the small town of South Toheeden, Ohio— right in front of me. I could barely believe it.

Brian began to speak immediately. "Okay, so we've agreed that 'Theater, ship, and paradise' are the three places we have to go. The three events in history we need to fix—"

"Rick's not here," Nick interrupted. "We can't go without him."

"Who is Rick?" Brian asked, looking perplexed. "I heard you mention him at the Red Bush Café, but I still don't know—"

"Rick is my brother," Nick answered. "My twin, actually." Brian looked a little surprised.

"So there are two of you?"

"Don't worry, he's nothing like me," Nick laughed. "He's my polar opposite, actually."

"Oh," said Brian. "Well, where is he?"

"We don't know," said Rebecca.

"What you're telling me is Rick isn't here, so we can't use the Stone of Discedo?"

"Yes," said Nick.

"This isn't like a dentist appointment that can be easily rescheduled."

"But—" And then it happened. The Stone of Discedo began to glow. At first, it was a subtle shimmer, and then it got brighter and brighter. It was almost blinding. The emerald color illuminated the entire room.

"What's happening?" I asked.

"I . . . I don't know," Brian said. "It's never done this before!"

"It's a sign," whispered Rebecca.

"It's a what?" Aaron asked.

"It's a sign," she repeated. "We have to use the stone. Now."

Nick objected, "Rebecca, just because—"

"It's a sign. I know it is," Rebecca interrupted. "Let's do it."

"But Rick—" Nick began.

"I know Rick isn't here, and we'd be better off with his

help, but this is a sign. The stone is telling us to use it," Rebecca interrupted. "Brian, what's the first terrible event we have to fix?"

"Abraham Lincoln's assassination." It wasn't Brian who said it, but Nick.

"Yes," Brian said. He looked at Nick, obviously a little surprised.

"How do you know that, Nick?" Aaron asked.

"Rick always babbles on about Lincoln," Nick said with a shrug. "I remember him mentioning that Lincoln was assassinated in Ford's Theater."

"Alright. Everybody, touch the stone," Brian ordered. I inhaled and closed my eyes. Then, unable to keep them closed, I opened them once more and glanced sideways at Rebecca who pursed her lips. We laid our hands on the stone.

"Ford's Theater, April 14, 1865, 8:30 p.m.," Brian stated. There was a rush of howling wind and color. I felt a sickening jolt as if being whisked away from the Earth. All I could see were flashes of things. People's faces, brick buildings, park squares, corn fields, cobblestone streets, everything was happening so fast, gone in the blink of an eye. I was spiraling around and around, immersed in flashes of colors, and surrounded by howling winds. My ears were filled with sound, people yelling indecipherable things, the sounds of horseshoes and hearty banter, the sounds of wind and water running, heels of shoes clapping on the stone, cheers for something or other, the sounds of carriage wheels and creaky wooden floors . . . all so much, too much, to take in.

My feet fell to the ground with a not-so-graceful thud, and I lost my balance. Rebecca and Aaron fell to the ground with me, but Tessa, Nick, and Brian landed gracefully.

"Wow," said Tessa. "That was . . . wow."

"I'm dizzy." Aaron's face was tinted with green.

"That was incredible!" said Rebecca, looking both amazed and excited.

As I got to my feet, I realized I wasn't wearing my own clothes. I was wearing a long light pink dress and brown lace-up boots with a small heel. Tessa and Rebecca were also in dresses, Tessa's red and Rebecca's purple.

"Ugh, I have to wear a dress?" Rebecca moaned. "Brian, you never said anything about our clothes changing!" She looked mad.

"Sorry, I forgot," Brian blushed. "Anything you have with you changes to fit the time period."

"Haha, you have to wear a dress!" Nick stuck out his tongue at us.

Tessa rolled her eyes and said, "I think I make this dress work." Tessa's red dress had a white strip around her waist. Rebecca's dress was fluffier than mine and had white frills all around.

Nick said, "My outfit isn't that bad." The boys were wearing starched white shirts with a tie, covered by a buttoned vest and old-fashioned suit coats. They also wore knickers, trousers ending at the knee, and sturdy brown lace-up shoes.

Aaron adjusted the tie that choked his neck. "I'm glad I'm a kid of the twenty-first century."

Rebecca patted down her poufy dress. "You're telling me."

"This 19th-century fashion is awful," said Tessa, wrinkling her nose.

"19th-century fashion? More like lack thereof," said Aaron.

Nick laughed and asked, "Where exactly are we in 1865?"

"Backstage at Ford's Theater," Brian answered. "C'mon. We've got to get out of here." He led the way out to the auditorium. The theater was vacant. It was eerie how quiet it was.

"Ah, here they come," Brian said as people began flooding the theater, chatting happily, oblivious to what was about to happen. The women wore fancy, elegant gowns, while the men wore suits and hats. Brian somehow knew the way, and we followed him to a little nook where I could see the theater in its entirety. Ford's Theater itself was a colossal building, elegant for its time, but now, well, now it seemed run-down and ancient to my futuristic eyes. Glistening golden bars divided the audience from the stage, whose beautiful red velvet curtains were the one truly gorgeous thing about this historic theater. My observant eyes were drawn to a massive painted sign that read: *Our American Cousin: A Comedy.*

"Oh good, I'm always in the mood for a comedy," Aaron jested, his eyes transfixed on the sign. "And I didn't expect their outfits to be this ugly."

"It's the olden days," said Tessa, "and besides, we've got more important things to worry about than the people's outfits."

"We've got to go. The show starts in about thirty minutes," Brian said, consulting his watch, which was now a pocket watch rather than a digital wristwatch. "We've got to get up to the Presidential Box before Lincoln. He'll be here soon."

"They'll never let a bunch of kids up there!" Tessa said.

"Aaron and I can distract the guard," Nick suggested.

"Yeah, I've been working on a few new jokes."

"The last thing we want to do is get into trouble," Brian said. "We need to get this right. We only have one shot. One chance."

FIFTEEN

"Who knows anything about Abraham Lincoln?" Aaron asked.
"Because I sure as heck don't."

Tessa beamed. "Finally, a chance for all this information to
come in handy!"

I was confused. "What do you mean?"

"I've retained so many things from history class, but they
never seem to come in handy, other than on tests of course." Tessa
paused, "The story goes like this. John Wilkes Booth gained entry
to the box by handing Forbes, Lincoln's footman, his calling-card,
which he had from acting at the theater. During Act Three, Scene
Two, he stepped in and shot Lincoln from behind at 10:15. Booth
had waited for a funny line so the crowd would laugh and it would
be harder to hear the gunshot. He'd shot Lincoln thinking slavery
was good for everyone, and therefore despised Lincoln. Booth
thought he was doing the country a favor by killing the president
who worked hard to abolish slavery."

"Where was Lincoln's guard?" I asked.

It was Brian who answered instead of Tessa. "Lincoln and
his party arrived late. Once they were settled in the box, Lincoln's

guard, Officer John Parker, left. He went to the first gallery so he could watch the play. During intermission, he went to get a drink from the Star Saloon, the bar next door to Ford's Theater. Most people believe Parker was still at the bar when Lincoln was shot by John Wilkes Booth."

"What's the point?" Nick said.

Rebecca stepped in to answer, "Point is, all we have to do is warn the guard and make sure he never goes to get a drink."

Tessa asked, "Aaron, what time is it?"

Aaron checked his wrist and frowned, "My watch is gone." He dug a hand into his pocket and pulled out a gleaming gold pocket watch engraved with the word 'Pilgrim.'

"What time is it?" I asked. Aaron sighed. "I think it's nine? No, that's the minute hand. It's . . . seven fifteen? No . . . ugh, this is confusing."

"It's 8:44!" Tessa said. "Did you ever learn how to read a clock?"

"Probably," Aaron shrugged. "I just don't remember."

Brian sighed and said, "The show starts in fifteen minutes. We should move and split up before they realize we don't have an adult with us or worse, that we don't have a ticket."

"Here's what we'll have to do," said Rebecca. "Nick, Sandy, and I will wait by the stairs and warn the guard before he leaves to watch the show from the first gallery."

"Then what do *we* do?" Tessa pointed to Brian, Aaron, and herself.

"Find somewhere to hide," answered Rebecca.

"Got it. Hold on . . ." Brian took out his watch and handed it to Rebecca. "Remember, Booth enters the Presidential Box and shoots Lincoln at 10:15."

Rebecca took the watch. "Thanks."

Tessa waved a hand. "Come on guys, let's go find a place to wait." She turned to Nick, Rebecca, and I. "Good luck."

"Thanks," I said as the other three left.

"Let's go over here," Rebecca suggested. She pointed to a small corner by the door to the stairs.

"Won't someone ask us if we have tickets?" I asked.

"I doubt it," answered Rebecca. "Technically you have to have a ticket to get in the door."

"True."

As the play started, I glanced up at the Presidential Box. It was still empty.

Like Brian had said, the play was in progress when President Lincoln and company entered the small theater box. As soon as President Lincoln and his guests entered the theater box, the play stopped, and the band began to play "Hail to the Chief." The audience stood up to applaud the president. He waved graciously and bowed before taking his seat on the far right. There were four seats in the box, for the four people attending. Looking up at the box, I saw President Abraham Lincoln sitting in his garnet upholstered rocking chair, watching the show below. He was tall, skinny, and bearded, just like I'd seen in history textbooks. To his right sat his wife, Mary Lincoln, and two guests, Clara Harris and her fiancé, Major Henry Rathbone. They were all enjoying the show, oblivious to the looming danger.

• • •

Smirking, Booth ran an idle finger over his single shot .44

caliber gun. The smooth metal was cold beneath his quivering fingers. His handlebar mustache shook with adrenaline. He had a murder to commit. And only one bullet in his gun.

* * *

If our plan worked, President Lincoln's life would be spared. It was hard to watch him, enjoying himself on a lovely night. I felt sick thinking his life was in the hands of a few kids.

After a period of uneasy silence, Rebecca murmured, "It's time. Let's go warn the guard." Quietly, we went up the stairs and moved towards the yellow door leading to the Presidential Box.

Outside the Presidential Box were two men.

"Which one of you is President Lincoln's guard?" asked Rebecca.

"That would be me," said the one on the right. He was a gangly, large man. He had a messy beard, cracked lips, a lopsided mouth, crooked yellow teeth, and a broad nose. I assumed the man on the left was Lincoln's footman, Forbes.

"What are you kids doing up here?" he demanded.

"Someone is here to kill the president," answered Rebecca.

"I assure you President Lincoln is in no harm," the guard said, crossing his arms over his chest. My heart turned to ice, and I gulped.

"Just don't leave," Rebecca warned.

"What do you think gives you the authority to command me? I am sure the president is safe. Now go back to your parents."

"Listen, you cannot leave your post," said Rebecca. "Not to watch the play, and not to get a drink."

"The president doesn't need me here," said the guard. "I'd like to the watch the play myself, and besides, I could use a good drink."

"Well, the barista told us to spread the word that the bar is closed."

"The who?" The guard frowned.

"The guy who makes drinks," Nick said, rolling his eyes.

"So the bar is closed?"

"Yes."

"Then I'll go watch the play from the gallery."

"No!" protested Rebecca. "You have to stay here. Please. The president is in danger!"

"Silly kids, move out of my way." The guard pushed past us. I gave Rebecca a look that screamed 'What do we do?'

"Sir, how would you feel if the president died because of you?"

"The president is safe," said the guard. "Nobody would dare to lay a finger on him." He paused. "How would you three know anyway?" I felt like I was going to pass out. My head was spinning. What were we going to do?

"Please!" begged Rebecca. "You have to believe us!"

"If this is some silly scheme—"

"It's not! The president is in danger!"

"Well . . ." the guard looked torn.

"Better safe than sorry, right?" asked Nick. Rebecca looked at him, surprised he'd spoken.

"Very well then. I guess it is my job," said the guard. "Go away now."

"Come on guys, let's go," Rebecca said. We went back down the stairs and waited in the same little nook, close enough to see the Presidential Box.

Act Two began, bringing with it an unpleasant shadow of panic. An assassin was lurking unseen around us, a gun in his hand, and a president's life in ours. Act Two Scene One concluded with tumultuous applause.

"Man," said Nick. "For a comedy, it isn't very funny."

Finally, the scene before intermission began, and I felt as though I was about to vomit. I was shaking violently, unable to control myself. If anything were to happen to one of my friends, it would be my fault.

"We should go make sure the guard is there," Nick said, breaking the silence between us.

"What?" I asked.

"We need to make sure he's still there! And if he's not, we need to warn the president!"

"What time is it, Rebecca?" I asked.

"It's 10:10. Five minutes away from the shooting."

"Then we have to hurry," Nick said. We went up the stairs and over to the yellow door that led to the Presidential Box. Parker, the guard, wasn't there. Lincoln's footman, however, was still outside the door.

"Where's Parker?" Rebecca asked.

"I'm not sure," said Forbes.

"We have to talk to the president!" Rebecca said.

"No one is allowed in," grunted Forbes.

"Please? This is important!"

"No."

Rebecca looked defeated, desperate. I'd never seen her like this before. For once, it seemed she had no idea what to do.

Then an idea hit her. She pulled out a twenty-dollar bill from somewhere in her dress. I noticed the bill looked different than the one she had at the café.

"Will this change your mind?" she asked. "Please?" she lowered her voice to a whisper and said something to the footman.

"We're just kids, what could we do?" Nick asked.

"We have to deliver a message!" Rebecca begged.

Forbes took the bill from Rebecca. "Very well."

"Thanks," she said. The three of us ran into the Presidential Box. "Oh no, it's 10:13," Rebecca said. At that, all four members of Lincoln's party jumped to their feet and faced the three of us.

"What are you doing in here?" Major Rathbone, the man on the opposite end from Lincoln, demanded.

"President, sir, someone is here to kill you!" Rebecca blurted.

Lincoln began, "What—"

"Is this some joke?" Rathbone demanded. "Get out of here!"

"I'm not joking, the—"

Footsteps. Coming closer and closer.

"Booth," Rebecca whispered. She looked at me with horror as we turned around to face the door. My heart raced, so fast I feared it would pound its way out of my chest. Booth's eyes widened at the sight of three kids in the Presidential Box and the fact that Lincoln's party were all on their feet facing him. With an evil glint in his eyes, he raised his gun to shoot. His face twisted into a maniacal expression as he aimed the gun . . .

If I hadn't seen it with my own two eyes, I would never have believed it. Rick suddenly appeared out of thin air and tackled his twin, who stood in front of President Lincoln. At the same time, Booth fired his shot. The bullet sliced through the air and hit Rick in his neck. Rick's scream cut through the stuffy air. His glasses, which were now 1865 spectacles, fell to the ground and broke into pieces.

Nick's eyes widened, and he rolled over onto his knees beside his wounded twin brother.

"SOMEBODY HELP! SOMEBODY!" Nobody came. We all stood there, in shock. "Somebody!" Nick called weakly. "Please." Nothing happened. The world seemed to stop. Even John Wilkes Booth paused for a second to gaze in wonder. How had Rick managed to appear out of thin air to save Nick? I knew the bullet had been aimed towards Nick and Lincoln, but if Rick hadn't done what he did, one of them would have been shot instead. Rick laid on the ground, still and motionless. His face was stony gray, his brown eyes—the only thing that really separated him and Nick—rolled back in his head. Nick was frozen, gaping at his twin in horror. I felt tears well up in my eyes, but I knew I had no time to cry. Rick was dead, and there was nothing I could do.

Suddenly Nick screamed, "You killed my brother!" His misery and nerves transformed into unfiltered rage. It was beyond anything I'd ever seen or felt. "YOU KILLED HIM!" "MY BROTHER WAS THE BEST AND SMARTEST PERSON I KNEW, AND YOU KILLED HIM! YOU KILLED HIM!" Booth ran past everyone and leaped out of the Presidential Box, onto the stage, and then through the curtains. Nick howled and tried to run after Booth, but I pulled him back.

I said in between sobs, "Nick, you c-can't go after him—"

Major Rathbone leaped to his feet and jumped out of the box onto the stage. He followed Booth as he ran backstage. The actor on stage screamed and ran away. Meanwhile, the audience erupted into screams and shouts. It was utter chaos. People in the theater were screaming, running this way and that.

At the same time, Brian, Tessa, and Aaron rushed into the box, all their eyes widening in pure horror. Nick struggled to break free of my hold. "Let me GO!"

"Booth has a knife, Nick, you'll get hurt!" Brian shouted over the din.

"I DON'T CARE! I don't give a damn if I get hurt, just LET ME GO!" At this point, it took the combined forces of Tessa, Brian, and me to hold him back.

"WHERE IS PARKER?" President Lincoln bellowed. "Forbes, go find Parker!" The footman ran away immediately. Meanwhile, Clara Harris and Mary Lincoln stood in the corner, shaking with fear. Their faces were drained of color, and their jaws were dropped in horror. Nick cried in despair and knelt beside Rick.

"Your brother was very courageous," President Lincoln said. Nick wasn't listening.

Nick was sobbing his heart out, soaking his shirt in tears. "He's dead. I never . . . I never got to say goodbye."

"He died to save you," I whispered.

"How did Rick get here?" Tessa wondered aloud, voicing what everyone was thinking. My eyes brimmed with tears. Sure, I hadn't known him as long as the others, but he was part of my new family. I couldn't believe he was gone.

"Oh, dears, I'm so sorry." Mary Lincoln laid a hand on my shoulder soothingly. I wiped my tears from my face.

I put my arm around Nick, trying to soothe him with kind

words. President Lincoln tore a bit of cloth off his own suit and wrapped it gingerly around Rick's blood-stained neck like a scarf.

"I'll kill Parker!" President Lincoln shouted over the din. "His incompetence is unacceptable."

He was still shaking. All of us were. It was no wonder to me why Booth had an easy time shooting Lincoln in the alternate timeline, there was no one there to protect him. At least Lincoln had been saved . . . but at too high a cost.

"We should go," Brian said. I could see he was trembling, everything about him screamed of anxiety, of fear, of terror. I could sense a feeling of loss, even though Brian had never known Rick. Brian's eyes found mine, seeming desperate for comfort, but I felt as though nothing I could say could mend the wound. Nothing I could do would soften the blow. All I could do was stare.

"Rebecca, can you help me lift Rick?" Nick pleaded.

Tessa wiped her eyes. "We can't take him with us."

"Well, we can't just leave him here!"

"Nick, you know, um, our parents are with grandmother helping her recover from her illness," Rebecca said. "They can't make it back in time to get his body." Nick, who was still crying, looked utterly confused.

"We will bury him for you," President Lincoln offered.

"I can't leave Rick," Nick protested, looking at his brother's body.

"We have to," murmured Rebecca, patting Nick with a soothing hand.

"But—"

"We don't have any other options."

"We need to get out of here," Tessa said. She lowered her

voice to a whisper so only we could hear. "Or else we'll be stuck here. We need to leave before anything else happens. If people realize we were up here during a murder . . . besides, we can't mess up anything more."

"Agreed," Brian said. "Let's go outside where nobody can see us."

"Good idea," Rebecca nodded, and the five of us left the box, Nick taking one final, fleeting look at the body of his courageous brother who had died for him. Rick was dead. The shock had not abated, and I doubted whether it ever would. We exited Ford's Theater and walked around it, the cobblestone road blanketed in darkness. I could only see my friends' silhouettes.

"This is too dangerous," I said. "We should go home."

"Once you start, you can't turn back." Brian shook his head. "You can't even try again. You only get one chance."

"Oh." I couldn't take it. This was all my fault. Rick was dead because of me—because I wanted to go back in time, because I wanted to save my parents and Skyler. And myself. How selfish was I? Guilt tugged at my heartstrings. How had Rick known where we were? How had he known we had time traveled? And how had he gotten here? I was snapped back to reality by Brian's voice.

"Let me get the stone," Brian said, digging a hand into his pockets. "The stone . . . isn't here."

Nick exploded. "Where did you have it last? I want—I NEED—to get out of this time."

"The last place I had it was when I was heading up to the Presidential Box." Brian looked intently at his feet. "It must have fallen out of my pocket when we were holding you back."

Tension thundered through my body. What if we never found

it? What if we were stuck here forever?

"We won't be stuck here forever, Sandy," Brian assured me.

"You did it again! How did you do that? How'd you read my mind?"

Brian shrugged. "I don't know."

"We should wait for everyone to leave," suggested Rebecca. "Then we can go back in and look for the stone."

"Good idea," said Aaron. We waited in the streets, watching people file out of the theater, most of them still looking shocked. We took turns hugging Nick and hugging each other. We all needed each other's support. We lost a family member. I was still in denial. Rick couldn't possibly be dead. Not yet. He had so many wonderful things left to do, places to go, people to see. He had to graduate high school as valedictorian, get a scholarship to Harvard, get a degree, and become a lawyer or a doctor or an author, whatever his heart desired. He couldn't be gone. It wasn't possible. At least, that's what I told myself.

Brian's voice cut through my thoughts. "Let's go back in and find the stone."

• • •

"It's not here," Aaron said. We had just finished searching the box. The president, his wife, and Rick's body were gone. "Maybe Lincoln took the stone?"

"Well, it's not up here, and nobody else was here other than Lincoln's party . . ." Tessa's voice trailed off.

"Then President Lincoln must have taken it," Rebecca said.

"How on earth are we supposed to get to the White House?" Brian wondered aloud. "It's getting late, it's almost midnight."

"We'll have to sleep here overnight," Rebecca stated, "and by here, I mean the 1800s."

"But won't regular time resume if we stay here?" Tessa remembered.

"Yes, it will," Brian nodded, "but there isn't anything else we can do. We don't have the stone, so we can't travel. There aren't any other options."

"Where are we supposed to sleep?" demanded Aaron.

"Could we stay here?" Rebecca suggested. "We could sleep in one of the boxes on the other side of the theater."

"It's not like we have anywhere better to go." I sighed and followed Brian and Rebecca. Every part of me ached—my mind, my heart, my arms and legs. Even my feet ached from the shoes they'd been forced into.

"Well, would you look at that! Our very own five-star hotel." Aaron forced a small laugh at his own joke. I knew he only wanted to lighten the mood, but none of us felt like laughing.

"There are three chairs in here," said Tessa.

"I'll be a gentleman and let the ladies sleep in the seats," said Aaron.

"Yeah, sure, me too," shrugged Nick.

"Actually, I think I'd rather sleep on the floor," said Tessa. "But thanks anyway." All of us laid down on the floor and listened to the eerie silence of the empty theater.

In the silence, my mind thought back to Nick crying over the body of his brother. And then the whole scene in the Presidential Box blossomed in my mind's eye, John Wilkes Booth about to shoot, his malevolent cackling, Rick's body as still as stone . . .

Rick was truly gone. I would miss his unique genius-worthy intelligence, his enormous vocabulary, and his help on homework. He was often the one who kept peace within our group. In such a short amount of time, Rick had become very close to me. Now, there'd be a missing spot in our group, a spot that no one could ever replace, an empty bed where there shouldn't be, a little hole in all our hearts that formed the moment the bullet was fired. Rick had been killed by one of the most infamous assassins in America. How had Rick managed to get back here, if we had the stone? How had he done it?

Ice-cold realization splashed on me, washing away all questions about how he got to the 1800's. Rebecca said there was a second stone, the Stone of Moraetas. Had he found it and come to save us, knowing we'd be in trouble? Had Rick discovered the meaning of the 'Theater, ship, and paradise in history' after we left? He would have read about this very moment in his book, *Honest Abe Lincoln*. I decided I would tell the others in the morning, it didn't really matter right now. Everyone was struggling with their own demons.

Was it my fault Rick was dead? That he had left us for good? Was he dead because I wanted to time travel to have one chance to change things?

No.

Yes.

No.

Yes.

No.

Maybe.

SIXTEEN

In the morning, I woke up stiff from having slept on the floor.

"We better go," Rebecca said as she stretched. We followed her down the stairs and out into the street. My entire body was aching, but I had to ignore it. There was no time to mourn or feel bad. Not now, at least.

"We need to get to the White House," Rebecca announced.

"How will we find it?" Nick asked. His face was still wet from crying. Nick's emerald eyes were bloodshot and underlined with purple bags; his hair wild and unkempt.

"It's the big house. And it's white," Aaron answered. "It shouldn't be that hard to find."

"Hmmm," said Brian. "I think I know the way." We followed him blindly as he lead us. As we walked, Brian continued to tell us about how Lincoln liked his privacy. He was the first president to separate the White House into living quarters and official quarters. He got annoyed that he could not move freely, mingle, or chat with the people. In the fall of 1864, four personal guards were assigned to protect Abraham Lincoln, and they tried to remain as inconspicuous as possible because he didn't like interfering security people.

After a left turn, a right turn, and another left, we arrived at the White House.

"It's about time," muttered Aaron. Tessa rolled her eyes, and we all looked up at the White House. It was magnificent-looking. It was large and beautiful, but much different from the White House I'd seen in the news. It wasn't the same design as the current-day structure, yet still incredible.

"There won't be much security," Brian said.

"Okay, but how do we get in?" Aaron asked.

"I'm not quite sure," Brian admitted.

Just then, we heard the familiar voice of President Lincoln. The president and his wife, Mary, were having a serious conversation.

I peeked around the corner and saw the two of them on the balcony, sipping tea and enjoying biscuits.

"There they are!" I said, pointing.

"Um, hello!" Tessa shouted.

"You are back?" Lincoln asked, looking surprised.

"Mr. President, sir, we were wondering if we could talk to you?" Rebecca asked.

"Of course, of course," Lincoln said. He turned and whispered something to Mary, then came down from the balcony, opened the gate, and allowed us to follow him into his private sitting room. Lincoln was extremely tall, making me feel even smaller than I usually did. It was almost unbelievable that here I stood, in the 19th century, next to one of the country's most famous presidents. Abraham Lincoln was a person I'd only read about in history textbooks. I'd thought of him as an article, a mere mention, in the history of the United States, in the timeline of the world, but here he was. Flesh, blood, bone. He was an actual person, not just a picture or a test question. He was real.

"Can I get you some biscuits?" he asked. It suddenly occurred to me that we had not eaten a single thing since we left on our adventure. My stomach growled as if replying.

"That would be lovely," said Rebecca. Lincoln left and returned a few minutes later with a basket full of warm, buttery biscuits. I took one and bit into it. It spread warmth throughout my body. It felt good to put a little something into my empty stomach. How strange it was to be eating at the White House, and even stranger to be eating in the presence of a president.

"We were wondering if you found a green stone?" Rebecca asked. "About . . . this big?" She held up her fingers to show a space the size of a tennis ball.

"Yes, as a matter of fact, we did," President Lincoln said. "We assumed it belonged to the boy. We thought it would only be right if it were buried with him. I placed it in his casket." Nick gulped at the word 'casket.'

"Can you show us where the casket is? We really need the stone. It's, um, a family heirloom," she said.

"Well, I don't see why not," Lincoln said. He led us to the small anteroom. In it was a wooden casket. "We were going to hold a small ceremony here at the White House," President Lincoln told us. Nick bit his lip to keep from crying. I, too, was on the verge of tears. Lincoln crossed the room and carefully opened the casket. Nick turned away, unable to look at his brother's body. I closed my eyes until I heard the casket closing.

President Lincoln held the Stone of Discedo with two hands and passed it to Nick. From one brother to the next. Nick held it for a moment, staring at it as if it was a connection to his brother. Then, he gave it to Brian who slipped it into his pocket.

"Thank you, Mr. President," Brian said.

"It's the least I could do. I am so terribly sorry. You must tell your parents he died a hero." Nick began to cry. I wrapped an arm around him and wiped away his tears.

"I'll always be here for you," I promised him.

"Me too," said Rebecca.

Tears streamed onto Nick's face, faster and faster. Rick's death was the first time Nick had dropped his protective outer shell, the first time he'd shown true vulnerability. Nick cried, and nothing I said changed that. He finally managed to calm down a bit, and when he did, he whispered, "I lost my other half."

Once everyone calmed down, and President Lincoln left the room after promising to "give us some privacy," Brian pulled the Stone of Discedo out of his pocket.

"Nick, magic exists," I whispered. "Magic exists. Maybe there is a way we can bring Rick back—"

"He's gone," Nick murmured. "He's really gone."

"Nick, there's still hope—"

"Sandy, I appreciate you tr-trying to make me feel b-better, but don't try and get m-my hopes up. I have to be tough. Rick would've w-wanted that."

"Alright, guys," Brian said. "We need to go to the second place from the note. The second word was 'ship.' I think it's—"

"The sinking of the Titanic," Rebecca whispered.

Brian nodded, "Exactly. It's the most famous ship in history."

"So all we have to do is get there early and warn them?" I asked.

Nick, who was still getting over the tears, sniffed and said, "That seems easy enough."

"Oh yeah," Aaron said. "Saving thousands of people from certain death is easy."

"Guys, just be quiet!" Tessa interrupted.

"Alright. Let's do this," Brian held out the stone, and everyone placed their hands on the smooth surface. "We'll arrive about one hour before the Titanic hits the iceberg."

"Titanic, North Atlantic Ocean, April 14th, 1912, 10:30 p.m.," Brian said. The volatile swirls of color and wind enveloped as we soared forward in time. Colors, lights, sounds and swirls, an overwhelming number of things to take in. I heard clanging bells, squawking seagulls, and shouting voices. I could hear the subtle clink of glasses and the pop of champagne bottles. I smelled the salty air of the sea, expensive lavender perfume, and the smoke of cigars.

I felt queasy, dizzy, and desperate for solid ground to appear beneath my feet. I clamped my eyes shut, but it didn't help. I wanted to throw up, and I would've if I weren't afraid the wind would throw it right back at me. At last, we landed with a thud on the carpeted and deserted corridors of the RMS Titanic, where all was calm . . . thus far.

SEVENTEEN

Tessa, Rebecca, and I were wearing scratchy dresses that weren't much of an improvement from those we wore in 1865. My dress was yellow and flouncy and went just past my knees. I squirmed uncomfortably.

Brian looked at us. "Good. First class."

"There's school on this ship?" Nick asked.

Tessa rolled her eyes. "No, Nick. It means we look like we're in First Class." Nick still looked confused, so Tessa added, "The rich people."

"Oh, I see."

"They had about fifty years," Rebecca said, tugging at her dress, "and they didn't improve these things at all." The boy's outfits were a little more formal, but basically the same as in Lincoln's time. Nick was staring at her with an eyebrow raised. "What?" Rebecca asked impatiently once she noticed Nick staring.

"It's just . . . I've never . . . never mind."

"Okay, let's see," Brian said. "We have about one hour before the Titanic strikes the iceberg at 11:40."

"I wish I studied this in school or something. I just, you know, have an uneasy feeling. All I know is that this ship sank and a ton of people died. I don't know, I wish I knew a little more," I admitted.

"Surprisingly, I wish I knew a little more too," Nick agreed. "The one time I want the facts is the one time when I can't get them. How ironic."

Tessa flipped her auburn hair over her shoulder. "Who said you couldn't get the facts? I read an article about the ship after I saw the movie, and I can tell you everything it said and describe the photos too."

"When did you read an article on the Titanic? And more importantly, why?"

"Reading can actually be fun, Nick," Brian laughed.

"Yeah, maybe you should try it sometime," Aaron said. Everyone, including Nick, gave a little laugh. "Of course, you'd have to get someone to teach you how."

"Shut up," Nick snapped, his face falling into a solemn expression. "Rick liked to read."

"Do you want to hear it or not?" Tessa asked.

"Yes, please, Tessa," Rebecca said. "Go ahead."

"Alright, it said 'Published by Sullivan Corporation, established 1932, copyright 2014—'"

"Very interesting," Aaron said. "Maybe we can shout dates at the iceberg and get it to move out of the way, that's a huge help." He paused. "Do you have a fast-forward button?"

Tessa narrowed her eyebrows, thinking hard. "Okay, I'm ready!" she declared. And without waiting for any of us to respond, she began, "The Titanic was designed by a man named Thomas Andrews. Andrews worked with Joseph Bruce Ismay, son of the founder of the White Star, the ship line that owned the Titanic. Ismay insisted there would only be sixteen lifeboats (enough for 1,178 people), instead of the forty-eight Andrews planned to have. 'People don't pay to see lifeboats' Ismay claimed. In the end, they decided to go with sixteen lifeboats, regardless of the fact the Titanic would carry over 2,200 people on most voyages. In the event of an emergency, they'd only be able to save about half the people."

"See, that right there is the logic of someone who's had a few too many drinks," said Aaron.

Tessa looked annoyed. "So anyway, Edward J. Smith, the most experienced captain in the White Star line, was chosen to be the captain of the Titanic. The Titanic's maiden voyage from Southampton, England to New York City would be his crowning accomplishment before he retired. Lots of people changed their travel dates so they could sail on a ship under his command. The sister ship, the Olympic, returned for emergency repair, and the work on the Titanic came to a stop, delaying its departure by an entire month. Some of the officers on the Olympic had joined the Titanic crew because of the unexpected delay. At the last minute, Captain Smith was forced to shuffle some of his crew. These last-minute changes included replacing 2nd Officer Blair so he would not work on Titanic's maiden voyage. When he hastily packed his stuff and left, he accidentally took the key to the locker in the crow's nest which held the binoculars for the lookouts."

"Excuse me, miss," a young gentleman said to Rebecca, who moved aside to let him pass. The man had a cigar between his fingers.

Tessa continued, "At nine a.m. on April 14, 1912, the Titanic received its first ice warning with the latitude and longitude of icebergs. Harold Bride, a wireless operator, recorded the message and gave it to John Phillips, another wireless operator, to give to the captain. Over the course of the day, the Titanic received six ice warnings, but the captain only read the first two. The second ice warning came a little after mid-day from the steamship Baltic giving the location for large icebergs and field ice. The message ended with 'Wish you and Titanic all success.'"

"Oh my gosh," I whispered. "So they had warnings."

Tessa nodded, "It wasn't until 5:30 that the captain finally decided to alter the route from southwest to due west. Smith believed he was heading in an ice-free direction, but little did he know he was on a direct course for the iceberg. Wireless Operator John Phillips finally finished with the messages for the wealthy passengers on board when he overheard a third ice warning. This one was from the Amerika to the US Hydrographic Office in Washington DC, which warned of icebergs directly in the path of the Titanic. However, this message never got to the bridge. At 7:30 p.m., Harold Bride overheard a fourth message from the Californian to the Antillian with the location of 'three large bergs.' Bride gave it to an officer on the bridge because he was unable to find the captain, who was dining with passengers."

Tessa paused again to collect her thoughts. Her brain was an encyclopedia. "Had this message been delivered to the captain, he would have been able to plot another change of course. None of the survivors remember seeing the message, and the name of the person to whom it was given is still unknown."

Tessa paused once more and scratched her head. "The windless night and the absence of binoculars made it hard to see any icebergs. The crew steamed on at 21 ½ knots, a reckless move. John Phillips received the fifth ice warning, arguably the most critical, from the S.S. Massaba. This one gave the precise location of icebergs which were only fifty miles away from the Titanic. The message came without the prefix MSG, so Phillips interpreted it as non-important and went back to sending messages for the wealthier passengers. The sixth message, from the Californian, overrode John Phillips's messages with a loud and powerful signal. It tells the Titanic that due to ice, the Californian stopped for the night. Phillips then told the Californian to stop sending ice warnings because he was busy with passenger letters. In response, the Californian turned off their wireless signals for the night. Unfortunately, that meant the Titanic lost contact with the only ship that was less than two hours away."

"So, in a way, it's really all John Phillips's fault," said Nick.

"There are a lot of people that, had they done one thing differently, the Titanic wouldn't have sunk," said Tessa. "Anyway, the lookouts warned the bridge—"

"Bridge?" Nick asked.

Brian answered, "Where the steering wheel is. It's like the control center of the ship."

Tessa continued, "Without the binoculars and with little to no wind to make whitecaps, the iceberg was nearly impossible for the lookouts to see until they were close to it. By then, it was too late. The collision was along the right side of the Titanic and was so gentle that most passengers slept through it. The ones who did notice remembered it as a mere glancing blow. The wrought iron rivets failed, and the Titanic began to take on water. The crew described it as splitting its seams, and water began to flood at 400 tons per minute. To stop the flooding, Captain Smith locked the water-tight doors, trapping hundreds of crewmen below to drown. The way the Titanic was designed, it would theoretically stay afloat even with four compartments flooding. Unfortunately, five flooded, and the Titanic began to sink.

Furthermore, it was the first time the crew had deployed the lifeboats because they never received the necessary training. Some of the lifeboats broke when being deployed, and some left at half-capacity. Believe it or not, in the beginning, even though they'd been told the ship was sinking, many passengers refused to leave the warmth of the ship. Only women and children were permitted onto the lifeboats. Most, but not all, of the deaths were men."

"Isn't that sexist?" Aaron muttered. "In the 21st century, it's women who are at a disadvantage but here it seems it's men."

"Anyway, after they realized the ship was going down, the wireless operator John Phillips tried desperately to contact the Californian, which was two hours away. The Californian was close enough to save all of them, but the crew had turned off their wireless signal. Finally, the Titanic got in touch with the Carpathia, who messaged back and said they were coming. Captain Smith reported they had two hours until the ship completely sank, but the Carpathia was four hours away. After all the lifeboats were loaded and lowered there were still 1700 people left on board."

"These people had terrible luck," Nick said. "I mean all the things that could go wrong, did."

"Wait, what happened to the captain?" I asked.

Brian was the one who answered, "Captain Smith was last seen on the bridge, and it was rumored he went down with the ship."

"Aw, that's sad," I said. "Tessa, how did you memorize all of that?"

"Tess, you're even more incredible than I thought!" Rebecca exclaimed. "That was amazing."

"Thanks," Tessa blushed. "Not all of it was word for word. My eidetic memory only allows me to picture the article, not really memorize it."

"Still incredible," I told her.

"What a happy story!" Aaron forced a wry smile. "I'll tell it to the toddlers back at the orphanage for a bedtime story." I felt my facial expression fall. The thought of ice-cold bodies, floating in the choppy ocean waters, the screams and cries of those left to die, the clinking and smashing of broken china, the angle at which the Titanic was pointing up into the night sky, the raw breeze that knocked the breath out of passengers, the stars twinkling down upon the shipwreck, the crew members trapped below deck, knowing death was just around the corner . . . Brian's business-like voice snapped me back to reality.

"The way I see it, we can do one of three things. The first option is to find binoculars for the lookouts. If they can spot the iceberg earlier, we're saved. One of the lookouts—I think his name was Fredrick Fleet or something like that—managed to survive the collision and claimed, during his inquiry, that if he had binoculars, he would have been able to save the ship. Our second option is to warn the captain directly. The last option is to find John Phillips and Harold Bride, the wireless operators, and make sure that the fourth message is delivered to the captain, who will be dining with the passengers."

"Which one was the fourth message?" I asked. With the deluge of information, I couldn't keep all the facts straight in my head. I had no idea how Tessa could manage all the information she had in her head.

"It was from the Californian," Tessa answered. "It gave the exact location of an iceberg in the Titanic's path."

"Oh," I said. "Right."

"The second idea Brian had is the easiest one. Let's warn the captain ourselves. I think we should do it that way," Aaron voted.

"Sometimes you have to do what's right, not what's easy," Brian said. "The captain most likely won't believe six kids about an iceberg. What he will believe is an official message. I say we go ask John Phillips where the message is. Tessa said Harold Bride couldn't find the captain and gave it to an officer on the bridge instead. All we have to do is get it to the captain ASAP."

"You're too smart," Aaron grumbled.

"Just like Rick . . ." Nick murmured.

"Any objections?" Brian asked. Nobody spoke. Nobody had any problems trusting him.

"Let's go," Rebecca broke the silence and led the way down the hall.

"Does she even know where we're going?" Nick whispered to me.

"I don't think so, but I trust Rebecca. She'll find it." It took us awhile to locate the wireless operator room, but at last, we did. The words "Marconi Room" were emblazoned on the door. I knocked, my hand shaking nervously.

"Who is it?" a man's voice, with a strong British accent, called out.

"We need to talk to you! It's urgent," Tessa responded.

"Nice subtlety," Aaron muttered.

"I'm busy right now," said John Phillips. "I'm sending passenger messages. Who are you, anyway?"

"Doesn't matter," Aaron answered.

"Oh, there are more than one of you?" he asked.

"There are six of us," Tessa said.

John inquired, "What class?"

"Sixth," Aaron joked.

"Very funny," John said. "I must get back to what I was doing if you don't mind."

"Alright, suit yourself," Tessa said. She placed a hand on the smooth, cold door handle, forced it down and pushed the door inward, revealing a man with mussed brown hair and brown eyes. His pale face, chalky complexion, and the lack of bright lights in the room gave him a ghostly appearance. John Phillips looked younger than I expected, maybe 25 years old.

It was hard to think that the power to save so many lives rested in his and his partner's hands. He jumped to his feet, dropping his writing utensil, his headphones still on. He had been working at a dark wooden desk in the corner of the small, cramped Marconi Room. The wall, a light cream color, had arches carved into it, and was covered in instruments I assumed were used for communication. The light came from a small lamp attached to the wall in the far corner, providing little light.

"What the bloody hell do you think you're doing?" John Phillips demanded.

"We, um," Aaron said.

Rebecca answered, "We need to make sure a message gets to the captain."

"That is none of your business," Phillips said. "Now leave me to my work."

"We need to know if you gave the message to Captain Smith from the Californian regarding the iceberg?" Tessa wasn't leaving without an answer.

"Bride gave it to an officer on the bridge," John answered. "The captain wasn't there."

"It might be urgent," Tessa said. "Did it not occur to you or Bride that the ship could be in danger?"

"We need to find the officer you gave it to, and get the message to Captain Smith," Rebecca said. "We think he's dining at the moment."

"Is he now?" John asked, suddenly interested. "And how would you children know?"

"We just do," said Tessa.

"Get out," John demanded. "Get out of here. I have messages to finish."

"Listen, this is important," Brian said, his voice serious. "Your life is on the line here."

"My life?" John repeated incredulously. "Is that a threat?"

"No, not at all!" I said. It wasn't a threat, in fact, it was the opposite.

"You don't know what you're talking about," John snapped.

"Now get out."

"No," Tessa refused, her arms folded purposefully across her chest.

"No?" John cocked an eyebrow. "I will call the Master of Arms—"

"The ship is in danger," Nick told him. "It's on target to hit an iceberg."

"Ridiculous!" John replied. "Captain Smith is the best captain ever to sail the seas—"

"Yeah, yeah, he's fantastic, the best," Tessa said, "but you need to listen to us. The ship is in danger."

"Doubtful," John leaned on his mahogany chair. Right then, a young man walked in. He looked even younger than John Phillips.

The guy began to speak, "Um, who are—"

"Bride! These kids want to know about the ice warnings from the Californian! They think the Titanic is on target to hit an iceberg. They won't go away or leave me alone—"

"The note you gave to an officer," Rebecca said, turning to talk to Harold Bride. "Do you remember who you gave it to?"

"None of this is your business," John snapped. "Now for the last time, get out, or I will call the Master of Arms!"

"No," Tessa refused. "Answer the question."

"If I answer, will you leave?" Bride queried.

"Maybe," Tessa said, avoiding a promise.

"Who did you give the message to?" Rebecca questioned once more.

"I'm not sure which officer," Bride admitted.

"Then I guess you'll have to take us to him," Tessa sighed.

"I really do have things to do," Bride countered.

"The ship is in actual danger," Tessa said in a serious voice, "and this message is crucial. We need to know who has the message, and figure out a way to get it to the captain."

"Could you re-write the message?" Rebecca asked.

"I don't remember what exactly was on it," Bride said. "So I guess . . . I guess I'll show you. I'll let the officers on the bridge deal with you." Bride led the way out of the Marconi Room and shut the door. For a moment, I considered suggesting we go and tell the captain in person, but reminded myself Brian had said the captain wouldn't believe a bunch of kids. He needed to see the note himself, proof that the information was true.

In all the commotion, I hadn't had much time to think, but now, my thoughts began to rush in. The fate of thousands rested in our hands. What if we failed? It was unthinkable. I held my breath. I dreaded the potential for failure. We only had one chance.

EIGHTEEN

The carpeted hallways muffled our footsteps as Bride led the way to the bridge, which was, thankfully, on the same level as the Marconi Room. I glanced at their name tags. Officer Lightoller was stern-looking, his face smooth, his features carved, and his white hat sat proudly atop his head. Beside him was Officer Hitchens, who looked to be the oldest of the bunch. He had a receding hairline, his face was round and impassive. Chief Officer Henry Tingle Wilde wore navy, his eyes sharp and focused, his face calm and serious. He was taller than his fellow officers and much more intimidating. Officer Wilde paced the floor behind them, holding an envelope embossed with the words Captain Smith.

The wooden wheel rested in the middle, in front of which stood Officer Hitchens, who was looking out at the ocean below. The bridge had a line of rectangular windows facing out to sea. The floor was interrupted by tall poles that stretched from the smooth wood surface to the barred ceiling.

"Here he is," Bride declared, indicating Henry Wilde. "I gave the note to him." Then Bride left the bridge with an unmistakable sigh of relief.

"What are you children doing here? Where are your nannies?" Officer Wilde demanded with exasperation, stopping to look at us. Outside, the opaque, freezing water was like a black sheet. The Titanic cut through the gloomy windless night with alarming speed, and it was frightening to think of it sinking to the bottom of the ocean.

"We need the note," Rebecca pointed at the message in Officer Wilde's hands.

"Why?" Officer Wilde inquired.

"It needs to be delivered to the captain."

"I am well aware," Officer Wilde said coldly, "but—"

"He's dining with passengers," Rebecca interrupted. "Look, you need to get that message to Captain Smith."

"What makes you think you can trust them?" Officer Lightoller interrupted, glaring at Officer Wilde questioningly.

"I don't know if I do," Officer Wilde admitted. "Especially this one here," he added, pointing to Aaron.

"Hey, I may be untrustworthy, but you can trust my friends!" Aaron said.

"Still," Officer Wilde shrugged. "We are the very best in the field. We've been trained in this. I assure you nothing bad will happen. We work with one of the best captains in the world, and he would know if something was wrong." It was strangely comical to hear those words since the Titanic was famous for sinking and the Captain hadn't been able to save it. Nick managed to stifle his chuckle, but Aaron laughed out loud.

"What's so funny, boy?"

"Children are not allowed on the bridge," Officer Wilde snapped when Aaron didn't answer. "Nobody is. Go back to your parents or your nannies."

"Sir, just give us the letter please," Brian pleaded. "We will take it straight to the captain."

"No, I don't think I will, thanks."

Rebecca's eyes lit up and her facial expression transformed into an 'I-have-a-plan' face. I felt relief flood my heart, soothing my nerves. Almost.

"I guess we'll have to tell the captain that we can't get it," Rebecca sighed, pretending to be disappointed.

"You are on captain's orders?" Wilde asked, suddenly interested.

Officer Lightoller said, "If you are on captain's orders, Henry has no choice but to give you the envelope. But we can't be sure if you are telling the truth."

"How do you plan to decide whether we are telling the truth?" Tessa squinted at Wilde, who looked taken aback by her demanding tone. Officers Lightoller and Wilde said nothing. The silence was like a piece of glass, so fragile it could break at any moment. It was broken moments later by the light-hearted banter of first classmen passing by. The absence of the frigid April winds was a little odd; and thus, the ocean was calm. Officer Hitchens, who was at the wheel, seemed not to be listening, at least until Officer Lightoller continued speaking.

"Henry, the word of a young lady is hardly reliable." Officer Wilde nodded at this.

Rebecca looked at me and winked. She then said, "We are

First Class passengers and should be treated with respect. As some of your highest paying customers, our parents and we demand that the note gets to the captain. My father is friends with the captain, and—"

"Enough!" Officer Wilde bellowed. "Let me think!"

Officer Hitchens said, "Henry, just—"

"Shut up, Robert," Officer Wilde said. "I know what I'm doing." He looked from me to Tessa to Brian. "Very well, then." He paused before passing the message to Brian.

Officer Lightoller scowled, "It has been a pleasure meeting you."

"I wish I could say the same," Aaron muttered to Rebecca and me. We left the bridge and hurried back into the hallway.

Rebecca bit her lip. "We've got to hurry. We've already wasted time. The captain may not be there much longer. I really hope he's still in the dining room."

"Where is the dining room?" Tessa asked.

"We should've asked John," said Rebecca.

"Should we turn back and ask Lightoller, Wilde, or Hitchens?"

"No. We've already overstayed our welcome on the bridge," Rebecca said. "It's up to us. Besides, if we ask, then they will know we lied."

"I guess we have to look around until we find the captain," said Brian. "I don't think we have another option."

We hurried down the stairs and ended up in a carpeted corridor. It was the hallway of the first-class staterooms.

"Where are we?" Tessa looked around.

"These are the first-class cabins," Brian said. "They match the black and white pictures in my book."

"Then the dining room must be near here!" I said.

"Let's go," Rebecca suggested. We broke into an urgent run, sprinting down the deserted corridor. At last, we came to the first-class elevator.

Brian stated, "We're on the Boat Deck. We have to go down to D level."

"Down it is," Rebecca said, closing the gate and hitting the button. The elevator lurched downward coming to a stop on Level D. Nick pulled back the gate, and we spilled out into the hallway. The six of us darted through the first class reception room, hoping to find the first class dining room. Panting, I stopped running.

"Guys, stop for a second," I gasped. "I need a break."

"Sandy," said Nick, not at all out of breath. "Now isn't the time for a break. We're almost there."

"Right, sorry. Let's go."

We finally entered the first class dining room. It was crowded with wooden tables surrounded by dark green chairs, most of which were occupied by rich passengers. Columns divided sections of the room from one another, aligning perfect rows of tables. The stained glass windows on the walls seemed dead without sunlight streaming through them. The carpet was blue with orange and gold patterns. Beautiful arches lined either side of the first class dining hall, and they were carved with special designs. It was magnificent. So pretty, even for a century ago. A beauty, a miracle on water.

And to think of—I shuddered at the thought—the laughs

becoming screams, the hands trying to hold on and forced to let go, the smiles wiped off faces and replaced by expressions of horror, of fear. To think that soon, if we failed, families would be torn apart, lives would be stolen, and screams of terror would pierce the silent night. I couldn't think about it any longer. I forced these thoughts from my mind, begging my mind to keep them locked away. I knew that if we failed, we too would go down with the ship. We had no choice but to succeed.

The elegant, relatively quiet room was clouded by smoke, and the faint scent of cigars wafted throughout the cool air. I saw well-dressed men sipping glasses of brandy, puffing cigars, and it crossed my mind that they had no idea how bad smoking was for them. The women in their elegant dresses adjusting their silk gloves and chatting, oblivious to the iceberg mere miles away.

The first class dining room was nothing like any dining hall today. No purses and smartphones. Nobody answering phone calls. No one texting a friend. No one playing games or watching videos. It was different. The people here were more attentive to one another. Maybe it was because there was no cell phone temptation. Or maybe that was just how it used to be.

"Where is the captain?" Rebecca asked, not to anyone in particular.

"The captain went to his room," said a gentleman to our left. "He's likely asleep by now, don't bother him."

"We won't," Tessa lied. Without another word, we left the first class dining room.

"Where is the captain's bedroom?" Aaron asked.

"Probably with the rest of the officer's quarters," I answered.

"If you think about it logically, the officer's quarters are probably by the bridge," said Brian. "Let's check there first."

"Now that you mention it, I think I might have seen the officer's quarters on the way here," Tessa added. Sure enough after searching for a while, she found a door with the word 'Captain' on it.

Nick banged loudly on the door. It took a minute or two, but the Captain opened it. His hair was disheveled, and he looked exhausted. Captain Edward Smith was a man of average height with an aged face, cloaked by a thick white beard and mustache.

"What do you want?" Captain Smith demanded. Brian handed him the envelope.

"This is from wireless operator, Harold Bride. It's a message from another ship," Rebecca explained.

"Why didn't he bring it to me himself?"

"Um . . . he was busy," Tessa said.

Rebecca added, "And his shift ended."

"You need to head up to the bridge. There is an iceberg in the path of the Titanic," Brian said.

"Why should I believe you?"

"You don't have to," Rebecca answered, "but you have to believe the message from the Californian. Or any of the other five messages with ice warnings. You only saw the first two."

The captain read the Californian's message and sighed again, "Oh my. I better head to the bridge." I felt relieved. Without a parting word, the captain rushed from the corridor.

"I'm surprised. That went a lot better than I expected," I said.

"Me too," Rebecca agreed, "but we don't know for sure if he'll actually do anything. If we can get binoculars to the lookouts, they'll be able to warn whoever is at the wheel earlier than before."

Aaron objected, "But—"

"As a precaution," Rebecca amended. "Just in case."

"But—"

"As a backup," Rebecca added.

"Yes, but—"

"Do you want to go down with the ship?" Tessa snapped. "I don't think so."

"We could always just leave," Nick said. "We'd fail, but we wouldn't die."

"Whatever," Tessa said, her voice filled with annoyance.

"We need to come up with a plan," Brian announced.

"Okay," I said. We waited while Brian thought.

"We need to split into groups. Three of us will try to go break open the crow's nest locker and get the binoculars to the lookouts. The other three need to make sure that not only does the captain actually go to the bridge, but also that one of the officers at the wheel actually turns the ship before it's too late," Brian said. "Okay, Nick, Aaron, and Sandy go break open the locker. Tessa, Rebecca, and I will go to the bridge."

"Where do we meet? You know, when we're done," Aaron asked.

"The Marconi Room," Rebecca said. "We can all find that by now."

"Alright, let's do this. See you guys soon," Nick waved goodbye as he followed Aaron and me down the carpeted corridor. Tessa, Rebecca, and Brian headed in the opposite direction and disappeared around the corner.

"How are we going to break open the locker? That Blair guy took the keys with him," I wondered aloud.

"I think I have a plan," Aaron said.

"Good. Now let's go find the locker."

• • •

The crow's nest was easy to find way up in the air, I saw the two lookouts, and inevitably, neither had binoculars.

"So what's your plan?" I asked Aaron.

"You mean the one that is as whole as a slice of Swiss cheese?" Aaron asked.

"Yeah, that one," said Nick.

Aaron turned to me. "Do you have any bobby pins?"

I reached a hand into my hair, happy to find the smooth metal of not just one, but two bobby pins.

Aaron slipped them into his pocket.

"So what's next?" I asked.

"Nick, you know how to pick locks, right?" asked Aaron.

"Yeah," said Nick.

"You do?" I asked. "How?"

He shrugged. "I grew up in a bad neighborhood, fending for myself most of the time."

"Good." Aaron turned to look up at the crow's nest. "HEY!" he shouted.

"Hello?" Fleet called back.

"How come you don't have binoculars?" Aaron shouted.

"They're locked in the locker," Fleet answered.

"We can pick the lock for you."

"How will you open it without a key?"

"Trust us!" shouted Aaron.

"Very well," said Fleet.

Aaron turned to me. "Wait down here, Sandy. Nick and I can take care of this."

"Are you sure?"

"Absolutely," said Nick. "There might not even be enough room for us."

"Okay." I agreed. The two boys ran over to the lookout tower, leaving me alone. It suddenly hit me how cold the night air was. The ship sliced through the dark ocean, causing ripples in the surrounding water.

Even Ohio's winter months were no comparison to this chill. The cool night carried the smell of the salty air. The breeze created by the ship's movement whipped my hair around me. I squinted off into the distance. The ocean was a murky black mass under a navy blue sky. The few silver stars cast little light. No wonder the lookouts couldn't see the iceberg ahead, I thought to myself, I can barely see anything

I heard the splashing of water on the side of the ship, and looking down, I started to feel queasy. I could imagine the screams for help, pleas for rescue, the air filled with breaking china and the splashes of people and furniture into the ruthless sea. Watching hundreds die in miserable agony. Unable to handle it, I clutched the cool metal railing and shut my eyes.

"Got it!" I heard Nick shout. I felt my heart soar, and relief seemed to thaw my whole body. Warmth spread from my head to my toes, and once again I was able to ignore the chill of the night air. I looked up at the crow's nest, and while I struggled to even make out their silhouettes, I saw the binoculars being held triumphantly up in the air, presumably by Nick.

I felt another rush of relief but realized the Titanic wasn't saved quite yet. The time of impact was just around the corner, and Fleet had yet to see the iceberg. Maybe Captain Smith had already changed the course. It was hard to tell if the boat was turning because there was nothing around to judge it by.

"Damn it," I heard Fleet curse. Then he yelled at the top of his lungs, "ICEBERG AHEAD!" He rang the alarm bell and called the bridge. Nick and Aaron scurried back down to the deck, while Fleet continued to ring the alarm. The clang of the metal rang through the night, loud and clear. "ICEBERG AHEAD!"

NINETEEN

We spotted Tessa, Brian, and Rebecca running towards us and we met them in the middle. All six of us were breathless.

"Will they have time to get out of the way?" Aaron called up to Fleet.

"Just enough," he shouted down. "Captain Smith already started turning the ship, I believe." I held my breath and crossed my fingers. I silently prayed we would make it, that we'd have enough time . . .

Soon after, the iceberg came into view. It was not as close to the boat as I expected, but still a thousand times bigger than I'd imagined. And to think that most of it was underwater. It was unfathomable.

"Get back inside," Fleet shouted to us. "It's too cold out here for you." None of us objected. We sprinted back into the hallways of the boat deck and stood in silence waiting and bracing for a collision we prayed would never come. The fear was palpable in the silence which only added fuel to the fire created by our uncertainty. I closed my eyes, unable to take it all in. We were on the Titanic, close to the iceberg that was famous for stealing hundreds of lives. There we stood, side by side. We had done our best. All we could do now was hope.

• • •

After a few minutes, Officer Wilde appeared in the hallway.

"I don't know how you knew about the berg, but thank you," he said. "Your service will not be forgotten." With that, he tipped his hat and walked away.

"We did it! We saved the Titanic!" I declared. We didn't know what specifically saved the Titanic. Maybe giving the note to the Captain or maybe it was the binoculars that did the job. It didn't matter. All that mattered, was we succeeded. The Titanic would make it to port, and all the lives of her passengers would be spared. In joy and relief, Rebecca, Tessa, and I embraced the boys.

"Ew! Ew! Get off me!" Nick wriggled out of our hug.

Tessa, laughing, said, "Man-up, Nick."

"Two down, one to go," I said.

"Where to next?" asked Tessa. "The third place on the note was 'paradise.'"

"What does that mean?" Nick asked as we all looked at Brian.

"Well, everyone thinks of Hawaii as paradise," Rebecca said before Brian got a chance to speak.

"Yes, but not what you're thinking," Brian said. "I think it means we have to help warn the people at Pearl Harbor." The smiles were immediately wiped from our faces.

"That'll be tough," Aaron said.

The hallway was now deserted, and Brian slowly drew the stone from his pocket. None of us felt like talking. We were more nervous than words could describe. Fear. The thing that silenced us, kept our tears at bay and our minds at attention. The thing that kept our adrenaline pumping.

We all placed a finger on the Stone of Discedo's smooth surface as he said, "December 7, 1941, Pearl Harbor, 7:00 a.m." The last thing I heard was Nick complaining about something. Then everything went black.

The inevitable stream of colors whirled around us, winds whistling in our ears, pictures of this and that, sounds of voices—shouting, conversing, whispering with words I couldn't quite make out. I heard the clap of ocean waves, the sounds of songs and the sea, the music of a band, the whistle of the wind, and the clanking of cups. Then came the chatter of voices, mostly men, as we raced forward in time. It was like every other time we traveled, at least until we landed.

TWENTY

66Where are we?" Nick asked so softly it was almost inaudible.

"What happened?" Aaron asked.

A horrible sound met my ears—a woman's screams. In confusion, the six of us whirled around. There, curled up on the ground, was a woman. She shrieked and convulsed, her body bent at an unnatural angle. You could feel her agony.

The woman was clothed in rags, tattered and streaked by dirt. They were draped carelessly over her, torn in places and blackened in others. The woman screamed again, eyes tightly closed. The woman had chipped teeth, and her gums were raw and bleeding. She shrieked once more in unbearable pain.

The woman was small, and her wispy gray hair stuck straight up from her dry scalp. It was as though all the moisture had been drained from her body. Wrinkles lined her face like a spider web. She was emaciated with sunken eyes and droopy eyelids. Again, she let out a yell of agony. Her eyes flew open and wide-eyed, she stared at us. We were in a dark landscape, nothing but her and my friends were visible.

"Water," the woman gasped, crawling towards us. "Food . . ."

Tessa, Nick, and Aaron, who were closest to her, backed away.

Nick looked horrified. "What—"

"We're lost," Brian murmured to me and the others. "Lost in time. We messed too much with the space-time continuum. We have to give the universe time to correct itself before we can return."

"So where are we?" Tessa asked, looking around at the empty landscape.

"Nowhere," Brian answered, "but at the same time, we're everywhere."

"Fantastic," Aaron muttered, his voice rich with sarcasm.

"What do we do until we can go back?"

"Wait," Brian answered.

"Even more fantastic," said Aaron.

I whispered, "What happened to her?"

"She's starving. She got lost in time and gave up hope. You can't die here because here is nowhere," Brian explained, "but at the same time there is no sustenance."

"That doesn't make a whole lot of sense," Nick said.

"She has no nourishment here, but she can't die because we are nowhere. We have been removed from the earth and the space-time continuum. So, this woman has no choice but to live in dehydration, pain, hunger, and illness."

"That's awful!" Tessa covered her mouth in shock.

"Kill me," the woman pleaded. "Put me out of my misery. Do it. Please." Her voice was raspy. It was clear she hadn't had water for ages.

"Should we kill her to end her suffering?" I asked, thinking it was the right thing to do.

"Please."

"Um, Sandy, do you know what you're suggesting?" Nick asked.

"I'll do it quickly," I said, as I held the woman's hand. Her skin felt like sandpaper. Her dry, cracked lips pleaded for death as her matted hair fell into her eyes.

The woman wailed, her voice shrill and pained as she begged for death.

"I thought she couldn't die. Couldn't we take her back with us?" Rebecca asked.

"She can't die, and we can't take her back because I don't think the stone works that way," Brian said. "Sandy, there's nothing you can do for her—"

I protested, "Maybe she can be killed. It's different than dying."

"Kill me," the woman begged. *"Please."*

I stared at her. After listening to several more pitiful pleas for death, I reluctantly agreed . . . The woman gave a little 'oh' and then was limp. Brian looked both shocked and confused.

"How did you—"

"You said she has no nourishment here because here is nowhere and everywhere," I explained, "so, therefore, she cannot die. I thought maybe she couldn't die on her own."

"Sandy, don't you realize you've killed someone?" Rebecca said in a small voice.

"I did it to help her."

"I'm not saying you didn't," Rebecca said quickly, tears in her eyes. "It's just that—you took someone's life."

"She begged us," I said.

"It's over now," Tessa said. "We can't change what Sandy did. But even if we could, we wouldn't because she did the right thing. She put a woman out of her misery. Who knows how long she's been here."

Rebecca said, "Sandy, I'm not trying to tell you what you did was wrong, I know she wanted to die. I just wish you thought it over more . . ."

My eyes started to tear as reality hit me with full force. I just killed someone. I took someone's life. It was me who watched the light leave the woman's eyes.

Sandy, you did the right thing, I told myself.

You killed someone, another part of me argued.

You would've wanted the same.

• • •

We were all sweating bullets and fanning ourselves with our T-shirts and hands. I could feel beads of sweat forming on my forehead and racing down my face. It was one of the most horrible feelings I ever experienced, like being trapped in a desert during summer with no water or way out.

My thoughts were broken by Rebecca's slightly nervous voice. "How long do we have left until we can go?"

"There is no telling how long the universe and space-time continuum will take to correct itself," Brian answered grimly. "It depends on how much of an effect our changes made on the future."

"So we could be stuck here forever?"

Brian's voice was grim. "That's a possibility."

• • •

We had been there, waiting for the space-time continuum to correct itself, for what seemed like an eternity. It was unbelievably hot, and there was nowhere to go, nothing to eat or drink. The woman's body had just disappeared when we weren't looking, leaving the six of us alone.

"Brian, why is it taking so long?" Aaron asked, wiping away sweat with his shirt.

"I . . . I don't know," Brian said. "I guess we made changes that had a big impact on the future. The space-time continuum has to correct itself—"

"You told us that already," Nick said.

"—I guess some of the changes we made had a bigger impact than I expected," Brian finished.

"Like what?" Rebecca asked.

"It's impossible to tell, really," Brian answered. "Going back in time and changing things has a ripple effect. One change can lead to thousands or even millions of changes. If Lincoln never died, Andrew Johnson wouldn't have become president. Reconstruction in the South after the Civil War might not have ended so quickly. Had Reconstruction been carried through successfully, there's a possibility the civil rights movement would have happened differently, and maybe someone else would start peaceful protests before Martin Luther King Jr."

"Wait, what's Reconstruction?" Nick asked.

"Basically, rebuilding the South after they lost the Civil War," Brian said. "Many changes could have taken place because of what we did. Maybe a passenger on the Titanic whose death was prevented by our actions started a movement or changed history in some way. All 1,503 people who didn't die because the Titanic didn't sink would cause changes too. You never know what might've been."

"I didn't really think about that," Nick said.

"All I've been thinking about is getting out of here," said Aaron. Just then, the Stone of Discedo began to glow a bright emerald green.

"We can go!" Brian said, relief washing over all of us like cool water on a warm summer day.

"Where to next?" Nick asked.

"Pearl Harbor," Tessa said.

Aaron objected, "That's going to be too difficult."

"The writer of the notes is helping us," said Rebecca. "We don't know why, but we followed the first part of the note, so we should follow the last part."

"We need to get out of here!" Tessa said.

Brian held the Stone of Discedo out in front of him so we could all reach it. He spoke loud and clear, "Pearl Harbor, Fort Island, Oahu, December 7, 1941, 7:00 a.m."

By now, I was somewhat used to the feeling. My feet were swept out from under me, and my entire body was whisked away from the world. Colors, pictures, sounds, so many, so fast, my brain was still unable to process them all. I saw flashes of red, white, and blue, the froth of ocean waves as they slammed onto the beach. I smelled the rawness of the salt in the sea and even the scent of something ocean-y that I couldn't describe. I could hear the music of amazing bands—trumpets and trombones, sousaphones and snare drums.

Moments later, we were standing on a large, cement dock. The cool air swallowed me, and the feeling of relief was indescribable. The greenish-blue sea laid out in front of us. The sun was up, illuminating the sky with an array of colors. The sky's reflection glittered magnificently on the glassy surface of the ocean. All was calm. Pearl Harbor, Hawaii, was at rest, not knowing the devastation that would soon occur.

Brian said, "The attack starts at about 7:55 a.m."

"We have to go warn the U.S. military," Rebecca said. "There is no way to prevent the attack, but if they can prepare—"

"That simple?" Aaron said rolling his eyes. "We just warn them?"

"Yes," Tessa said. "I read an article about this recently. Kermit A. Tyler was on duty at the Fort Shafter Radar Information Center. It was his first time on the job. While he was on duty, a radar operator reported seeing a large number of aircrafts quickly approaching Pearl Harbor. Tyler told them not to worry because Pearl Harbor was expecting a group of American planes coming from the mainland."

"So they knew planes were coming into the harbor?" I asked, raising an eyebrow.

"Yes, but they didn't think they were enemy planes," Tessa answered. "Kermit Tyler had to live with this mistake for the rest of his life. Can you imagine feeling responsible for 2,403 people dying?"

"I wouldn't be able to cope with it," Nick murmured.

"People ridiculed and hated him because of this," Tessa said. "If we can find him and warn him, then he won't make the mistake."

"They could've prepared and evacuated people. They could've fought back," Rebecca said.

"Tessa, Rebecca, and I are the fastest," said Nick. "We'll go to the base and try to warn them."

"You know, I'd argue with that, but if you guys want to do all the work, that's fine by me," Aaron said with a shrug.

"Where are you going to go?" I asked.

"We'll figure it out," said Tessa.

"C'mon, let's go," Rebecca urged. The three of them took off running towards some buildings.

The military was here, going about their daily duties, unaware that this very day would soon be recalled with sorrow and sympathy. To them, it was a regular Sunday. They had no idea the Japanese were about to commence a deadly surprise attack. They didn't know this day would be burned into Americans' memories as "a date which will live in infamy."

Large ships sat in the harbor, like immense gray mountains protruding from a sea of blue-green. Slight ripples cut through the otherwise calm surface, and a light layer of mist hovered above the water.

Far off, the water became murkier, a sheet of darkness obscuring what lay below. The glimmering water was so calm, so peaceful . . . the serenity would soon end with a brutal splash of reality.

It was then we heard the music. I spotted the band on the deck of one of the many colossal ships. I saw the instruments glittering in the sun and heard the beat of the snare drums. The music was rich, each instrument blended and balanced with one another, not one sticking out, but not one lost. Each instrument had a part, a place, a role in the band. Each instrument relied on the one beside it. Each instrument worked with the next to form the wonderful harmony. It reminded me of our group, each of us with our own specialty, our own part, our own role to fill. I relied on them, and they relied on me. It just worked. We stood there for a while, distracted by the beautiful sound of the band.

Brian looked down at his watch. "Oh no," he whispered.

"What's wrong?" I asked.

"That's not possible . . .," he said, staring wide-eyed at his watch.

"What?" I repeated.

"It's 7:50 a.m. For some reason . . . we didn't get here at 7:00, the time I said. I don't know what went wrong."

"So—"

"It's 7:50. It means we're too late."

Shouting, Aaron pointed at the sky. "I see something!" I looked to where he was pointing. A small black dot was set against the sky.

"We're too late."

TWENTY-ONE

We had missed our chance. Something went wrong. We arrived here 45 minutes late. The attack was about to begin, and we had done nothing to help the innocent lives of the military and civilians, now in imminent danger. Despite the danger, to which they were oblivious, the marine band continued to play.

"ATTACK! THERE'S AN ATTACK!" Aaron screamed, pointing at the distant horizon. Nobody heard him.

Adrenaline coursed through me, thundering through my veins and energizing my heart. Squadrons of Japanese planes soared into view, and bombs began to fall like rain. The sky was soon clouded by more than 350 Japanese planes which appeared over the island of Oahu as a big black cloud.

A large battleship, the USS West Virginia, was engulfed in a merciless fire. Minutes later, a bomb was dropped onto the USS Arizona which erupted in flames. Shrapnel from the explosion flew in every direction. Smoke colored the sky black and filled our senses with the acrid smell of burning metal and ashes. The saltiness of the sea was masked by the ugly scent of a hungry fire enveloping the ships in the harbor.

All we could do was watch.

We failed to fix this. How could I have thought we could pull this off? How could I have been deluded into believing we'd succeed? Most of all, how did I think I had even the slightest chance of getting my parents back?

A large metal something broke the water's smooth surface. From what I could see, it was long and slender, with a large bump on the top like a shark's fin. I realized it was an enemy submarine.

"We need to get cover! Head for those trees." Brian shouted over the noise. Aaron, Brian, and I ran for a small group of trees. we huddled together beneath the trees, waiting. Wondering where Rebecca, Nick, and Tessa were. Somehow this had gone from solving to surviving.

"I can't just sit here and wait," Aaron said at last. "We need to go find our friends."

"We'll get killed!" I shouted over the roar of the planes. "We have to stay here, where we're out of sight."

"No way," Aaron got to his feet. "I'm going to find them."

"The attack has started, there's nothing we can do to stop it. Aaron's right, we need to go find the others so we can leave," said Brian firmly.

"We'll get killed!" I yelled again.

"Fine. You and Aaron stay here, by the trees. When Rebecca, Tessa, and Nick realize what's going on, they might come back. I'll run the way they went and try to find them. We have to get out of here ASAP," Brian shouted. He was just a foot away yet most of his voice was drowned out. Brian ran off in the direction the other three had gone earlier.

A minute after Brian ran off, Rebecca, Tessa, and Nick came sprinting into view from a different direction. Relief flooded through me. Aaron and I ran to meet them. Suddenly, shrapnel from a nearby explosion pelted the sand. I grabbed Nick's arm and seized Tessa's wrist, pulling them away from it. Rebecca leaped backward on her own but, unfortunately, Aaron was out of reach.

Aaron cried out, reaching for his foot. Blood was quickly soaking through his shoe. He fell to the ground, unable to move.

"Aaron! Nick, take off your shirt." He didn't argue and handed me his T-shirt. He stood there, shirtless, helpless, and terrified, watching me as I desperately tried to help Aaron. I wrapped the shirt tightly around his foot. Nick knelt, scooping his best friend up in his arms. Together we made our way back to the shelter of the trees.

"Brian's hurt!" Tessa shouted as loud as she could, pointing to Brian, who was limping back to us from about 50 feet away. Thundering planes drowned out her voice, and I couldn't hear the rest of what she was saying. She and Rebecca raced off to help support Brian. Nick set Aaron down so he could lean against a tree.

Aaron's eyes were closed shut as tears slipped down his face, leaving tracks on his sweat-drenched cheeks. Aaron tried to suppress a scream. I paid no attention to anything else; not the yells, gunshots, or explosions of mammoth battleships. The only thing that mattered in the entire world right now was Aaron, Brian, and the others.

"Nick, you stay with him. I need to go help Rebecca and Tessa support Brian."

"Alright." Nick cried as he tried to console his best friend and apply pressure to the wound. I ran over to where Rebecca, Tessa, and Brian stood.

"Sandy, help us with Brian," Rebecca gasped as they stumbled over. She and Tessa flanked Brian, who limped on one leg. "He hurt his ankle and can't walk," she explained. The three of us carried Brian over to the trees where Aaron and Nick waited.

Rebecca's eyes were drawn to Aaron. "How bad is it?"

"Bad."

Rebecca knelt beside Aaron and tried to soothe him. "We need to get back to present day. Soon. We need a hospital."

Brian reached into his pocket, and his eyes widened in shock. "We need to find the stone. I don't have it. I think it fell out when I tripped." My heart began to race. What if the stone was gone? What if we couldn't find it? What if it got blown up or buried or swept out to sea?

"You lost the stone again?" Nick asked in disbelief.

"Tessa, Sandy, c'mon," Rebecca beckoned for us to follow, ignoring Nick. "We'll go find it. Nick, stay with Aaron and Brian."

"Got it," Nick nodded.

Pewter gray smoke hung over the harbor, and black planes still soared over the scene. I could hear earsplitting explosions. Fire and clouds of black smoke emanating from battleships that listed below the water's surface. The piercing sirens and alarms rang in my ears and filled the air.

At that moment, I didn't care that we failed. All I cared about was my friends and I surviving. It was no longer about succeeding, about saving my parents, or Skyler, or any of that. It was about getting my friends home alive. I had put my friends in danger and would never be able to forgive myself. It was my fault.

My head buzzed, and I wanted more than anything to disappear, to make this go away. The noise, the screams, the terror, and the fact that the blame fell solely on me. All my fault— all my fault . . .

Many of the Japanese planes had exploded or been shot down. Some of their parts sunk, while others bobbed around in the water. The occasional enemy plane swooped above us, making my heart skip a beat.

Rebecca and I followed Tessa to a point where she shouted, "I saw Brian trip and fall around here. The Stone of Discedo should be close." Fortunately, it didn't take us long to find it. The stone's emerald green color set it apart from the ground. Tessa grabbed it, and we started running back towards the others.

"We've got to get out of here," I muttered, not expecting the other two to be able to hear me. I took one last look at what was left of Pearl Harbor. For a moment, it seemed as if the Japanese had retreated. Just as the thought crossed my mind, I heard snapping, popping, and sizzling loud and close by. The trees were on fire, and the others were still under them. Nick, Aaron, and Brian were shouting for help. Nick scooped Aaron into his arms and struggled to carry him away from the fire. Brian, unable to walk, hopped slowly on his good leg over to where we stood.

Aaron was still silently sobbing, and Brian had a look of mingled shock and terror on his face. Then I heard a crack. I felt a searing, burning pain. The only thing I saw was black, everything was black.

TWENTY-TWO

Three weeks later at South Toheeden
General Hospital

The cold hard metal shook beneath my fingers as I moved forward. It was still a new feeling, something I had yet to get used to. It felt as if I was gliding languidly down a lazy river or rollerblading on smooth tile.

I glanced down at my leg. Or rather, where my leg used to be. The doctors were forced to amputate it when I was brought to the hospital with a massive hole in my leg. I had one and a half legs now. According to Rebecca, shrapnel blew a hole in my leg. When Rebecca, Tessa, and Nick briefly visited me, I asked them how they kept me from bleeding to death. According to them, Rebecca took Brian's belt and used it as a tourniquet to stem the blood flow until they could get me to a hospital. At least that's what I'd been told. The time I spent at the hospital was both painful and clouded in my memory. With all the anesthesia and the procedures, I often hadn't a clue what was happening.

I was yanked back into reality by the wheelchair's stiff metal sticking into my shoulder. Mr. Phillips had offered to drive me to the Red Bush Café for some sort of gathering. Rebecca, Tessa, and Nick had promised to explain everything at the café. Fortunately, Brian had fully recovered, and Aaron had been discharged two weeks ago. Aaron was now on crutches but was told he would make a full recovery. All of them would be at the café, waiting for me.

• • •

Mr. Phillips's car came to a halt in the parking lot of the café, and he wheeled me in. I didn't like the feeling of not having both legs. It was weird. Unnatural. Awkward. I was missing a part of my body, but I was alive, and for that, I would be forever grateful.

Miss McLaughlin, the receptionist at Mountain View who was also a part-time waitress at the cafe, opened the door for me, her eyes were warm and caring. The café had a closed sign in the window. Had they really closed the café for me?

All the tables were pushed together to form one long table that was filled with the strangest assortment of people. Bright, colorful balloons were tied to the chairs. It was a large reunion, a way to congratulate me on finally getting out of the hospital. There was an empty space at the head of the table in between Tessa and Rebecca. Looking around, I saw the boys. And to my surprise, Ms. Evelyn, Ms. Abigail, Jade, Katie, and Allison were even there. I could also see Coach Simpson from Rolling Hills sitting at the opposite end of the table. Wow! Ida, my friend from Mountain View, had come.

When they saw me, everyone began to clap. Aaron's goofy smile immediately spread across his face. I saw happiness dancing in Rebecca's eyes and relief in Nick's green eyes. Everyone seemed happy to see me.

I smiled and looked at my friends. I noticed Brian trying to avoid Ms. Abigail's gaze. There was no doubt it was awkward between the two of them. Rebecca came up to me, smiling as she wheeled me over to the empty space. Mr. Phillips went to sit by Coach Simpson.

"I suppose you would like an explanation of everything that has happened?" Rebecca asked as she sat down.

"Everything?" I was stunned. "Does that include—?"

"Yep," Tessa nodded, a smile breaking across her face.

"First, I want to apologize, Sandy," Ida said. "I was out of line that day in the band room, and I'm sorry."

"I'm sorry too, Ida." We exchanged smiles before I said, "Now, how about the explanation."

"Right." I expected one of my friends to say this, but instead, it was Coach Simpson. "Sandy, take a good look at me. Do I look like someone else?" he asked.

I stared at him, thinking hard. "Uh, not really."

He took off his glasses. "How about now?"

"No, sorry," I said, shaking my head. What was going on? Was Coach Simpson more than just Coach Simpson?

"Think about it," he said. "Look at my eyes."

Utterly bewildered, I looked at his face. And then it hit me. There was something about his hair, his height, his build, his face.

"Oh, my gosh," I whispered. "You look like Coach David from Mountain View."

"Yes, in fact, I am Coach David. My full name is Mark David." My mouth fell open. So Coach David and Coach

Simpson were the same person? My gym coach from Mountain View was the same person as my gym coach from Rolling Hills? But how and why?

"I think you better start at the beginning," Aaron said, "she looks lost already." Bewildered, I looked around at all the familiar faces. Was I the only one who didn't know what was going on? And why were they all smiling?

"Sandy, I think I should start by saying I was the one writing the notes," Coach David said. My mouth fell open again.

"Y-you? R-really? Why?"

"I wrote those notes to warn you, to protect you."

"But why did it matter to you? I'm just one of your students."

"You, Sandy, are much more than that. You are my daughter."

"I-I'm y-your . . ."

"Daughter, yes. Please let me explain—"

"You left me! You left me, and you never came back!"

"I know, and it was the hardest thing I ever did—"

"YOU LEFT ME AND NEVER CAME BACK!" I wanted to turn away and run out of the café, and never return. I wanted to scream and shout and cry, away from all of this. "Did you even love me?

"Of course, I loved you! Sandy, please let me explain—"

"No! No explanation can be good enough!"

"Please, listen," Coach David said.

"Fine," I said as I crossed my arms over my chest. There better be a very good reason for this, I thought to myself. Rebecca reached over and put her arm around me.

"There is a man named Charles Moon. He is, well, the best way to describe him is, he's a villain. Most of what he does and why he does it is a mystery, but your mother and I spent a few years on a team of gifted—"

"What do you mean, a team?"

"I'll get to that. Let me start a little further back. My childhood friend, Alex Supter, and I were twelve when we along with six of our friends were chosen to be Questers. A new group of Questers is chosen every twenty-five years, and it is their job to stop evil. Each Quester, when chosen, receives a weapon and a power."

"A power? Like a magic power?"

"Correct. Questers have two types of powers, elemental and skilled. Four of us were Elemental Questers, and four of us were Skilled Questors. We spent a lot of time investigating Charles Moon, kind of like detectives. We found out he was planning something more evil than ever before, something that could destroy the country or even the world."

"What was it?" I asked.

"You'll find out someday," he said. "Anyway, while investigating him your mother and I fell in love, got married, and had you. Over time, we realized Charles Moon needed to be eliminated. Your mother, Julianne, and I volunteered to go on the mission to kill him. It didn't work out the way we planned. They were prepared for us, and it went badly. During the fight, she was . . . your mother

was . . . killed in the fight. I'm so sorry."

My father looked at me with sadness in his eyes and then

continued. "I managed to escape, but not unharmed. At the time, I was in no condition to be a father to you, and Charles Moon and his men were still hunting for me. I was in danger, and by returning home, I would put you in danger too. I knew you would not be safe if you were connected to me in any way. If Moon figured out I had a daughter, he would kidnap you or harm you to get to me."

"I . . . wow," was all I could manage. I gulped and stared at him through tear-filled eyes.

Coach David (Dad, I guess) continued, "Most of my close friends were also fighting against Charles Moon, so I contacted Ms. Evelyn. She was the only person I knew who had nothing to do with him and could take you in as a foster child."

Ms. Evelyn picked up the story, "Your father told me about everything that was going on and begged me to take you in and paid me well. He insisted I change your last name to 'Marsh.'"

"Why?" I asked.

"We tried to keep you off Moon's radar, and to cut the ties between you and me," my father said, "so you would stay safe. I didn't want you growing up in danger."

"Why couldn't the Supter family keep me? Eight years ago when you and mom dropped me off, did they know you might never come back?"

"Ah, I knew you would ask me that," he sighed. "As far as keeping you, Alex Supter was a single mom, and she couldn't take on the full-time responsibility of another child. I also thought you'd be safer with someone who could not be connected to me or your mom. And yes, Alex knew there was a chance we wouldn't return."

"Oh, but if Ms. Supter was a Quester too, then how come her kids were not in danger? How come her daughter, Lara, could stay with her?"

"Alex wasn't as involved with Moon. She's not on his radar like your mom and I were."

"So she has powers too?"

"Yes, Alex has powers."

"Has? Meaning she still has them?" I asked.

"Questers have their powers for life."

"Does that mean—"

"Yes," my father answered, knowing what my question would be. He grabbed Ida's drink and waved a hand over it. Her lemonade froze solid.

"WHOA!" Nick leaped up, knocking over his own drink.

"Settle down, settle down," my father said chuckling.

"Uh, can you unfreeze my lemonade?" Ida asked.

"Of course," my father laughed and tapped the glass. The frozen block of lemonade immediately melted.

"Freeze something else," Nick begged.

"Okay, last time." He pointed at the window, which immediately froze over. He waved a hand, and the window defrosted, although droplets of water remained on the glass. Everyone marveled at his magic.

"Wow," Nick murmured. Miss McLaughlin came around the table, refilling everyone's drinks. When she got to my father, she placed a supportive hand on his shoulder. What was going on? He looked up at her with a smile and their gazes locked for a moment. Then my father looked back at the table, regrouped, and continued.

"When I recovered and was physically and mentally capable, I wanted to watch over you, even though I couldn't have you in my custody. I couldn't live without seeing you, no matter how rarely I spoke to you. I had a teaching degree, so I decided to put it to good use. At your elementary school, Dry River Elementary, I took a job as a fifth-grade teacher. When you graduated to middle school, I took the only open position, gym coach. While I was teaching, I continued to work against Charles Moon every moment I had to spare—every moment I wasn't watching over you. At school, you always looked happy and self-confident. To me, it appeared you were constantly surrounded by friends, and it never occurred to me you weren't happy."

"Well, I—"

"I understand now how difficult it's been for you," he told me. "I wanted to make sure you were safe. When I noticed you befriending Brian, I got nervous you'd be in danger or get into trouble. I left the notes so you would not get involved with Brian or the Stone of Discedo."

"How did you know he had it?" I asked.

"It's a long story, but I'll do my best to shorten it. Charles Moon had a partner in Europe, Simon Moreno. Remember my group of Questers, the ones fighting Charles Moon? We also worked against Simon Moreno. We knew Simon and Charles were planning to steal the Stone of Discedo, thinking it would make them the most powerful people on this planet. The Questers and I figured out a way to track it. Moon has partners in Europe, and so do we. About twelve years ago, our European partners were able to sneak into Dr. Ava Petris's lab in Germany and place a tracer on the stone—"

"What's a tracer? And wouldn't someone notice if there was something stuck on the stone?"

"Tracers are invisible. They show the owner of the tracer the location of the object that it is attached to. They're like a very, very small sticky tac that clings to an object. The only person who can remove it is the person who attached it. A tracer is about as big as the point on a pencil. And no, nobody can notice or feel a tracer unless he or she knows it's there. Our European partners and we wanted to let Dr. Petris activate the stone before we stole it. Dr. Petris is one of the best scientists this world has to offer. We figured if anyone could activate it, it would be her. However, we learned that Simon Moreno, Moon's partner in Europe, had other plans. He and his men stole the Stone of Discedo from Dr. Petris's lab, they killed the Chancellor of Germany and Dr. Petris's bodyguard. They would do anything to get the stone. Because we had the tracer on it, we knew right away what had happened. We contacted our partners in Europe, who broke into his hideout but didn't find the stone. They tipped off the police, who then arrested Simon Moreno and his men. When we looked at the tracer tracker, we still couldn't find the location of the Stone of Discedo. It seemed to have disappeared off the face of the earth."

"How is that possible?"

"Oh, my dear Sandy, I thought you would've learned by now there is more than just this earth. There are places in time that are neither here nor there. Places that are both everywhere and nowhere. The Stone of Discedo disappeared into what we call a Totum, derived from the Latin word for 'all' or 'everything.' It stayed there for twelve years."

"Is that where we went when the space-time continuum had

to correct itself?"

"Exactly," my father nodded. "About four months ago, I received a text from Alex, who monitors the tracer tracker for our team. She told me the Stone of Discedo reappeared after twelve years and was now in South Toheeden. She sent me the stone's location, the home of the McCormick family. At first, we suspected Brian's parents, but the next day Alex texted me the stone was at Valley Heights Middle School. A few weeks later, she texted me again saying it disappeared again. At that point, we knew it had gone to another Totum, or someone used it. The Stone was gone for another three months."

"When I got stuck in the 1980s," Brian murmured.

"Three months after the Stone of Discedo went missing, it showed up again in South Toheeden. Within a week, we noticed it was at Mountain View Middle School, the day Brian transferred there. As a teacher, I have access to kids' records. I noticed there was a blank period in his file of three months. It's normal for kids to miss school for a week or two sometimes if the flu is going around, but three months is almost unheard of. The three months he was absent from school were the same three months the Stone of Discedo disappeared. That was when I knew for sure Brian had it. By asking the librarian to see Brian's library account, I was able to see he had signed out two books about time travel."

"That was probably a dumb thing to do," Brian muttered.

"But how did you know he told me about the Stone?" I asked. There was something I was missing. There had to be.

"I saw Brian talking to you when I was in the library making copies, and I saw the two of you talking again at lunch. When you asked me for a tardy pass to seventh period, I was concerned you were getting too involved with Brian and the Stone of Discedo. You're not the best liar, Sandy. You get that from your mother."

"She couldn't lie either?" I asked.

"There were a lot of things she could do, but lying wasn't one of them," my father chuckled. "I left the first note hoping it would keep Brian from you, and the second one to keep you away from him, but it didn't work. Instead, you got even more involved. All the notes were my attempt to keep you safe."

"Why did you write them that way? Why didn't you tell me exactly what you wanted me to do?"

"I wrote them cryptically in case anyone else came across them."

"How did you leave all the notes?"

"The first and second notes, 'Stay away from the girl' and 'Don't get involved in trouble' were easy. As a gym coach, I have a master locker key. I left Coach Bates in charge and went to go leave the notes.

Then it became much trickier because you changed schools. The reason you were kept home for a week was so I could transfer from Mountain View to Rolling Hills. I was friends with Principal Higgins growing up, and he owed me a big favor. He allowed me to work there temporarily under a derivation of my name since I had the proper paperwork. From my Quester work, I had several IDs for various aliases. I used 'Mark David Simpson' so I could teach at Rolling Hills. I was afraid you'd recognize me, so I shaved my face, dyed my hair light brown, added a pair of glasses, et cetera. I totally changed my appearance. However, keeping you at home for a week presented a problem. You were not at school, so I couldn't leave you notes. Because I didn't want to involve Ms. Abigail more than I already had, I needed to find a way to sneak into the orphanage. I got the blueprints from City Hall and came up with a plan to get in. For the third note, 'Watch your back,' I visited the orphanage during my lunch break and delivered a box of food claiming it was a donation from a local church. I brought it to the kitchen, and then snuck upstairs."

And to think, so many times I'd been within feet of him and didn't even know he was my father.

"How did you know which bed was mine?" I asked.

"Easy, your crimson bag, and I was delighted to see Jessie again, by the way," my father said with a small smile.

"What about the fourth note?"

"I left the fourth note, 'Don't underestimate the power of a small object' because I thought you didn't fully understand the extent of the power of the Stone of Discedo. I saw you and your friends at lunch on your first day at your new school. You all were in serious conversation, and I feared you were telling them about the stone, so I left you another note. It was easier to leave that one because I was able to slip it into one of your textbooks in your locker using my master locker key."

"What about the fifth note, the one left the day the cleaners came?"

"Yes," my father nodded. "As you figured out, I created a fake cleaning company, Julianne's Cleaning Services. Julianne was your mother's name. I activated one of my disposable cell phones, made up the fake business cards, and a flyer with a discount price. I knew that would appeal to Ms. Abigail. When she hired me on Friday to clean on Tuesday, she told me the place needed to be finished by 12:00 because the state inspectors were coming at 1:00. By the time Tuesday came, I was more worried than ever. Even though I'd left a note the day before, I realized I needed to be more straightforward. I took the morning off from school that day to work with the cleaners. When I planted the envelope with the fifth note, telling you I knew about the stone, I saw the piece of paper with Brian's name and number. I threw it away because I wanted you to stay away from him."

"How did you leave the envelope?"

"When I came to clean your room, I put it on your bed—"

"Then why was it in the trash?"

"What do you mean?" my father looked genuinely confused.

Ms. Abigail jumped in, "Oh, I think that must've been my fault. I went around with a trash bag to make sure everything was perfect before the state inspectors came. I saw the envelope, thought it was trash, and threw it away."

"You did?" Coach David, or Coach Simpson, or Dad, or whoever he was, raised an eyebrow and then turned back to me and asked, "Then how did you get to read it?"

"We were searching the trash for Brian's number, and we found it," Tessa explained on my behalf. I was dumbfounded.

Finally, I said, "So, that was the fifth note, but what about the last note? The sixth one that said 'Theater, ship, and paradise in history,' how did you leave it?"

"Well, I waited for the middle and high schoolers to go down to dinner, knowing the upstairs floor would be empty. I picked the fire exit door lock to get into the orphanage and planted the sixth note. In my rush to leave, I must have accidentally left the door ajar. Rebecca and the others told me you found it open and called the police."

"Yeah," I said, thinking about the note. "Why those three events in history?"

"I knew you guys would know about those specific events because you would have studied them in school. I felt they would be the easiest to fix. There were a lot of mistakes that caused each of them."

I thought about the places we'd gone using the Stone, and it made sense. What didn't make sense is how Brian got the stone in the first place.

I asked, "So do you know who planted the stone in Brian's locker?"

"I'm sure Brian told you this already, but when Simon Moreno's hideout was found, a note was discovered that said 'by one with a pure heart and even purer intentions.' The theory is that once the stone is activated, it appears in the possession of someone who needs it or could use it with good intentions. So nobody planted it on him."

"Wow," I said. There were hundreds of questions flying around in my mind, and it was as though I reached up and picked one at random. "Why did I have to go to the orphanage? Why couldn't I just stay with Ms. Evelyn?"

"I'm not well," Ms. Evelyn said. "I was recently diagnosed with breast cancer."

"Oh my gosh, I'm so sorry," I said.

"We caught it early, and I'm going through treatment.

Hopefully, everything will work out."

"Well, that's good," I said, unsure of what exactly to say. That was all I could think of.

Ms. Abigail continued the story, "My sister, Evelyn, asked me to take you in but the orphanage was full, so we had to wait for an opening."

"How come Moon never came to hurt me or kidnap me once he figured out I'm your daughter?"

"Like I said, Questers, when chosen, get powers. Alex has power over light, an elemental power, and I over ice, another elemental power. Certain elemental magic, when combined, can produce specific charms. It just so happens that ice and light create a protection charm."

"So you—"

"Yes. When I got back from my mission with some of the other Questers, Alex and I created a few protection charms. We cast a protection charm on Ms. Evelyn and me. As long as you are within a mile radius of either of us, you cannot be harmed by Charles Moon. The protection charm also protected us, the people it was cast on. And the combination of all the things I did to protect you worked perfectly, up until recently."

"How were you able to leave school? Wouldn't I be unprotected then?" I asked. "Like when you went to the orphanage to do the cleaning and leave the note."

"I also placed a protection charm on Principal Higgins in case I ever had to leave," my father answered. "And I placed one on Mr. Phillips while you were at Mountain View." I turned to look at Mr. Phillips with a look of gratitude. Here I thought I was all alone, but really, all these people were watching out for me and keeping me safe.

"I set up your community service with Mr. Phillips because I knew he had a protection charm," Ms. Abigail added. "I would've rather you worked with someone less soft, but—"

"Being soft isn't a bad thing!" Mr. Phillips said.

Ms. Evelyn added, "Sandy when you asked me that Saturday to go to the Red Bush Café to meet a friend, you might've noticed I checked my phone. I was checking to see exactly how far away it was. Because it was just under a mile away, I let you go, knowing the protection charm your father cast on me would keep you safe at the café." It was tough to believe, after all this time, Ms. Evelyn was looking out for me.

My father said, "I just happened to call Ms. Evelyn that day to see how she was feeling. She mentioned you had gone to the Red Bush Café to meet someone. I decided to put on a disguise and go there for a couple of reasons. I was afraid you were meeting Brian and discussing the stone. And since it was your last day living with Ms. Evelyn, I thought I might need to protect you because her charm might be diminishing. Protection charms don't last forever. They last about ten years, and they can diminish when the person they were cast on is weakened or sick. Since we had already agreed that it would be best if you moved to Ms. Abigail's, I reconnected with Alex Supter to renew the protection charm on myself and place one on Ms. Abigail and one on Principal Higgins.

I sat there trying to take it all in and then asked Ms. Abigail, how come she let Deputy Brute take me to the police station if she knew I wouldn't be protected.

"I was foolish to assume that you would be safe surrounded by police," Ms. Abigail admitted. "I was wrong. Charles Moon isn't scared of the police or anyone else."

"How was I safe on the bus ride to Mountain View to do my community service?" I asked.

My father said, "I planned to follow the city bus to Mountain View every Friday. I knew you'd be safe once you were there because you'd be with Mr. Phillips, who has a protection charm. Your first day helping him, I followed the bus. When I got there, I was surprised that Mr. Phillips's car wasn't in the staff parking lot. I decided to stay to keep you safe. Suddenly, my Julianne's Cleaning Services phone rang. Imagine my shock when you pretended to be 'Sandra Hopkins' and asked me for my name."

"That's the name you used?" Nick laughed.

"Yeah, I know," I said, laughing a little. "I started saying my own name. And when I realized I couldn't do that, I just used 'Sandra Hopkins' instead."

"I recognized your voice right away, it didn't matter what name you used," my father told me. "Nobody else in the world has that phone number. When you called and asked me for my name and to come by that night, I quickly hung up and ran the phone number you called from through my regular phone. I saw it was Ms. June's. Even though I was worried about you, I felt a sense of pride when I realized how clever you are," he paused. The café was silent. My father said in a soft voice, "Just like your mother—

"When Mr. Phillips arrived, I planned to leave since now you were protected, but my gut told me to stick around. I couldn't believe it when you and Mr. Phillips emerged after your 'community service' with none other than Brian, the person I'd been trying so hard to keep you from for weeks. I didn't know why Brian was going with you and Mr. Phillips, so I decided to follow you. I was confused and surprised when you went to the Red Bush Café. Then I began to wonder if you had gotten Mr. Phillips involved, but realized that was unlikely when I saw Mr. Phillips sit by himself. I was still sitting in the parking lot when a deputy's car pulled in. I was beyond shocked to see Deputy London arrive with what looked like the rest of the kids."

"Does that burglary have anything to do with the story? Or was that just a coincidence?" Aaron asked.

"He explained that to us when we talked to him last week," said Rebecca.

"I'll explain it again for Sandy," said my father. "Somehow, Moon figured out you were my daughter. And somehow, he knew you were going to take a walk that night. He's always been very skilled at predicting the future. Unfortunately for Moon, you stayed within a mile of Ms. Abigail, and could not be harmed by him. We think he knew there was a deputy nearby and if he robbed the nearest store, you would become a suspect. Then you'd end up at the police station and be more than a mile away from Ms. Abigail's protection charm. And at that point, he could get to you."

"Wait. Something strange did happen at the station. The lights went out, and there was a silhouette of a person in the hallway, and then a man came into the room and said my name. Was that Charles Moon?" I asked. The puzzle pieces were finally coming together. My heart began to race. Had I really come that close to the person who murdered my mom and Skyler? To the person who tried to murder me?

With a grim look on his face and graveness in his voice, my father said, "I believe so."

"But then . . . he disappeared."

"Hang on," Ms. Abigail interrupted. "Didn't I arrive a few minutes later?"

I thought about that for a moment. "Yeah, actually, you did. That's when you came with everyone."

"The moment Ms. Abigail was a mile away, you were once again protected by the charm and Moon was left with no choice but to leave," my father said.

"Talk about good timing," Nick said.

My father looked at Nick and said, "Unfortunately, because Charles Moon discovered Sandy is the daughter of his enemy, he figured out who her friends are too, meaning you might be in danger as well.

"When Charles Moon wants to kill someone, he makes a plan. Often, that plan involves using the victim's biggest weakness, their Achilles' heel, to destroy them. Mine . . . well, mine is Sandy. Moon will likely come after the people I love to get to me. Which, as you know, is why I couldn't raise Sandy or be connected to her in any way. Yet somehow, he recently realized her true identity."

"How?" I asked.

"We don't know," my father answered looking grim. "We do know Skyler's murder was committed by Charles Moon. Thursday was the morning I decided to drop off the Julianne's Cleaning Services business card and discount flyer. It was the morning after Skyler was killed and when I drove up, I saw yellow crime scene tape and deputy's cars in the driveway. Nobody would tell me anything. I was terrified something had happened to you. When I got to school, Principal Higgins told the whole staff Skyler had been killed. I looked in her file and was paralyzed by fear. Skyler looked almost exactly like you. I knew then that Charles Moon was the one who killed her thinking she was you."

"Ms. Abigail, where were you the night Skyler was murdered?" I asked. "I went to look for you, and you weren't there."

"I got a call around midnight and had to go pick up a child," Ms. Abigail said. "Normally Jade does that, but she was sick, so I had to go. I thought you'd be safe for the fifteen or twenty minutes I was gone, but I was wrong."

"Somehow, Moon figured out Ms. Abigail had left the orphanage, leaving you unprotected. He went there and killed Skyler, thinking she was you. Later he discovered it wasn't you that he killed."

"Why would he have wanted to kill me?" I asked my father nervously. "Wouldn't it make more sense to kidnap me to get to you?"

"Moon is incredibly powerful," my father said. "He has ways to revive the dead. His magic is beyond anything you can imagine."

"Oh," I said, and then the café fell silent.

"I'm confused," Brian admitted, breaking the silence. "All of the notes you left except the 'Theater, ship, and paradise in history' note were your attempt to protect Sandy. Why did you suddenly change your mind and encourage us to travel back in time?"

"That's a little more difficult to explain. It's kind of . . . a long story."

"I've got time," I said. A couple of people chuckled.

"Kids I want you all to listen," my father said in a serious voice. "Despite my praying that Sandy didn't tell you about the stone when you called the Julianne's Cleaning Services number, and Tessa spoke with me, I realized Sandy had told her new friends everything about the Stone of Discedo and my notes. From seeing you all at school and hearing about you from other teachers, I learned that amongst you, there were special talents like Tessa's eidetic memory and Nick's natural athleticism. I realized there were six kids, seven with Brian, and you were destined to use the Stone of Discedo. I knew I could not stop you and must help you instead. I needed to change my strategy, so I left the 'theater, ship, and paradise in history' note. There was no choice but to help you do the very thing I'd been trying to keep you from doing. Why? Because you kids are the Children of the Prophecy."

"The children of who-what-now?" Aaron asked.

"Listen carefully, there's a prophecy called the Children of the Prophecy. We've only heard part of it, but enough to know the prophecy is about the six of you and some others."

"What does it say?" Rebecca asked

"If it's about us, we deserve to know," Tessa said.

"Unfortunately, we were only able to hear the first two verses—"

"What do they say?" This time it was Aaron who interrupted.

My father pulled a piece of paper from his pocket and read it aloud:

"*I foresee ten kids,*

Six of whom have traveled far, far away,

But soon on this world,

Only five shall stay.

They shall fight in the war,

Alongside rulers and men,

And out of the war,

Will survive all ten."

There was dead silence. Tessa's mouth fell open, and Nick's eyes were wide. At first, nobody spoke, but a few minutes later, we all swamped my father with questions. It was clear my friends were hearing this for the first time, too.

"What does it mean?"

"What are Rulers?"

"So are we the six kids?"

"We must be the six kids who have traveled far, far away."

"Who are the other four?"

"What war?"

And then the magic question. In fact, it wasn't even a question at all. I said it as a statement. "Only five of us will survive."

"It says 'only five shall stay,' not 'only five shall survive,'" Brian corrected.

"I will not let anything happen to any of you. You will be safe with me," my father promised.

I nodded, feeling slightly reassured.

"But it also says, 'will survive all ten,'" Nick said.

"It ends with all of us surviving. That's good enough for me," Aaron added.

"Well, that's not the end of the prophecy," my father said. "We don't know what else the prophecy says. There is more to it."

"We'll have to fight in a war?" Tessa asked.

"I don't know."

"What do you mean you don't know?" Tessa exclaimed, jumping to her feet. "We're at risk of dying, and you can't even tell us why?"

"Sit down, Tess," Rebecca whispered. But Tessa wouldn't listen.

"We're going to be fighting in a war, and you can't even tell us why or what it's about?"

"I told you everything I know—"

Tessa interrupted, "But—"

"Tessa, dear, please have a seat," Mr. Phillips spoke up. "We all understand why you're upset but nobody here is keeping anything from you." Tessa looked at him, studying his face for a moment, thinking, and then sat down. The frustration and indignation in her eyes, as blatant as the sky.

I was curious why it was Mr. Phillips who told her to calm down? As far as I knew, they didn't even know each other.

"Is there any chance the prophecy isn't referring to us?" Aaron asked.

"I'm afraid not," my father said. "The prophecy is definitely referring to you. You were destined to use the stone, and now the first part of your destiny has been fulfilled. There is undoubtedly more to come."

"Great," Aaron muttered.

"Your destinies have been written, outlined, like a page in a coloring book, waiting to be filled. You are destined to do so much more than average kids."

"Great," Nick muttered.

"This prophecy is one of the reasons Moon might go after one of you. But, I can promise you, we will keep you safe. We have enormous resources, powers, and skills. There are very smart people who are going to help us, and it's going to be okay. In the history of Questers, evil has never triumphed. We will win, in the end." I saw Tessa nodding her head.

My father cleared his throat breaking the silence. Was I supposed to be saying something? I looked around, confused. And then I saw. A ghost-like figure, a silvery-blue apparition, floating out of the restroom. It was Rick. But how? For a second, I tried to figure it out, but then I realized it didn't matter. All that mattered was that he was here. Alive. Kind of.

"Rick?"

"In the flesh," Rick smiled at me, then closed his eyes and shook his head. "I mean, not in the flesh . . . I mean . . . I'm still getting used to this."

Coach David, or Dad, or whoever he was, began to say, "When I let Rick use the Stone of Moraetas—"

"You had it?" I questioned in disbelief. My brain was on overload.

"I got it when I attacked Charles Moon, eight years ago. Getting the Stone of Moraetus was part of the mission."

"He has partners in Europe who stole it, and its brother, the Stone of Discedo. I'll continue this part of the story from the day you used the stone. I was shocked when I saw Rebecca and the others arrive here at the Red Bush Café with Deputy London. I didn't realize Rick was missing."

"You saw the more handsome twin," said Nick with a chuckle.

"I knew you wouldn't dare use the Stone of Discedo while at the café with so many people around and Deputy London there. I figured you would go back to the orphanage and use the stone in the privacy of your room. While you all were at the Red Bush Café, I had a flash of intuition and decided to go home to get the Stone of Moraetus to help you even more. I wanted to tell you everything so you could be successful. When I finally got to the orphanage, I found the fire exit door ajar and got in that way."

Rick picked up the story, "When I got home, Deputy Sphinx said you guys were upstairs. However, when I got upstairs, I couldn't find anyone. Now I know you had left through the fire exit door. When I went into the girl's room Mr. David was there," he said. "He had this burgundy-colored stone with him, the Stone of Moraetus. I immediately wanted to go get Deputy Sphinx, but instead, your dad confessed everything. He told me about the notes and about being your father. While he was explaining things, he got a text."

Continuing my father said, "Alex had texted me letting me know that the tracer tracker went off. The Stone of Discedo had been near the orphanage, then in the abandoned building, and then it completely disappeared."

"That's when we knew that you guys used the stone," Rick said. "We agreed you might need my help."

"I helped Rick split his body from his soul. His body went back in time, and his soul remained here. I did this so he could protect you if anything were to happen. It turns out, it was a good thing I sent Rick. When his body died, he became a Vaporized

Soul. He is not quite a ghost, but he is not dead either because his soul survived."

"How did you split his body from his soul?" Nick asked.

"It's a complicated process. But, in short, the Stone of Moraetas enables the essence of a person to be extracted from their body."

"Why couldn't you go?" I asked my father.

"When someone uses the Stone of Moraetus to split their soul from their body, they have to pick a person to be the Keeper of the Soul. When Rick went back in time, I was his Keeper of the Soul, which meant I had to stay behind," my father answered. "We decided that between the two of us, he knew much more about history. Also, had I gone, it would be confusing for you kids, who only knew me as Coach Simpson."

"Yeah, I guess that makes sense," I said.

"I knew I'd come back as a Vaporized Soul if anything happened," Rick said. "We felt it was worth the risk."

My father added, "I intended to split all your souls from your bodies, which is why when I left the café I went home to get the Stone of Moraetas before going to the orphanage. Unfortunately, you had already used the stone by the time I arrived at the orphanage."

"So where is the Stone of Moraetas now?" I asked.

"With me. Unlike the Stone of Discedo, you don't have to be in direct contact with the Stone of Moraetus to use it. I was able to send Rick back in time and hold onto the stone. I figured he would come back with you and I could put his soul and body back together."

"Wow. That's . . . wow." I said.

"That's one way to describe it," said Nick, glancing up at his brother. He laughed. "Now I really am the more handsome twin."

"Ah, you can dream," said Rick. Everyone laughed.

"So . . . is the world much different because of what we did?" I asked. Silence. My friends exchanged looks.

"Well, the thing is . . . it's all or nothing," said Brian at last. "If you don't change the outcome of all three events, then history remains the same. It doesn't change."

"Are you saying nothing changed?"

"Unfortunately, yes," he said. "Because we failed at Pearl Harbor, all the changes we made with Lincoln and the Titanic were erased. Nothing has changed."

"Oh."

"In a way, it's probably a good thing," said Tessa. "There's no telling what could've been affected." We believed the changes we made would be positive ones, but Tessa was right. We don't know how the world as we know it would have changed if we were successful. Even though we'd had pure intentions, our changes could have resulted in making things worse.

Maybe the universe would have worked out. Maybe if Lincoln hadn't been assassinated, he would've died some other way. Maybe if the Titanic didn't sink, another ship would have suffered a similar or worse fate to teach the world a lesson about boat safety. Maybe the universe has a way of getting what it wants. Maybe everything was the way it was because that's how it was always supposed to be. I'd never been one to believe in fate, but up until a few weeks ago, I hadn't believed in magic either.

Magic. Magic was responsible for my leg being amputated. It was responsible for Aaron's injury and Brian being trapped in the 20th century. Most of all, it was responsible for Rick's current situation.

And then it came to me—"But wait," I said, "if nothing changed then why isn't Rick . . . human?"

"We don't know," said Rick. "We think that is because I used the Stone of Moraetus, which has different rules than the Stone of Discedo, but we don't really understand it."

"Do you know why we got to Pearl Harbor more than 45 minutes after the time Brian said?"

My father said, "From what Rebecca and the others told me, you were in a Totum for quite some time. Essentially, I believe the amount of time you were in the Totum was added to the time Brian said. Would you say you were there for about 45 to 50 minutes?"

"Yeah, about that," I agreed, even though it had felt like an eternity.

"All of this is speculation, of course," my father added. "Nobody knows for sure exactly how time travel works."

"Hold on a second," I said. More puzzle pieces were coming together. "There was a woman there, in the Totum. Does that mean she used the Stone of Discedo or the Stone of Moraetus? Does that mean someone has tried time travel before us?"

"It's a possibility, but there is more than one way of getting trapped in a Totum," my father explained. "There is a lot we don't know."

"Right." An awkward silence wrapped around us. My mind

was buzzing, filled with so many thoughts I found it difficult to focus on just one.

"So I'm still in danger?" It seemed unreal.

"Well, now that Moon has figured out you're my daughter, you'll be safer with me. You will officially be in my custody."

"Wait . . . really? So my last name will be . . . David?" I asked. My father nodded.

"Sandy . . . David," I whispered. I tried on the name, like a new T-shirt, seeing if I liked it, if it fit right. "Sandy . . . David. Sandy David." I loved it. The last name felt right. It felt as though it was mine. And it was. "Sandy David. Daughter of Mark David." My heart swelled with happiness, but then something occurred to me. "But if you adopt me then I won't see Rebecca, Tessa, Nick, Aaron, or Brian again!" I protested. "They're like my family—"

"Yes, you will," Rebecca said with a huge smile. "You'll see me every day . . . sis."

"Sis? As in sister?" I exclaimed, euphoria rushing through me. This couldn't be real! "My dad is adopting you?"

"And me," Brian put in, grinning.

"And me, too!" Aaron added.

"Brian, I thought you had, you know, parents."

"My foster parents are moving out of the state in the fall, so I was scheduled to go back into the system. My foster parents worked it out with your dad, and they agreed to let him adopt me. They want what's best for me."

"That's great!" My heart swelled with happiness.

"Oh, and one more thing," Mr. Phillips added. "I've been considering adoption for a while now, and . . . well, I decided to adopt Tessa, Nick, and Rick," Mr. Phillips announced, smiling at Tessa who beamed at him.

"Rick too?" I asked.

"According to my records, I'm still alive," said Rick. "I, well, just can't leave the house again."

"Oh."

"Don't worry, there are plenty of things I can do from home. I can enroll in virtual school and read and get a job. I think I might even try my hand at writing."

"That's good," I said. "This is all so . . . amazing. I can't believe I have a family now!"

"Yes," said my father, a smile stretching from ear to ear. "And while you are still in danger, you will be safer with me."

"Hey, if Charles Moon does stop by, can you kick his butt for us?" Aaron asked. We all laughed.

"You will all be protected by a newer and stronger protection charm. Alex and I have been working on it, and we think it will be the strongest protection charm ever produced." It was silent for a while. Maybe they were giving me time to take it all in.

"We know it's a lot, but you'll adjust to it," my father assured me. "We've had weeks to sort it out and get everything in order. And Sandy? I want you to know that I love you so very much. Everything I did was for you. I had your best interests at heart every step of the way."

"I know," I whispered. "Thank you." He'd sacrificed his own happiness for my safety, his heart for my security. Even though I'd never gotten to know him, I owed him everything. My whole life I'd wished I was somewhere else, with someone else, when all this time . . . I was exactly where I was supposed to be. Safe and loved, even though I hadn't known it.

"No 'thank you' necessary," my father said. "You are my daughter, and I love you."

"Aww," Rebecca put a hand to her heart.

"I love you," he told me again. My father got up and walked over to me, then pulled me into a hug. I looked up at him. 'Tall, dark, and handsome,' my mom would have said. I began to cry, letting years of fear, anger, and sadness pour out. I let it all go. The world around me disappeared, and the only thing I cared about was my family and friends. Rebecca. Tessa. Nick. Rick. Aaron. Brian. And my dad. The dad who had left me because he loved me, who sacrificed so much to give me the best life possible. The dad who would now take care of me, and who I would get to see every day.

"I packed all of your bags and put them in Coach David's car," Katie announced to Rebecca, Aaron, Brian, and me, as we went outside to the vehicles.

"And Allison packed Tessa and the twins' bags and put them in Mr. Phillips's car." I noticed Katie's eyes were watery. "I'll miss you, sis," Katie told Rebecca, pulling her into a warm embrace. Rebecca began to cry. The two sisters hugged each other tighter.

"I want you to have this," Katie pressed her tablet into Rebecca's hands.

"No, I-I can't," Rebecca protested. "Mom gave that to you b-before she died."

"So it's mine, and I can decide what to do with it," Katie insisted. "Take it. You can text Allison's tablet. I already put her contact info in there. We can stay in touch that way."

"Are you s-sure?" Rebecca said, eyeing the tablet.

"I'm sure," Katie nodded and hugged her sister one last time. "I'll miss you."

"I love you, Katie," Rebecca whispered, wiping away her tears.

"I love you too, sis." Katie gave her sister a kiss. She and Allison waved goodbye as they, Ms. Evelyn, and Ms. Abigail climbed into Ms. Abigail's van.

Ida gave me a good-bye hug and a parting wave before she left. Tessa, the twins, and Mr. Phillips piled into his car.

"I'm sorry Sandy," my dad said. "I know this has been hard for you, but there is a silver lining. If I had never done what I did, you wouldn't have met your friends."

"Yeah, you're right."

"I want you to know I never wanted to leave you. "

"I know."

"I did what I thought was in your best interest. I was trying to keep you safe."

"I know," I said again. I understood. My dad had been trying to help me, not hurt me.

In the end, we hadn't been able to help warn people at Pearl Harbor. As Brian said, it was all or nothing to make a change in my own timeline. We blew our one and only chance. We didn't get the chance to stop my parents from leaving me, the chance for me to have both of my parents, but yet I still ended up getting one of them. I had my dad.

I knew it would take time to get used to the fact my mom was dead. Not that the thought hadn't crossed my mind, but now that it was confirmed, it was real. In the back of my mind somewhere, I'd always thought I had a chance to get both my parents back. I guess it hurt a little more to know I couldn't. But at least I had my father. My dad had come back for me. I was no longer an orphan. Not only that, but I had three siblings who doubled as my best friends. I realized how very lucky I was.

The birds chirped happily in the distance, and the puffy, cottony clouds floated along, prominent against the clear blue sky. The truth had come out at last, and I was relieved. I finally understood why my parents didn't return. I had the answers I searched for my whole life. I knew the reasons behind everything that had happened to me.

A whole new life would start for me today with a new family and a new home. I felt happiness I was sure would never leave me, and although I lost part of my leg, my life had taken a turn for the better. I hoped I'd be able to get a prosthetic and be up and walking again soon. For now, I might struggle with my new disability, but with friends and family by my side and love in my heart, I knew I could still do anything.

• • •

I pressed my face against the cool, smooth glass of the window. A single tear glided down my cheek as I watched the cars drive away and be swallowed up in the distance. I used to think we only had one chance at happiness, but I now realized we all had many chances, and this was the start of a new one.

Jen Bravo

SARAH FRANK began writing stories in first grade and hasn't stopped since. Her first story was about a girl who could become invisible. To thank her elementary school teachers, she published *What Really Happened in Elementary School! Super Silly Poems Scribbled in a Notebook*. Sarah started writing *The One Chance Series* when she was in fifth grade. She completed the first book in the series, *One Chance*, for publication when she was 14. Sarah lives in Florida with her family. She attends Howard W. Blake High School of the Arts as a creative writing major. You can visit her online at www.SarahFrankWrites.com.

CPSIA information can be obtained
at www.ICGtesting.com
Printed in the USA
FFOW02n1757130318
45568315-46351FF

9 780999 092415